Praise for The Rabboni

"The Rabboni is a captivating journey through history, offering a compelling blend of biblical scholarship and storytelling that will resonate very well with readers interested in the early Christian era." K.C. Finn

"I was deeply touched by the book, moved to tears. It renewed the Sermon on the Mount for me and brought out Jesus' sense of humor." W. Elston

The Rabboni

The Lost Mission Journals of St. Matthew

Dr. Bill Senyard

Dikaio Press

This book is dedicated to my surprising Patron Benefactor Jesus who came close when I needed it and gave me real worth.

Thanks also to all who helped with the writing, editing, and publishing of this story. May God use it for His Kingdom in surprising ways. Special thanks to my wife Eunice for all of her work and sacrifice. Thanks also to the many friends and family who encouraged me in this project. It is better because of you.

Contents

The Rabboni

THE LOST MISSION JOURNALS OF ST. MATTHEW

DR. BILL SENYARD

Dikaio Press

1

Day 170 of the Axum Mission

"I tell you the good news, society's former unenviable disenfranchised ones are now enviable, because God is theirs and they are God's."

Welcome again, my friends. I am continuing my expanded journal of my Rabboni Jesus and his life, his passions, his love for unlovables, and all the unbelievable things he did. It is hard to find the right words to communicate the swirling of feelings in my gut. My memories are still sharp even these many years later. What I write is true.

He was the Son of God, the Messiah, no more and no less, but even saying that, how can one describe all that entails? I can't, but I will attempt to say more than I did in my first concise account.

In my first work, the Gospel of Jesus, now a decade old, I spent a lot of time on his teachings in northern Galilee. His words were so scandalous and new then. To be sure, he made many enemies everywhere he spoke. But he could also gather crowds, the poor in spirit, he referred to them lovingly. So many lives were irreversibly changed. I am one of them.

I have never witnessed anything like it then or since. I miss my teacher and friend so very much.

I must say I am humbled by the response to the Gospel. I never thought of myself much of an author. I am so much better with numbers.

I remember the week I completed it. The Romans had already begun to lay siege to Jerusalem. Anxieties were high. Many people were starving to death. I still shudder to think about it. It would only be a few months before the Romans razed the Holy Temple to the ground.

So many of my dear friends and acquaintances were either crucified, a horrific death, or sold into slavery. Tragic and preventable. I will say more about this later. May God bless our people again.

My, how the time flies. All our lives were upended then—again. Who would have ever thought it would come to that?

There was a sense of real urgency to write the original Gospel. Credible eyewitnesses, many of them my dear friends, were being hunted down and martyred. Our core group had been scattered and were less and less available to approve accounts. Also, fictional misrepresentations of Jesus' life were becoming popular—some quite laughable. Something needed to be done.

All I am saying is there was a sense of urgency among the disciples to get the Gospel down on papyrus. Be assured the leaders, the remaining disciples, and even the surviving family members of Jesus checked every word I wrote.

The elders in Jerusalem gave me a very modest budget. Writing supplies were very expensive. But good news. Where writing biographies doesn't tap into my natural gifting, managing money does. My team was able to finish the Gospel project on time and more or less on budget. There was a final gracious gift from a surprising source. I am indebted to her.

To give credit where credit is due, mine was not the first attempt. There were a couple of incomplete manuscripts covering some of Jesus' life and words. Many of the Tarsian Paul's letters are quite helpful. Dr. Luke's work and John Mark's are each excellent in their own way. I made sure we used the authorized ones where we could. Praise God! I completed the Gospel and received the full support from my colleagues.

But now, two things have encouraged me to expand on my early work. First, I can't tell you how many questions I get as people read the original Gospel. What did Jesus say next? Do next? Was he joking? Being tongue in cheek here? How did the people respond? How did Jesus handle that? How did he pray? What were the religious leaders really like? And my favorite, whatever happened to Lazarus?

So, I am excited to expand my original account. I want to do it while there are still some eyewitnesses. I work hard to get their input and sign-off again.

Second, I now have the same gracious benefactor who has assured me money is no object for this new codex. Gamilah is a member of the Nabatean royal family, and she is a gracious gift from God. I ask God to bless her, her family, and her business.

As you have noticed, I am doing the project in a journal format. I find here on the mission field; I can't seem to set aside a regular time to write. The journal format allows me to be more flexible. There are days, often many days when my hands are full of caring for the Ethiopian mission. We are surrounded by so many needy people. I am sure you understand.

I hope you have already seen my first journal project where I expanded on Jesus' birth and early childhood. I did a great deal of research about Herod—including interviews with many who knew him well—and would not have been willing to risk talking about him while his children were still alive. He was a frightening king—one not to be messed with.

This manuscript picks up with Jesus' adult ministry some thirty years later. If you could only read one of my books, I recommend the original authorized Gospel to you before you pick up this newer journal account.

Praise to God from whom all blessings flow. Amen.

2

Day 175 of the Axum Mission

I mentioned in my last entry I can't seem to carve out dedicated time for this project. Even I am surprised that it has already been five days since the last entry. Nevertheless, I will persevere. So much has been happening here, nothing tragic or out of the ordinary, just day-to-day running of a mission compound.

I think I will start there. Let me tell you about the Ethiopian mission. When I wrote my Gospel, I was an old man living comfortably in Capernaum, surrounded by a thriving community of Jesus followers, and witnessing new believers every week. I did take a few odd trips to Jerusalem for a variety of meetings, not so many since the Temple was destroyed, and a couple of excursions to Antioch to encourage other missions. But generally, I am a home body. I am comfortable sitting on my porch telling stories to whomever might listen.

The other day, my beautiful wife Deborah joked I am becoming more and more like one unnamed character from the Writings.

"In old age, your body no longer serves you so well. Muscles slacken, grip weakens, joints stiffen. The shades are pulled down on the world. You can't come and go at will. Things grind to a halt. The hum of the household fades away. You are wakened now by bird-song. Hikes to the mountains are a thing of the past. Even a stroll down the road has its terrors. Your hair turns apple-blossom white, Adorning a fragile and impotent matchstick body. Yes, you're well on your way to eternal rest, While your friends make plans for your funeral."[1]

We laughed of course, but it is true. I have become a white-haired, old, and slightly pudgy Jewish curmudgeon. I recently realized I have outlived my Lord and dear friend Jesus by over 40 years. I am in my mid-70s and experiencing more and more old-man aches and pains. There are only two of the original disciples still alive. At least as far as I know. Maybe I am the only one left. Time fears no man.

But everything changed in the last six months. As I write these words, my team is dwelling in a rugged mission compound on the outskirts of the growing town of Axum in Ethiopia, on the Eastern side of Africa, near the Red Sea. Axum is glorious. It is located some 2,000 meters above sea level, on a magnificent plateau. We are surrounded to the north by great mountain peaks, so different than in Galilee.

Not bad for a white-bearded, muscled-slackened old Jew, eh?

I don't want to complain, but I am not ashamed to say the journey from Jerusalem to Axum took a great deal out of me. I joked to Deborah I will certainly soon see the Rabboni again face-to-face. "Old tax collectors never die," she quipped back, "They just need fewer bribes."

I love her dearly.

I do need to share some horrible news. We started off in Jerusalem with twelve stalwarts. Now we have ten. I am struggling to make sense of it. These were people under my care, and I was powerless to do anything to stop the tragedy. I have mulled it over time and again. It is my fault.

I know—I know the Rabboni said we would be persecuted. That's the last of his two beatitudes. Still, why these two colleagues? Why, my Lord?

One of my lost friends, Sorkatti, had been helping me with this journal. I know if she were here still, she would want me to express myself—my feelings. I am not good at that. My father was not such a model for me. But in her memory, I will try. Please forgive me any offense.

Jesus, why? Where were you? You said it to your Father when you perished, 'Why have you forsaken me', us, Sorkatti and Gallio—the very best of us?

My heart is shredded—again. No, I am angry. I felt the same way when Jesus died. I had committed everything to him, to follow him, to be speak of the Father's love for the most unlovable. And then in a moment, he was gone! My dreams were shattered. Honestly, I felt betrayed. I felt like a fool for believing this story. I felt like a disappointment to my family. I was sad—but mostly I felt angry at myself. I am feeling that same ball of emotions now wedged in my gut.

When we got to Axum, we had an appropriate service for them. But since we didn't have the bodies of either, what could we do to honor them? There was no washing or wrapping their hands and feet with strips of cloth. There was no funeral procession. We tore our cloaks and mourned for seven prescribed days. It did us little good. Only sadness and anger remain unabated.

I know they are in the arms of the Rabboni now. I can imagine them there. And yet, I feel like I let them down. Honestly, I would have preferred God take me instead.

May God resurrect them into His arms quickly and bless them for all eternity. We miss them so much.

With your permission and patience, I would like to tell you about the remaining team, my friends, and missionaries of the Gospel of the Rabboni.

I have long thought my own team reflects the new gift of the Rabboni, which is not a thing, but an expression of the one who has changed each of us.

I would be remiss to not start off mentioning again my beloved wife, Deborah. I will say much more about her later as time allows. In spite of her warped sense of humor, she is a source of great joy for me, and I will humbly say, one of the true leaders of our group. We have three adult children and two grandchildren, all who have stayed behind in Capernaum.

Then there is Bernice, a woman from Galilee, and her husband Hanno. Bernice manages all our funds almost single handedly. I do not know what we would do without her. She was there, on that hillside in Galilee with her aged father. You will hear her story, I promise.

She is a true Jewess, faithful, forthright, and a woman of noble character. As the teacher says, "Her children arise and call her blessed; her husband also, and he praises her" (Prov 31:28). She is quite tall—easily a head taller than me—though as Deborah says, I am quite height-challenged.

Hanno is Phoenician and comes from generations of seafaring merchants. He has been a godsend on our long journey to Axum. He is of the uncircumcised—no judgment from me at all. In the community of the Rabboni, foreskinned or no, neither is a source for disrespect or judgment anymore. It is just another adjective of little import.

All I am saying is he is more Greek than Jew. He is learning our culture and religion, in fact a voracious student consuming anything that is written in his native tongue Greek. He came to me in Capernaum after someone had purchased my Greek Gospel for him. He wanted to know more. It wasn't long before he became an enthusiastic disciple of Jesus. Praise God.

His story is tragic. After his conversion, his family disowned him and left him destitute. Remember again, Jesus promised persecution. So sad.

We pray for reconciliation. We also pray that his family would be embraced by the Rabboni. No movement so far.

Unfortunately, Bernice's family didn't respond much better. Her father died 50 years ago, but her mother and brothers are staunch Torahic Jews. They deeply resented her marriage to a Gentile. I wish her father were still alive. I know he would have been far more supportive.

We were very surprised they were actually helpful to her when she joined our mission. Maybe something is happening in her family? Sadly, neither Bernice nor Hanno are welcomed in the Jewish synagogue here in Axum. Jesus' Spirit has such a power. Afterall, he raised the dead.

They brought their two adult children, Te'oma and Mago, both tall and swarthy men and their brides, Ruth, and Sophie (short for her full name Sophonisba, named after a legendary Carthaginian queen who killed herself rather than be captured by the Romans). We just heard the joyous news. Ruth is pregnant. Praise God.

There is old Ninos from Parthia. He came through Capernaum as co-owner of one of the many caravans bringing silk and exotic spices from the far East. He understands Greek, but he is familiar with many languages, including the Arabic dialect spoken by the Nabateans. God has richly provided for our team.

Ninos has no family. Sadly, they perished in a raid of a caravan years ago. Pirating of caravans and merchant ships is very common. Not a week goes by here without new tales of Nabatean pirates who have sunk unsuspecting Roman or Egyptian vessels in the Red Sea.

Ninos came to our doorstep after being left behind by his business partner due to his out-of-control addiction to opium—not uncommon in caravans from the far east. One of our people took him in, nursed him to health and told him about the God who loves unlovable addicts and outcasts.

Before this, he served many gods, or in his own testimony, failed to serve many gods. There was Mithra, the god of the rising sun and business ventures. There was Ahura Mazda the creator and sustainer god of the Zoroastrians, and then the myriad of Greek gods and goddesses. Truth told, he still falls back to superstitions and his many addictions as well.

Ninos is tall and wiry, bald with a narrow face dominated with piercing blue eyes. There is something about him. How do I describe it? People tend to trust him and feel comfortable with him. But on the other hand, there is also—sometimes—an obsessive intensity bearing witness to the ongoing inner struggle with addiction.

That said, Ninos is a respected and invaluable part of the team, helping us communicate to such people groups, ones we Jews have spent our lifetimes avoiding.

There are always addicts who come to our meetings—all struggle with shame and falling short of expectations, and a wide range of mommy and daddy issues. Ninos can tell them truthfully about the undeserved honor he has experienced in the arms of Jesus—about a 'new addiction', he calls it, to God's love. He tells them it is "even better than opium." Amen.

At first, when he said the thing about opium, I cringed. But he's right. The message resonates with lots of people.

I mentioned our late friend, Gallio. I will say more about his tragic demise. He was one of the most accomplished men I have known. He was called Gallio, but his full name was Marcus Aurelius Libertus Gallio. As you can see by his name, he was a freedman, a former slave of a wealthy Roman patrician Marcus Aurelius.

Gallio could not remember a time before his service in the Aurelius family. He believed he was from Armenia but could not be sure. He quickly rose in position and responsibility in the Aurelius family and was eventually given his freedom for exemplary service rendered. The Aurelius villa was just outside of Tiberius on the southwest coast of the Sea of Galilee. The name Marcus Aurelius demands great respect among both Jews and Romans up and down the western coast of the lake.

After Gallio had heard so many stories of Jesus, his first act of freedom was a trip to Capernaum. There, he met Peter. The rest is history. He went back to Tiberias and before long, the rest of his family were disciples of the Way. The Way is how some refer to this new Jesus-movement to separate it from other Jewish groups. I am not totally comfortable with the moniker, but it is out there.

Gallio had no family other than us. He was made a eunuch long before he could remember. He was by far the most educated on our team—with the possible exception of Reuben. I miss him dearly. His smile, his endearing confidence. Rabboni, may I introduce you to my dear colleague, the intrepid Marcus Aurelius Libertus Gallio. Enjoy him.

Reuben is our resident Torah scholar and actually a former member of the Sanhedrin. Reuben is my age and was a strident disciple of Rabban Gamaliel until his death and then a student of the great Rabban Zakkai for twenty years. You may or may not know, it was Rabban Zakkai who was used by God—almost single handedly—to save Judaism.

How? So many diaspora Jews, like those here in Axum, are just not familiar with the recent history of our people. Judaism of today is quite different from the Judaism of only a decade ago.

It was then, during the great siege of Jerusalem, Zakkai negotiated with the Roman General Vespasian for the safety of a few Jewish scholars, at least from the school of Hillel. The future of Judaism was on the brink. If the troops on the ground had their way, all the scholars of Judaism would have surely perished in the destruction or sold into slavery.

Rueben has help me understand how significant this was for our people. He was there on the frontlines. There have been only two times when the Temple was destroyed, first by the Babylonians in 586 BC and then by the Romans a decade ago.

What were we Jews to do again, when there was no temple, no sacrifices, no Day of Atonement? Rabban Zakkai was able to forge a new consensus among surviving Jewish scholars. I say consensus, but there were many who disagreed.

This began a crisis of faith for many of our people, including Reuben. He spent months of personal study and searching for truth. His testimony is of how he depended upon temple sacrifice to relieve him of his guilt and shame. While he would admit it was largely ineffective, without it, and its hope of earning even some of God's favor, he was lost.

He fell into despair and depression until he 'accidentally' stumbled into an argument among Thomas' disciples in Jerusalem.

We joke about the irony. Who could imagine anyone worse than the skeptical Thomas to answer Reuben's questions? But God is indeed a mystery and certainly has a celestial sense of humor.

Reuben was baptized into Jesus just days after his first awkward audience with Thomas. He was never the same.

Oh, I should mention Reuben was present at two events in the life of Jesus. First, after Jesus raised Lazarus from the dead, it was Reuben who was the lead prosecutor appointed by the Sanhedrin to consider whether the now formerly deceased Lazarus was guilty of some sin and should be cut off from Judaism and his soul deprived of the afterlife.

The charge? Lazarus and many other witnesses claimed he had died and after three days had been brought back to life by the pretender and false Messiah Jesus of Nazareth. This raised so many legal questions not covered by any legal precedent.

Reuben argued two charges before the court. First, the now-living Lazarus is ritually unclean due to his immersion in death. This was more than touching a dead body, he _was_ a dead body. There are no Torah prescribed sacrifices to remove such an impurity. Therefore, Lazarus should be considered eternally unclean and unworthy of entering the presence of the holy. It was the "better safe than sorry" persecution.

But far worse was the Reuben's second charge. It was widely suspected in scholarly circles, the Rabboni was in cahoots with the demonic realm and so Lazarus' life has been bought and paid for by the dark elements of creation—and again, making him impure and subject to the rules of karat ('cut-off' in our language). He must be cut off from his people, all fellowship, all community, and all worship.

The Sanhedrin agreed, not unanimously, I am told, and so Lazarus lived the rest of his short life in disgrace and isolation. His daughters shared with me how the emotional well-being of my friend deteriorated into deep depression over the next days and weeks. In short order, he died once more. His daughters said it was from a broken heart. So sad. Very few in the history of humanity have experienced both life and death twice.

When Reuben tells his story you can hear the sadness and shame in his voice. He so deeply regrets his part. He would do anything to take it back. But of course, it is impossible. Jesus' death paid for that, and so many others. Praise our Lord.

But, for Reuben, there is even more shame. He was there that evening, the tragic final trial of Jesus before the Sanhedrin. He did nothing to stop them. In fact, he was complicit in the Lord's murder.

I will make sure Reuben himself adds the account to this journal at some point. It must be recorded for future generations. He gives an eyewitness account of the uncontrollable rage effusing the room, like an evil spirit. These men hated Jesus and to a person, wanted him to die by any means—at any cost, whether the Torah was followed or not.

Reuben swears Jesus looked directly at him at one point—face to face and eye to eye. I asked him what he felt. He said it was a swirling rage in his heart, a deep growing shame, about to burst open inside of him.

He did what most men do and buried it—but like Lazarus, it would not remain in the grave for long.

Again, the beauty of having Thomas tell Reuben of Jesus' acceptance and love for betrayers—and cynical doubters, was special. You can't make this stuff up.

Reuben joined our team after first joining Thomas' mission to the far east. Unfortunately for Thomas, but so fortunate for us, Reuben fell ill just before Thomas launched his caravan. When he heard of our mission to Axum scheduled a couple of months later, he immediately came on board. We are so glad to have him with us.

One last thing. Reuben was a disciple of Gamaliel at the same time as Saul of Tarsus. You may know him as Paul the Apostle. Reuben laughs when he thinks of what Jesus has done with the former, very angry, young man. "If Jesus can use him, he can use anyone, including me," chuckles Reuben.

Lastly, but first in our hearts and minds in so many ways, is Sorkatti, our Nubian princess—well, technically at least. There was so much tragedy in her life. She was a niece of Candace the Queen of Nubia and should have been raised in splendor and glory, but alas it was not to be. Her father, Candace's brother had been exiled after being accused of mismanaging the treasury. Disgraced, her mother and father walked away from the palace and moved into a modest village compound some distance away.

Tragically, her mother died in childbirth. Sorkatti was a sickly baby and was not expected to live. She was dangerously underweight and non-responsive for a time.

She was also 'touched by the gods'. Her black Nubian face was noticeably marked by a light brown birthmark descending from above her right eye to her left jawline. In her culture, this was understood by some to be a curse from the gods. Shortly after, her father hung himself in his shame. The orphaned, sickly, and god-marked infant was then adopted by the midwife and her merchant husband and raised as their own.

Sorkatti became a follower of Jesus from the testimony of the eunuch missionary Simeon Bachos. You might remember him. He was an Ethiopian ambassador to the Roman government in Jerusalem and had arrived there only days after Jesus was crucified. The stories he heard fascinated him and so he investigated the Jewish writings more.

On a trip back to Ethiopia, Simeon happened upon the Evangelist Philip near Halhul in southern Judea. Again, this is God's marvelous sense of humor. I know no one bolder than Philip. Many would have just left Simeon alone. But not Philip. He was always up in people's faces.

Simeon happened to be reading from the scroll of Isaiah when Philip inserted himself in Simeon's business and asked him if he understood what he had read. Simeon was very curious and allowed Philip to say more—not that Philip needed an invitation.

Philip was one of my dearest friends and one of the twelve who were first called by the Rabboni. He spoke to him of Jesus and Simeon Bachos believed.

Simeon returned home and many in Africa became followers of Jesus, including Queen Candace and of course, her erstwhile orphaned niece Sorkatti. So many of those we minister to in Axum come from the legacy of the eunuch evangelist Simeon Bachos.

At some risk and personal expense, Sorkatti, still quite small for her age, her birthmark there for all to see, travelled to Jerusalem to learn more at the feet of James and Philip. After a few years, she felt God's call to go back to her people—the very people who shamed her family. Believe me, Sorkatti could be unbending—and that's the understatement of the century. When she got something in her head, the best thing to do was to get out of her way. I told her this might get her into trouble. Sadly, I was right. May God bless her.

Her name means 'writer' and that she was. To give credit where credit is due, she had been invaluable in the research and editing for the last journal. I miss her smile, her laugh and even her flashing anger.

Spirit, make me feel forgiven for not protecting Sorkatti and Gallio. Make me feel your honor again. Make me hear, 'Well done, good and faithful servant' again. Make me feel less sad. Fill them with unspeakable joy in your arms. Make me laugh again. Amen.

This team is something to see, a strange and wonderful reflection of the Rabboni's passion and calling—his transformational message to those people on the hillside in Galilee now forty years ago. Of the original twelve persons in our core leadership team, five were women, and all in leadership roles, all were irreplaceable. Only five of our team come from a purely Jewish background—though I rejected mine at a young age. To make the point even clearer of the seven men, only two of us are circumcised, just saying.

Though he knows better, Reuben still would prefer we circumcise converts. Old traditions are so slow to perish. All of us have been publicly baptized into Christ.

Only two of us knew the Rabboni face to face. Neither of us are very proud of our connection to him. Reuben was a part of the wrongful prosecution and death of the Rabboni. Me? I wasn't able, or willing to even stand with the Rabboni during his most difficult trial. I ran—to my great shame still—I ran in fear of my own life and reputation. To be perfectly honest, I was terrified I had once again put my fatherly hopes in a fraud.

That fear lingered even after Jesus was resurrected and walked among us again. He never expressed anger or disappointment at us, or toward me in particular. He just loved me as no father ever had.

I still need the power of Jesus' Spirit to feel, to know his adoration for me—the failure—as I am. I must ask His Spirit virtually every day to make me know Jesus still cherishes me even after my betrayal. I believe there will come a time when my shame will be excised by the Rabboni's Spirit. Until then, I walk by faith.

So, look at us. Rueben and I are walking failures, men who should be objects of God's wrath, not his devotion.

Sorkatti had spent her entire life proving she has worth and value. She perished trying to get others to experience the same.

Ninos still struggles with addictions.

I would admit I too am addicted to father figures. I so want to hear my father say, "You are my beloved son with whom I am well pleased."

My wife Deborah wrestles with past shame.

Gallio poignantly felt the second-class status endured by eunuchs. He wondered if he was less of a man. For most of his life, until his demise, his value and worth was only borrowed from his master. He spent too much effort looking for compliments and needing credit. I suffer the same emotional affliction for a different reason. Rabboni, make Gallio feel the honor which has eluded him until now.

Hanno must deal with poverty. He had spent so much of his life despising the poor. I remember when he once told me, "If only they weren't so lazy and would get to work. Then they would not need to beg." All sinners have a past. Amen?

All of us came into the presence of Jesus unenviable and though his touch has been unique to each of us, we would agree something has definitely changed. Now we are enviable because God is without hesitancy our King, our patron benefactor, our great husband.

That is our message to others. The honor of this world is fragile and fleeting. Yet, there is a new status with the risen Rabboni—freely given to us who did not deserve it. This world can quickly turn and rob us of so many things. No one can take away this new relationship we have with Jesus.

I will boast of one thing—all to God's glory. Our original team could speak or read over a dozen languages—some with more difficulty than others—including Greek, Latin, Aramaic, Hebrew, a variety of Arabic dialects including Nabatean and most importantly for us now in our immediate context, Ge'ez, the mother tongue of so many in Axum.

I must pick this up later. I have been called to work. Apparently, there has been another revolt among our herd of goats. They remind me some of Sorkatti, obdurate and unyielding. They hate fences. This is the third time this month there has been a breakout. Their leader, who we named Barabbas, always leads them to a very dangerous rocky ridge just to the west of the camp. Though I try to argue, I am too old to chase livestock, Deborah will not hear it. She has so helpfully brought me my cane. God bless her.

Farewell for now.

---

1. Ecclesiastes 12:3-5 MSG

3

Day 176 of the Axum Mission

Two days in a row. Sorkatti wouldn't believe it. I want to pick up where I left off in my last journal entry. By the way, we were able to gather all of the rebellious goats. We put Barabbas in isolation—none of us believe he will change. He is a goat after all.

Let me take you back to the beginning of our mission to Axum. Our team left before the break of day, almost six months ago now. We paid to join a large caravan headed from Jerusalem to Alexandria. These days, it is not safe to travel alone. There are bandits and robbers lurking throughout the region. Though it is more expensive, larger caravans have armed warriors with swords and bows.

As I said earlier, I am in my 70s, the oldest one on our team, but I am in fairly good health. I will admit by the time we made the port of Gaza late on the fourth day, I was exhausted, and my joints ached—every single one of them. I spent much of the journey on a donkey—which did nothing for my back, but I am not one to complain.

There we boarded a Roman trading ship bound for Alexandria in Egypt. Our veteran sailor, Hanno knew exactly where to go and who to ask.

This portion of our journey also lasted a little over four days. Fortunately, the winds were low, and the seas were quite gentle. That didn't stop me from becoming seasick. I am not now, nor have I ever been a sailor. Too many storms suffered on the Sea of Galilee, I suppose.

Alexandria is a wonder to behold. Our plan was to spend a few days there waiting for optimum traveling weather for the next segment of our journey.

The Red Sea, Hanno informed us, is a very dangerous body of water, subject to strong swirling winds and narrow sea lanes. The bottom of the water is riddled with wrecks of even the most experienced captains.

The optimum time to be at the Roman Red Sea port of Berenice is during the month of May. That gave us a week or so to recuperate in Alexandria—to be clear, to get rid of any residual sea sickness before we must get on a boat again.

We were welcomed with great hospitality into the large Jewish community there. I was able to spend valuable time with John Mark. We had spent much time at his mother's house in Jerusalem as we prepared for this journey. Mary had sent us with letters for her son.

It was great fellowship. Mark, as you may know had spent much time with the Evangelist Paul and has also written a most marvelous account of the Rabboni. I am very much indebted to it. He did not know Jesus personally, but frequently interviewed Peter. His work is special. He tells the Jesus story in a very unique way—very powerful. I have learned much from him as a writer.

We gathered together as a mission team to pray for his continued safety and success within the Jewish community in Alexandria.

On the 14th day there, we boarded a barge large enough to take all of us down the Nile to Copta. From there we joined a short caravan to the Roman Red Sea port, Berenice. After some delay, we hired a Roman merchant ship headed to ports south.

This is where our trip began to unravel. Our very meager quarters were below aft deck. They were filthy, stank of old spilt wine, sweat, and stale urine. I spent as much time as possible topside, watching the sailors pull on the yard ropes to make sure the large single red sail was full.

According to Hanno, this was a medium size vessel. It had the capacity to carry as many as 3000 amphorae of wine and olive oil when full. Its singular red square sail topped by two smaller triangular jib sails, was not ideal in the Red Sea where shifting winds often blew in the wrong direction. It was far more suited for commerce on the Mediterranean with its predictable winds.

For decades, those who controlled the trade to India preferred the 'lateen-type' ship with its large triangular sail. It is smaller and faster but of course carries less goods.

On the third morning, there was a loud shout from a sailor who had climbed high into the riggings. He was yelling and pointing to the southeast, raising a great alarm, alerting all aboard.

Within moments, armed Roman soldiers with spears and bowmen lined up on the port side, saying nothing but clearly sending a message to whatever or whomever was the source of danger. By that time, I was able to see the source of the emergency.

Passing us northward was a sleek, much smaller, and clearly much faster lateen ship. It had a large white triangular sail and it appeared to be controlled by a single sailor manning a rear rudder assembly. They were over 100 meters away from us—far out of bow range and seemingly paid us little attention. Danger averted.

I found out later it was a Nabatean merchant vessel. The Nabateans were considered dangerous pirates by the Romans and Egyptians. For centuries they had controlled the Red Sea—that is, until Rome conquered Egypt and set its sight on the lucrative incense spice trade. They are the reason why this ship was filled with armored soldiers and bowmen. The Romans had learned from experience you can't outrun the Nabatean vessels, but they could be scared off by greater armament.

Then I heard loud arguing on the lower deck, a woman's scream, and gruff angry voices. A chill went down my spine. As far as I was aware, we were the only passengers on this ship, except for a dozen or so bedouin slaves who were on their way for the harem of some King in distant India.

I hurried down the stairs as fast as I could. It took a few seconds for my eyes to adjust to the darkness. Then I saw Sorkatti, our Nubian princess, shoved on the floor, held there by a rotund Roman soldier who had his fat knee shoved hard into her tiny back. She was spitting, screaming, slapping the floorboards, and cursing, with no effect at all. The fat bearded soldier, whose belly uncontrollably bulged out from his thin undersized wool tunic, just smiled exposing the few rotted teeth remaining in his mouth.

I didn't know what to do, but I found myself running over to her and feebly tried to pull the flabby armed man off Sorkatti. For such a heroic act I received a painful backhand across my left jaw. Bright lights flashed before my eyes, and I fell back onto some amphorae stacked along the side of the ship's wooden wall. Then I experienced a sharp pain in my shoulder rivaling the dull throbbing in my jaw.

When I gathered my senses, I saw a Roman Centurion had joined the ruckus and was demanding a report.

The overly stout soldier awkwardly rolled off Sorkatti and started spewing complaints and excuses to his superior. He said he was inspecting the lower hold—likely taking a drink from one of the cracked Laodicean amphorae of wine—when he came upon this woman—as he pointed his fat stubby fingers into her face—acting strangely and upsetting the precious cargo. He pointed to the iron bars of the brig which was filled with emaciated and terrified brown men and women. Precious cargo? Really?

The Centurion, immaculately dressed in metal armor on top of a red knee length tunic and a bright bronze helmet topped with a red transverse crest signifying his rank as a Roman officer, reacted with outrage. Looking back, I wondered if his nerves were still on end from the sighting of the sea pirates up top.

By then Sorkatti had ungraciously stood up dusted herself off. She spit at the boots of the guard who assaulted her. I happened to notice the act of defiance caused a slight smirk to appear on the Centurion's face. I guess the Centurion had no love for the soldier—and Sorkatti—say what you will, she is royalty incarnated. I have told others, "You can take the woman away from the crown, but you can't take the crown away from the woman." She oozed respectability. The Centurion noted it.

Sorkatti went into a long angry rant about what she had discovered in the brig. She said those men and women had been kidnapped unjustly by evil men and were being inhumanely forced into this place. They were piled upon one another, subjected to thirst and malnutrition, and had to perform bodily functions in a dark corner in what appeared to be a shallow cracked amphorae which, judging by the horrible smell hadn't been emptied for some time. She further laid out her case to the Centurion. "It is unbearable to treat humans in this manner." She was right, of course. But what galled her the most, these innocents, perhaps distant relatives of hers, had been kidnapped in the first place.

Then she moved intentionally and regally, firmly planting her small feet in front of the cell. It was clearly a challenge to power.

The Centurion listened more than patiently as Sorkatti said each of their names aloud, in their own language, a language related to Nubian. She was not done. She had saved the most convincing argument to last. She pointed to the two emaciated young adults whose faces were squeezed against the tall iron bars of the brig--and who clearly had white raised bumps on their neck and arms, and cried out for all to hear, "Smallpox!"

She looked fiercely into the Centurion's grizzled eyes and said it again. "Smallpox—very contagious! They need care, immediately or all of us will be sick."

Well, that did it. When she said "smallpox" the Centurion eyes became quite large. He took a huge step away from the brig and paused to consider what to do. He ordered the fat soldier away with a mere wave of his right arm. The soldier obeyed, gladly.

Then the Centurion turned and left the scene. The last we saw were his red boots climbing the ladder.

Sorkatti looked at me inquisitively and shrugged her shoulders. I could tell she was pretty proud of herself. The Queen had emerged and apparently won a battle—or so she thought. I rubbed my face gently over the swelling in my jaw, surely noticeable under my beard by now. I suspected this was not over, not by far.

The next person who climbed down the stairs was the captain, followed by two heavily muscled sailors. By the looks of them, they were very serious and very loyal to the captain.

Without uttering a single word, they grabbed Sorkatti and dragged her away—against my objections. What could I do? We were strangers here. I had no authority whatsoever. My cries fell on deaf ears.

I have never felt as helpless. No one told us where they had taken Sorkatti. My guess is she was being held in the captain's quarters. Hanno believed the captain was desperate to protect his investment, meaning the kidnapped slaves. Shipping ventures are largely funded by wealthy and powerful investors, demanding men and women who expect no difficulties, no excuses, and no failures. It is all about return on investment.

I was shocked as Hanno explained, and Ninos agreed, "Few things are more valuable an export than slaves." He added, "There are numerous Kings and Sultans in the far east who will pay dearly for them, no doubt much incense will change hands. In those cultures, King's and Sultans worth is partly measured by the size and breadth of their harem. Slaves are each worth many amphorae of wine or olive oil."

If he was right, there is no greater priority for this captain than to get these kidnapped bedouin to India in one piece, alive if not healthy. Sorkatti's actions were not acceptable. She had threatened the very success of the captain's charge. Her fate was in his hands.

"But what about their health?" I argued. "What good does it do to ship dead slaves?"

Hanno agreed. He looked down thoughtfully for a time and then said, "My guess is Sorkatti brought the captain some very bad news. It will be seen as his fault if any perish on the way. His profit is at great risk, maybe his reputation, maybe even his ship. He will be looking for a way to pass the blame on to someone else. Maybe even Sorkatti? Maybe us?"

We prayed.

They moved us to the other side of the ship, furthest away from the captured bedouin. I say moved, but in fact they just tossed our goods out of our original small hold and motioned for us to carry our few belongings with us.

No one would say a thing about Sorkatti. I wondered once if the captain was going to replace one of the infirmed slaves with Sorkatti? That would be evil, but who could stop him. The captain is a god on the boat.

In a few days, we dropped anchor at Ptolemais of the Hunt, the last Roman port on our journey south. We were instructed to stay on the ship. We helplessly watched as Sorkatti was bound and taken to shore in a small boat along with the two sick bedouin, a young teenage man and woman.

It was then, Gallio urgently demanded to disembark as well. "Matthew, I will watch over her. I will protect her. Pray for God's blessing over both of us."

He refused to listen to all our objections. Again, I didn't know what to do. I am a tax-collector, not an international ambassador. What Gallio did was a gracious, heroic, and costly act. He reflected his savior so much. But selfishly, I couldn't bear losing two of our friends in only a few days.

That was the last we saw of both Sorkatti, our Nubian princess, a woman of compassion, a sense of righteousness and justice for others who were in need, and Marcus Aurelius Libertus Gallio, Roman Freedman, hero, and servant to the oppressed and enslaved, more of a man than the rest of us put together. Both, like their Savior and Lord, Jesus, were willing to die to save another. I am so proud, and so sad.

Our ship set sail the very next morning. There was still no sign of Sorkatti, Gallio or the slaves. The tension on the ship was very high. I chose to stay below deck—though I could barely breathe due to the stench. I didn't want to risk any more confrontations or to give the captain any excuses to do something even more rash. Nothing was said to us at all. No one would answer any of our questions.

"Rabboni, Sorkatti and Gallio are in your precious care as always. May your Spirit guard over them and give them peace. Save them from harm and further injustice. Our hands are open to you. I also ask for freedom for the bedouin. May they ultimately come to follow you. Speak to them and make them enviable in you as you did for us. Your incongruous love for unlovables is for such as them, and us. Amen."

We didn't dare to pursue the matter further. What could we do? They are in God's care now. Surely, he has some good plan for them. We know we will see them again, here or in the Kingdom future. My heart is breaking.

In our mourning, we pressed on.

We disembarked the cursed ship at the next port, Adulis and after a few days, joined a small caravan made largely of camels carrying wine and olive oil up to Axum. It took five days to climb the high plateau and arrive at our new home.

Once in Axum, it didn't take us long to find our contact. Obodas was very well known among the community. We gave him the letter of introduction from our sponsor, Gamilah.

He was so sorry to hear of our great loss. He could only shake his head and say regretfully, "Things are in such turmoil these days. So many are scared and stressed, and your people got caught up in a very dangerous power struggle. It is unfortunate. Your presence here though, will hopefully be a healing balm for many. Their loss does not need to be in vain."

He promised to contact his agents in Ptolemais on the Hunt to try to find out what has happened to our people. He wasn't hopeful.

"The Romans takes this merchant business very seriously. No disruptions are allowed. You saw the Nabatean pirates, yes? See, there is no margin for error. You are fortunate you didn't see others."

He shook his head and shrugged his shoulders. "You stay with me and my family until your compound is ready. For now, get some rest."

And so, we did.

4

Day 181 of the Axum Mission

Incense. It is all about incense.

What do I know about incense? I am a missionary, not a priest or Levite. We missionaries don't spend our time on politics or the international shifting of power, but having said that, such things affect the lives of real people, people who we are charged to tell of the Rabboni.

In Galilee, we were quite sheltered from the shifts. The economy was steady with long caravans from the far east transporting silk, spices, and incense to the wider Roman Empire. It was my job to garner tariffs for Rome. Those who passed through our region paid dearly for the privilege. For precious goods, I would gather as much as a 25% tariff.

The caravan owners were reasonably pleased to pay us. I am told there was at minimum a ten-times markup on most spice and incense. It's all about business.

You may know there are a variety of types of incense. There is the golden-brown frankincense imported from India in the far east. This poor-man's incense is relatively inexpensive and typically burned in homes and houses of worship for its aromatic qualities and has some medicinal values I am told.

Here in the street markets of Axum, we generally see a local variety, a more transparent and oily incense—quite cheap—sold for only a few denarii a pound.

There is another mid-range quality frankincense cherished for its lemony scent from parts of Arabia. This is what we used in Capernaum. It came from Nabatean caravans from Arabia along the Transjordanian King's Highway then across northern Galilee.

But, the highest quality, and by far the most expensive frankincense grows exclusively in the southern Arabia kingdom of Hadramaut, the 'Country of Frankincense' many call it. The demand for this very expensive product extends from the courts and temples of India and China to the Emperor's palace in Rome.

As you can imagine, Hadramaut is a very wealthy country. Until recently, it held the monopoly for the supply of this frankincense and the price for it has only continued to rise.

They have been very strategic about it. It began with the demand for its frankincense in India and China. They formed great shipping fleets harbored in Cana. Then they expanded their market north and west by creating what we know as the Spice Road, making their product available to Egypt, Rome, and the entire Mediterranean region.

How did they do this? They entered an exclusive trade relationship with the Nabatean Kingdom which includes the northwestern section of Arabia, the southern wilderness of Judea and much of the Transjordan region east of Judea and Galilee.

Up until recently, this was virtually the only way one could purchase this cherished product. Frankincense from Hadramaut and high-quality myrrh from Qatab were exclusively transported north along the western Arabian steppes by heavily guarded camel caravans, sold to Nabatean traders in Dedan. They then transported the product along their secret desert trading route to Petra and then on to the port of Gaza—to burgeoning markets in the Mediterranean region. The two largest customers are Alexandria and Rome. Both seemed willing to pay just about any price.

I am fascinated by this topic. I am told only a few Hadramaut families may grow frankincense trees. The right is considered quite sacred by law. No one else may cultivate the trees, upon punishment of death.

During the harvest seasons, the men must avoid all 'pollution', by which they mean having sex or touching the dead. Not to be cynical, but this certainly enhances the resin's perceived value for use in holy religious ceremonies throughout the world.

All the raw resin is then brought under guard to the capital city Shabwah where the workmen are closely watched and are even stripped naked and searched at the end of the workday.

The finished product is then shipped along a single road to Sabota, sold to other merchants who travel along the western Arabian plateau for many days to the city of Dedan. There it is transferred exclusively to the Nabateans who take the precious commodity to Petra then to the coastal port of Gaza or Alexandria for distribution to the rest of the voracious Mediterranean market.

I am quite familiar with the Nabateans since one of their queens has recently become an avid Jesus-follower. After the death of King Malichus II, his only son Rabbel ascended to the throne and is in control of the amassed Nabatean wealth and power. He is still a child, so his mother, Shaqilath, effectively is running the Kingdom for now.

But Rabbel's older sister Gamilah has become a follower of Jesus after a recent audience with Thomas' people, I heard. She has become quite a supporter of our Kingdom work and has almost single handedly made the way for us to come to Axum. The letter from her—our gracious sponsor—continues to open doors.

Gamilah is highly educated and speaks and reads Arabic and Greek. She is a huge devotee of all Christian writings, especially my Gospel along with the writings of Paul, John Mark, and even Luke. She is very gracious and financially supporting other missions like ours to many other regions.

She not only supports us financially, but her name opens many doors. Nabatean agents still do business throughout the region—including here in Axum. Even though the Kingdom of Axum is aligned politically with Rome, it is all about business.

So much has changed in the last few years. Like I said, it used to be the Nabataeans would at great cost travel across the desert by camel caravan to exclusively collect frankincense from the inland cities and move it back up Arabia to Nabataea in the north.

But new technology has caused a shift to more maritime distribution. Once a year, Nabataean boats now sail south to collect the frankincense harvest from their two ports in Luce Come and Aila and move it north. It is so much cheaper to ship the product. For a time, they enjoyed a monopoly in both land and sea distribution.

The Nabataeans would land their frankincense and myrrh at the Egyptian Red Sea ports, where they were transported overland to Alexandria. From Alexandria, these incenses were sold throughout Europe.

They even expanded their merchandise to include other high demand goods such as cinnamon, ginger, and vanilla, glass beads and Chinese silks. It wasn't long before Alexandria started to become a clearing house for most goods from the Orient, despite Damascus's direct connection with India and the east via the Silk Road.

The Nabateans were not messing around and worked hard to sustain their power in this shipping lane. They maintained a fleet of warships at the port of Aden, fast lateens attacking any ship daring to pass beyond the southern end of Red Sea.

All of this changed when Rome decided to attack the key Nabatean port of Aden with the entire Red Sea naval fleet. It was a critical victory. The long envied Red Sea shipping lanes were now open to Roman ships. Perhaps it is more accurate to say the shipping lanes were now shared by two embittered enemies.

It took some time for the Roman captains, who were used to the gentler winds of the Mediterranean, to master the Red Sea and the Erythraean Sea lanes to India and beyond. Now the Roman captains have surpassed the Nabateans for the first time in a generation and are bringing frankincense and myrrh to the Mediterranean market at less distribution cost than ever before—not that the savings are being passed on to the users. The price is only going up.

Rome also controls the export of Mediterranean goods such as red coral, certain grains, wine, and olive oils to high demand markets in India and China.

What happened to cause this historic shift? I am no sailor, but I am told by those who are, only a few years or so ago, a single Roman merchant ship, a new design, was finally able to successfully sail down the Red Sea. Before this evolution of merchant ships were launched, existing vessels had to hug the dangerous shoal-ridden coasts and suffered dearly. Few would dare attempt the journey, virtually no sponsors would pay for it.

Now the newer ships can follow a route which takes them down the deep middle of the sea, safe and sound.

In addition, the Roman captains discovered—what likely the Hadramautians already knew. There were annual trade winds called the Monsoons, which, once mastered, greatly expedited voyages to India. It didn't take long for Rome to control the new shipping lanes. The Nabateans are seeing the writing on the wall and are quite worried.

Don't mistake what I am saying. The Nabatean pirates remain a force to be reckoned with, as we clearly saw on our trip. The Romans have never been able to conquer the Nabateans, though many times they tried. It seems now though; they are about to put them out of business.

Have you heard the adage, "It is the already-wealthy who become wealthier." Rome is regularly the beneficiary of this truism.

Currently Rome controls Alexandria on the Mediterranean and the important Red Sea ports of Berenice and Ptolemais of the Hunt. At each of these trading stops, Roman agents charge very expensive tariffs on all goods passing through. This is exactly what I did in Capernaum. Romans are quite adept at this.

Ships must stop and be refitted at both ports and take on fresh water, wine, produce and meat, and other goods if room allows. There they will get a visit from the taxman. It is just how business is done.

Adulis, the port city of Axum is the first port ships can reach after they enter the Red Sea from the Erythraean Sea. It is the last port before you must deal with the Romans. Axum is not a Roman colony but is allied with them—strictly business. So, Rome does not mind a little tariff taken there for their friends in this city. As a result, the Kingdom of Axum is becoming one of the wealthiest non-Roman countries in the region.

Whatever country frankincense touches becomes wealthy and powerful beyond imagining. Not long ago, it was Hadramout, the Nabateans and to a lesser degree the port owners in Gaza. The story of frankincense has shifted to Axum, Alexandria, and Rome.

It is a major shakeup of international import. The Nabateans are very concerned and wondering what their next move might be. While they deal in a wide variety of products, like bitumen and horses, by far, most of their wealth and power was from the distribution and sale of frankincense from Hadramaut.

Enough about politics and incense. My desire is to tell you more about the Rabboni and his love for the unlovables.

In this world, one's worth and value is determined by so many things. I do not judge. I get it. Your worth-capital might be political power, or your return on investment, number of ships in your fleet, your closeness to a crown, or even the size of your harem.

Now, God has cast a new gift of the Rabboni to the world. This gift is freely given to those without regard to our present appearance of worth or the absence of any perceived worth. This grace is unconditional and incongruous. It doesn't match the worth of its recipients but creates it anew. The life, death, and resurrection of the Rabboni has redivided history and redefined the whole of reality.

It begins at the Rabboni's provocative and wonderful teachings one day on a gentle rising slope in northern Galilee.

Let us begin.

5

Day 190 of the Axum Mission

You may wonder why our team has traveled so far away from Judea and Galilee? It is because this gracious gift of the Rabboni belongs to no subset of humanity but is destined for all. It is far more value than incense shipping control.

Since no one is granted this gift on the grounds of their ethnic worth, no one of any ethnicity is excluded from its reach. And so, we have come to speak to Berbers, Arabs, Nubians, Romans, Greek, and of course, Jews. What is this gift? This grace? It is the person, Jesus himself. The Christ-gift.

I have been asked by a surprising number of people if I could put Jesus' message in a nutshell? If you had just a few sentences, can you put the infinite into a box? I will give it a shot.

I am sure Jesus couldn't have been clearer then at his home synagogue in Nazareth. While I was not there, I have this from a very credible, very close source.

He was a young man, only thirty or so. He was invited to share by the synagogue ruler, as is our common practice. He unrolled the Isaiah scroll and read aloud,

"The Spirit of the Lord is on me, because he has anointed me to preach good news to the poor. He has sent me to proclaim freedom for the prisoners and recovery of sight for the blind, to release the oppressed, to proclaim the year of the Lord's favor."

Say what you will. He stayed true to that prophetic charge for the rest of his tragically shortened life. Maybe, just maybe, it could be boiled down into the simple first beatitude, "Enviable are the formerly unenviable, because God is theirs." What do you think?

On that hillside, made up of the unenviable refuse of the population—the poor, our society's marginalized, the prisoners, the blinded, the oppressed—he gave each access to the favor of God, as they were, not as they should be or could be.

In a sense, they became God's chosen and God became theirs. They, the chronically unenviable became, in a moment of time, enviable.

This was not at all what we had heard before—no matter whether you were a Jew or from some other tribe. This message was dangerous and revolutionary. If I could be honest with you, I am surprised he wasn't murdered sooner.

I remember being with him on that sloping hillside on the north bank of the Sea of Galilee. He told the hodge-podge of desperate disempowered people, men, women, boys, and girls alike, God's patronage and benefaction was theirs, here and now.

In fact, the God of Abraham and Moses was pursuing them—not to shame them further or remind them how badly they failed—but to dance with them. No one had ever heard anything like it before.

I am often asked about who really was there. I could have been clearer in the Gospel for sure. The people came from all over. It was a cacophony of cultures, people groups and tribes—different languages, dialects, and mother tongues—the circumcised and uncircumcised alike.

We know Jews from Judea were there, of course. That is where Jesus had been earlier when he was baptized in the Jordan.

In Jerusalem and Judea, there was growing discontent among many of the people, particularly the middle class and the poor. If you were to ask most Jews, "What did it mean to be a Jew?", or a "Torah Jew", the answer would of course be wrapped up in the Temple and the preserved ancient ritual there.

But the people were becoming disillusioned with the priesthood and even began to question their validity, especially the high priests after the corrupt and highly political appointments of Annas and Caiaphas as High Priests. It was becoming a crisis of faith in Jerusalem.

Many were openly asking the question without respect to the temple, "How can I enter the Kingdom of God?" And "What must we do to know the favor of God, to have his face shine upon us?"

The historic answer, "Come to the Temple" was less and less satisfactory.

I will give you one of many examples of disputes between the Sadducean party, which included the priests and Levites, and the growing populist Pharisaic party that was undermining the unity and faith of the Jews.

For centuries the laws of ritual purity were strictly enforced in accordance with a literal rigid interpretation of the Law. The priests, who spent most of their time in the Temple, found it easy to avoid ritual contamination.

But if you lived outside the temple on the narrow, crowded, and international streets of Jerusalem, it was a real problem. How could you possibly avoid contamination. How could you, for instance not touch an 'unclean person', when you are bumping into people all the time? How would you even know?

Most people ended up just not caring about the purity laws. This included those Jerusalem tradesmen who daily prepared produce for use in the Temple's sacrificial service. You see the problem? The priests were ritually pure, but the produce used in the ritual had suspect provenance.

Please be patient if you are getting lost in the weeds here. I just want to shed light on the foundational fractures and cracks in the Judaism Jesus incarnated into.

This was the fractious *tevul yom* debate. According to a strict interpretation of Leviticus 15:5, one who has become unclean must take a prescribed ritual mikvah bath and then they remain unclean until sunset. Meaning, if you become unclean, you can't bring your supplies to the temple. Unless you can prove cleanliness, you can't work, and you can't get paid—and your family can't eat.

For those who made a living supplying the temple, which was a lot of people in Jerusalem, what were they to do? It was terribly burdensome to try to prove you were 'clean'.

Until recently. Pharisaic sages have taken a more populist interpretation that the person who has become ritually unclean and then takes a mikvah is no longer unclean until sunset. They are only <u>partly</u> unclean. They, say the Rabbis, can continue to work their livelihood without risk of making others unclean. They just cannot go to the Temple until sunset. Reasonable? You tell me.

Of course, the Sadducees and the priests were enraged and immediately rejected this new teaching. But they couldn't stop it from being embraced. What were the people to do? You can hear the confusion, right. So many of the city were very frustrated. It was a tinderbox.

So, due to this and other populist Torahic interpretations, the Pharisaic party was rapidly gaining support among the large middle class and the poor. They were forming rabbinical schools, some small and some quite large, usually meeting near the Temple to teach and discuss the Torah. All could see they were gaining popularity and influence.

I will say more about this later, but it was a time of serious transition among our people. Old institutions were being questioned.

Nowhere was this more obvious than by the crowds of Jews who flocked to be baptized by John in the Jordan River. This was a populist rejection of much of institutionalized religious Judaism. By the way, most of Judean Jews who joined us on the hillside in Galilee had also gone out to be baptized by John. There was a growing discontent with the Temple among the people.

Let me see if I can explain their mentality. To go out to be baptized by John was implicitly an affront to both the Sadducees and the Pharisaic party.

John's baptism had nothing to do with the Temple. No sacrifices were required. No offerings, no mikvahs, no tithing. No priests. It was an invitation to experience God and God's Kingdom apart from the Temple and the Temple cult. John was indeed of the priestly tribe, but the Temple priests certainly would not have seen him as an avid supporter by any stretch.

The Pharisees also did not know John. He was not a disciple of Hillel or Shammai and so had zero pedigree. None. He even demanded the Pharisees get baptized. Outrageous. He called some of the Rabbis a 'brood of vipers'. Many of the people there quietly agreed and some even chuckled under their breath.

Some had suggested John was aligned with the Essene movement. The Essene communities had also rejected the Temple and the Sadducees as being apostate and cursed by God. "If you really want to become right with God," they said, "to gain his favor, you must align with one of our prophetic communities and strictly adhere to our laws and interpretations."

John did no such thing. He didn't try to form any new community whatsoever. John proposed no new laws or teachings. He was about the need for all Jews to repent in order to receive God and His Kingdom.

Many of the Jews from Judah who came to Jesus had already publicly repented in the baptism of John, at great social and personal cost. Yet, most agreed their lives had not significantly changed. No noticeable experience of God's favor, or acceptance. No voice saying to them, "This is my beloved child, with whom I am well pleased."

You can imagine the disappointment, the shame, and crushed expectations. These wounded and increasingly cynical Jews just weren't expecting much from God anymore.

They came to the Rabboni primarily for healing, relief from their immediate pain and isolation. Where else would they go? They had burned bridges with the Rabbis, with the Priests, and often with their own families.

These weary Jews pretty much huddled together in protective pockets, anxious not to soil themselves with an unpreventable touch from the supposed unclean ones. Or perhaps, they were the unclean ones to start off with?

But to their credit, they showed up on that rocky hillside near Capernaum. There they listened. Many, oh so many, were healed in the most intimate way possible. So many of them became Israel that day.

There were other Jews and a multitude of Gentiles from Galilee, the very Roman Decapolis, pagan Syria including those coastal cities Tyre and Phoenicia, Damascus and even the more secular regions east of the Jordan. There were city dwellers, slaves, bedouin and sheepherders. There were the wealthy who came in caravans, and beggars who brought nothing. There were the educated and then those not so educated. There were widows and orphans, the divorced and the abused. Thieves and sex workers—and at least one former tax-collector. What a day.

I think for many today, it is easier and safer to imagine it was strictly a Jewish crowd. True, there were Jews, so many, but what makes a Jew? Aren't the Jews from Jerusalem very different from the Jews of Nazareth and both are different from the Jews who live in the very Roman villages in Galilee and the Decapolis? It is well known the religious Jews of Jerusalem think quite highly of themselves and their righteousness. God smiles upon Mt. Zion, right?

They tend to look askance at their Galilean brothers and sisters. It is sad. Words like impure, secular, uneducated, traitors, and even uncircumcised are inconsiderately bantered about. You've heard the saying, "Can anything good come out of Nazareth?" Laughable.

The Jews of Galilee who dwell outside of the shadow of the Temple with its strictures, purity laws and rules, thought differently about faith. Someone referred to their Judaism as more 'spontaneous'. They honored Torah—in their own way—but they also demanded miracles, signs, and wonders—daily. They were not satisfied abiding by the ancient rules defined their Jewish forefathers and foremothers. They wanted to know how they could individually inherit the Kingdom of God today. They wanted assurance of Paradise when they died. They wanted to know how they could experience the favor of God.

The Jerusalem Rabbis considered this childish and ignorant. One leading scholar famously quipped "Galilee hated Torah." It was another world.

I would be remiss if I didn't mention the powerful underground independence movement alive and well among the circumcised of Galilee. It is nowhere more evident than in Nazareth, the Rabboni's tiny home village. It has only been a generation since Judas the Galilean ignited a revolution that King Herod violently crushed. There is not a family there or in Capernaum for that matter who didn't lose a father, brother, or son. Anger against Rome and Herod is always just below the surface.

So, in their own way, they despised the Judean Jews as much as the Judean Jews despised them. Many of them had stopped going to the three annual festivals in Jerusalem. Why keep going only to be shamed again and again, to be told how disgusting you are to God, how irreparable your situation is?

I have attempted to study what has caused such a division among the sons and daughters of Abraham. I have a theory. If I had to boil it down to just one thing, I would say it was the Via Maris.

One of the things the Romans do very well is to create grand roads and highways slicing across their vast empire culturally and economically joining the silk and spice markets of the far east and the gold and precious metal mines from Arabia all the way to Rome in the east and beyond.

If you are fortunate to be near the Via Maris, you most certainly will benefit financially.

Galilee is a case in point. The Via Maris cuts through the villages of northern Galilee, heads northwest through the Valley of Megiddo to the Mediterranean then to Rome if you turn right or Egypt if you go left.

Capernaum is one of the many burgeoning hubs on the international trade route. My home village has grown so quickly. It was only a small settlement of a couple of hundred not so long ago. When the Rabboni launched his mission from there, it was maybe 1500 people. Even more now.

This is in huge contrast to the small Jewish enclave at Nazareth. While it is geographically fairly near the Via Maris, it is hidden well up in the Galilean hills, and chooses to largely be unaffected by the international peoples who traverse it. One friend used a helpful metaphor. Nazareth is like frightened mice hiding away from the large cats who hunt on the Via Maris.

Jerusalem is much the same. You must really want to visit Jerusalem to get there. You need to take winding and dangerous mountain passes which some have unfairly referred to as goat trails.

You can see in places like Jerusalem and to a lesser degree, even Galilean villages like Nazareth, it is easier to maintain your Jewishness, your strong culture, and your languages. You can remain more "pure". You can speak the ancient tongue more at home. Your children can be raised to be good Jews.

But in Galilee, you must also know Aramaic and Greek. You will be around pagans who eat pork and unclean fish. You will need to do business with people from all over the world. Your children will be exposed to religious philosophies from as far away as China, India, and Arabia and people who worship a cacophony of gods and goddesses and who live their lives holding to this or that superstition. If you want to be successful in Capernaum, you learn to blend in and get along.

On that hillside in Galilee, then and throughout the Rabboni's ministry there, the people who gathered were truly a collection of weary people from all over, a variety of types of Jews—the entire spectrum of Judaism, from religious to Jewish in name only—and of course Gentiles from many tribes.

They were desperate humanity, broken flesh who had one thing in common. They were at the end of their ropes, lost and for most of their day, joyless. They couldn't fix their lot. No culture has the exclusive hold on lostness and hopelessness.

All were relationally disconnected from God, celestially isolated. Few there expected anything from God anyway. We have an idiom in Greek that captures these people. They were the *ptochoi to pneumati* —the poor in spirit.

But I digress.

6

Day 196 of the Axum Mission

These are the Rabboni's beatitudes, or proclamations, or *'makarisms'* in my native Greek. On papyrus, they are hardly as stunning as they sounded in person. Writing them down does not bear witness to the life changes occurring right in front of our eyes as Jesus was speaking. It was very special. It was the opposite of John's baptism where nothing of note resulted. In Galilee, so many people came to be embraced by the God they had denied for so long. I have made the makarisms 2nd person for a reason. They are meant to be personal.

Enviable are you who were formerly unenviable because now God is your benefactor/husband.

Enviable are you, the inconsolable because I bring you close and comfort you myself.

Enviable are the humiliated—the disinherited, you will experience the fulfillment of all the promises of God.

Enviable are you who are obsessed with fixing all the brokenness and disparity in your own selves, relationships, culture and in the world around you, particularly related to restoration to favor with God. You will experience that and more—I will see to it.

Enviable are the merciful to others. That is to say, if you are being merciful to others, you are necessarily experiencing His mercy for you over and over. It's a heavenly formula.

Enviable are you who rest dependent in God's arms like a new-born child, you will see his face smiling upon you and know He is there for you.

Enviable are you who lean into being reconcilers, versus dividers. If this is you, you must have the new heart of a child of God.

Do you know just how enviable you are—you the persecuted ones—when others have systematically organized programs to harass and oppress you because you are doing good to others instead of just yourself – reflecting my HEART to a beat up marginalized, every-man-for-himself world. Hear this. They can't take the Kingdom of Heaven away from you.

O your enviable situation whenever people unjustly speak disparagingly of you, intentionally harass you, to purposely make up and say evil things about you, they are deceivers, all this is done strictly because you are with me.

Rejoice and even greatly rejoice because your wages (what you didn't earn but were earned perfectly for you by Jesus—and so it is as if you really did earn them) are vast in heaven waiting for you. Don't be surprised the so-called righteous—the self-proclaimed religious moralists will persecute you— for in the same way they persecuted the prophets who were before you.

I should say up front, I have chosen to present only nine of the so-called "blessed be's" (Note to reader: I am convinced we must be careful designating them the "blessed be's". I will regularly refer to them as 'macarisms' from the Greek word *makarios*). These nine macarisms I included in the Gospel; I believe best represent the very heart of his message. But to be clear, there were literally dozens more. All of them said the very same thing ultimately. God's Kingdom is filled with those, circumcised or not, who were not welcomed in this groaning world. The Kingdom of God is for the disempowered and disenfranchised.

The Rabboni was very clear, resolute and spoke loudly enough for everyone in the swelling rabble on the sloping hillside in Galilee, just a short walk from his new ministry home base in Capernaum on that remarkable cloudless summer day.

"Enviable are those who were formerly unenviable because now God is their benefactor/husband".

His typical way was to look intensely over the crowd, gazing into one face, then another, so all would feel he was speaking directly to them. Then he would smile, pause—so endearing—then go back to being intense, his eyebrows deeply furrowed as he waved his hands over the crowd and said at the top of his voice, "*Makarioi* are the *ptochoi* in spirit, theirs is the Kingdom of Heaven." Then he would repeat it slowly to make sure everyone heard.

"Enviable are you who were formerly unenviable because now God is your benefactor/husband."

I can't communicate just how crazy it sounded to everyone there. I will parse it out more, but in a nutshell, he said, "Enviable are the unenviable!" It was then and still remains, jarring.

A paradox beyond paradox. He could have just as easily said "white is black", or "wet is dry" or "circumcision is uncircumcision". Nonsense at first blush, then to tell them the Kingdom of Heaven is theirs? These people never owned any heaven. No heaven has ever pursued them, or embraced them, or gave them a shred of any hope. Truth told; these tragic people were not comfortable with the heavens at all.

Many were denying the very existence of heavens.

This horde was made up of those nameless men and women who had been summarily rejected and shamed by just about every institution around—religious or secular—including the heavens. Even many of their own families went through ridiculous machinations to keep them at a safe distance. It was the way things were in an honor-shame culture. These were a shoddy collection of humans who had the stuffing beaten out of them by life. No Kingdom of Heaven had ever intervened—or showed them any notice at all.

As I said, this was an honor-shame culture. People were careful to avoid losing face at any cost. There was shame that happened to you, shame from choices you made, but there is also an insidious shame coming from being seen as one who associates with objects to whom shame is due. I am not sure which of the three is more destructive to people.

At the end of the day, people like these get herded into the life-sucking shadows where they can't be seen—where no one else dares to venture. I understand. Who needs a reminder of what can happen in this often-cruel existence?

They are the *ptochoi to pneumati*—the poor in Spirit. For you not familiar with our idioms, he wasn't referring to money and he wasn't speaking only about their soul or spirits either. The Greek idiom is just saying that every aspect of their lives and world—physical, emotional, relational, and spiritual—was permanently broken—was lacking somehow in a way they just knew. They were relegated to chaos and void.

These *ptochoi to pneumati* were social lepers. "Unclean, unclean!" Never openly said, but everyone understood.

You are not *ptochoi to pneumati* because you botched up a little and feel like you fell short of expectations. It is not referring to a failing which can be fixed with just a little more effort. No, you are *ptochoi* in spirit when you have messed up so badly for so long and your sense of being a failure so deeply entrenched there was no way out. Or you have been abused, mistreated, despised, objectified, treated unfairly for so long, you just become that. You are an empty cup—or an emptied cup. It ultimately feels the same.

You are not a *ptochoi to pneumati* due to some recent financial downturns. You are *ptochoi to pneumati* when financially, you are so far underwater there can be no path out.

You are not *ptochoi to pneumati* when you catch a cold—but when you have chronic debilitating diseases, rashes and sores, leprosy, bleeding, seizures, depression, and are facing the imminent shadows of Sheol—or the damning judgement "Unclean!" uttered from the tightly pursed lips of religious leaders.

Are you oppressed by evil spirits? Blindly enslaved by drink, opium, gambling, or sex. Maybe you have sinned so much for so long, you can't bear to think of Yahweh, or any other deity. You haven't just disappointed others, you have become that disappointment. When you are labeled as that person, unclean, unrighteous, ugly, and untouchable, then you are *ptochoi to pneumati*.

Have you been wrongly divorced and forced to live on the street doing whatever vile thing you had to do to survive and feed your family? Your own family turned on you? *Ptochoi to pneumati*.

There is no heaven made for you. No land either—no home.

On this unimpressive hillside on the shoulders of the Roman international highway, Jesus had convened the non-community of the *ptochoi to pneumati*. Anyone else would have been troubled by such a first assembly—a horrible way to launch a ministry to change the world. But not Jesus. This <u>was</u> his strategy. This reflected his heart as a compassionate rescuer.

So, what do you say to tragic people like this? Something positive? Something uplifting? "I know it has been bad and unfair, but there will come a time when you laugh again. Then you will be accepted and restored. You will feel honor again. Loved again."

Everyone wants such hope. Right? But wait, that's not true. These were the *ptochoi to pneumati*. The *ptochoi to pneumati* have given up all hope—a little or a lot. Whether they had at one time wanted to laugh again, that thin possibility had been hammered out of them by their life's cruelness.

Consciously or subconsciously, the *ptochoi to pneumati* have learned that while others may feel happiness, they might never experience such emotion again. It is a depressing subhuman realization that their lot was to suffer, to live in shame, to be the butt of jokes, to be overlooked again and again. They suffered daily under the downward gazes of family members, former friends, and of course the religious officials who had the final word always. They are hungry ghosts.

Now you can begin to see they didn't come to Jesus to change their lot. No, they were resigned to think "I deserved this treatment, this life—but, if Jesus could just heal me of whatever was strangling me, right now—even temporarily—I could survive my miserable life a little longer. That would be enough."

They would sell their very souls for even temporary relief of pain.

Sad, isn't it?

To my point, these people hadn't come to be rescued by some heaven. They weren't expecting a Messiah—or if there was one, they would never have imagined he or she would be interested in them either.

They weren't on the hillside to fight for themselves, their rights, social justice or equality or reparation, for empowerment—not on anyone's mind as even a small possibility. They had little in common except for this maybe: each man, woman, boy and girl were resigned to this lonely existence. This was the mount of the mortified.

They just came to get some, any relief from their immediate anguish. They didn't want a lecture. They weren't here to be circumcised. They were not going to trust their lives with anyone again—especially someone religious.

There was no more unenviable group then the *ptochoi to pneumati*.

But then Jesus.

He had a different vision. Jesus came for each one—as a jewel merchant would hold up each precious yet flawed stone to the light, gaze at, cherish and appreciate each individual gem.

And with the Rabboni came a power beyond our comprehension to rescue we *ptochoi to pneumati* —a new light which by nature attacks overwhelming darkness, releasing its immediate hold on real souls.

In the presence of Jesus, the unenviable *ptochoi to pneumati* experienced something new and totally enviable. They experienced the Kingdom of Heaven—more than so many others who had sought and failed.

This is as good as any place to clear up one of the criticisms of my first book. The question has been raised several times, "Who was Jesus addressing the talk to?" As I re-read my words, I seemed to imply he was teaching his disciples at the beginning and the crowd at the end. Let me clear this up.

In some ways, as I have thought about this more, it is the wrong question.

The right question is this, "Who is Jesus referring to as the *ptochoi to pneumati*?" The answer? All of us! We men, and women disciples remain chief among the *ptochoi*. I haven't always seen that. I try very hard to <u>not</u> see myself as a *ptochos* in spirit, but alas, I only deceive myself.

The truth is I am Matthew, a *ptochos to pneumati*, who is still learning to rest in the adoring embrace of my God and King.

So, who was he speaking to? He was speaking to all of us. It just so happened we disciples happened to sit closer to the Rabboni. He had come to rescue the *ptochoi to pneumati* —including me.

As I have pondered the event and the Rabboni's message more, I have my own questions.

Who knew, other than Jesus, the one thing we *ptochoi* most desperately needed was the experiential favor of the Lord. There are so many other needs too: health and relational matters, community, justice, equity and fairness, physical things like food, shelter, and clothing—the list goes on and on.

What we most desperately needed, and for the most part were unaware of, was our celestial disconnection from our final source of meaning and value.

We Jews, for instance, had come home from exile almost 600 years ago and yet in a very important way remained in exile from our Celestial King, our great patron and benefactor. We remain the celestially isolated and lonely—functional orphans.

Until Jesus.

In Jesus, God's shekinah glory has finally returned to the land. I will say much more.

Here is another question I get a lot. When Jesus healed the sick, did they stay healed? Short answer. No.

Were the *ptochoi* reunited with their families? Some.

Were they re-embraced by their religious leaders? That is a complicated matter. We will get to the last beatitude in a bit. Jesus predicted persecution for his new followers. He was right. It's too bad.

I will say more when we get to it. But you can ponder this until my next journal entry. You can be in the embrace of God's favor and still hang on a cross.

More to come.

7

Day 240 of the Axum Mission

Praise the LORD. Praise God in his sanctuary; praise him in his mighty heavens. Praise him for his acts of power; praise him for his surpassing greatness (Ps 150:1-2).

We can't believe it! I can't believe it!

I can't explain my unhindered joy. I must share the great news with you. It would be inhuman and indifferent to be silent.

We have just finished our morning prayers; our growing Ethiopian family joined us in the courtyard of our compound seated around a beautiful large fountain. We have about fifteen families now who gather with us, people from different nations and tribes. Someone counted six mother tongues represented.

After prayer we break bread. Hanno and Bernice make the flat loaves in the clay oven built in the wall of our largest facility. We also purchase some local fruit which we slice up and hand out. It is a time of fellowship, joy, and thanks.

All in our community are invited to our fellowship feast. We call it our *Todah*, a Jewish meal of thankfulness to our God. The locals are very open to speak about the gods and are curious to know of this one who has sent us so far from our homes and tribes. We talk about the Rabboni and his life and tragic death and how he has changed the world—changed us. It resonates with real people, and it captures their attention.

Today I shared about the first macarism, "Blessed are the poor in spirit, for the heavens are now theirs". Or in my translation, "Enviable those who were formerly unenviable, because now God is their benefactor/husband"—or "God is theirs."

It is a jarring start to Jesus' words and mission. It generates so many questions, wherever I share this beatitude. By far, the most common is this, "What does it possibly mean that a God is owned by any person?" How can I unpack such a confusing concept?

I was stalling a bit to gather my thoughts, how to answer this great question. In fact, I was handing a piece of warm bread to an older woman when I felt a tap on my shoulder. It was Obodas, our host and provider here in Axum. He was the one to whom we handed the introduction letter from our Nabatean angel, Gamilah. He was grinning ear to ear clearly looking like a child with a vast secret.

I must give a little background. Gamilah had instructed us on the nature of hospitality in Axum and among most of the tribes in Eastern Africa. This was also the Nabatean way.

When we handed our introduction letter from Gamilah to Obodas, we made a point of praising her as a faithful and gracious provider and benefactor. This is the custom. Then we bowed to Obodas. This was the appropriate way of showing our public appreciation for Gamilah's care so far. To not do so would be to our shame and reflect ungratefulness.

Sorkatti told us, under no circumstances were we to offer to pay Obodas for his help. That would have been offensive. It would be saying we did not expect he had the substance or character to be a gracious host and provider like Gamilah.

When Obodas welcomed us into his home and later gave us free reign in this very large compound, we were very quick to thank him and to tell him how we feel secure and provided for in his care. We publicly gave him honor.

From that moment on, he became our *karim*. In Arabic, there is a word for hospitality and gracious generosity. It is *karim*. It is also the word for honor. It is also the name of one of their many gods. The *karim* is typically very wealthy and very respected. Under their care are many others who depend upon his or her graciousness and protection.

To be a *karim* is a source of great honor among the people. Generosity is not an act of charity here; it is an expression of the character of the *karim*.

How is the *karim* repaid for their graciousness? The recipients of their care are expected to "repay" with loyalty and gratefulness. That social capital is worth more than coin or even incense here in Axum.

The Roman philosopher Seneca wrote "Ingrates are the worst of a very bad lot."

"Murderers, tyrants, adulterers, robbers, the sacrilegious and traitors there will always be, but worse than all these is the crime of ingratitude."

On our trip, we were under the care and protection of the Nabatean princess Gamilah. Gamilah was our *karim*. If we needed anything or felt in danger, Gamilah would bend heaven and earth to make us well and secure. Gamilah was also the *karim* for Obodas and so he was more than pleased to honor her by caring for us now. Make sense?

You can be sure we have been very open with our praise for Obodas, our great Axumite *karim*.

We are learning we honor him when we ask him to help us with a need, even great ones—especially great ones. He welcomes ways where he can prove his character as a great *karim*—which he certainly has. We are grateful.

Back to my story. When I looked over my shoulder, I saw Obodas grinning from ear to ear. He was a thin man, maybe in his 70s, bald with wispy strands of white beard on his chin. His skin was very brown, almost black. His muscles sagged from age. His eyes were cloudy, but the man was full of so much energy and joy.

"I have a special gift for you Matthew ben Alphaeus" he spit out from the few teeth he had remaining. He regularly used my full name as a gesture of honor. "Two even. Maybe five." He laughed, his whole body shaking with joy.

It made me smile to watch my new friend enjoying the moment so much. We had grown close and though he had not followed Jesus—not yet—he was very curious.

He pointed behind him.

I couldn't believe my eyes.

There in the gateway stood Sorkatti and Gallio. A couple of months have passed, and we had long given up any hope of seeing them on earth. We assumed they were dead. But there they were.

I dropped what I was doing and ran to hug them. It didn't take long for the other ten to join us. It was a joyous reunion. We were dumbfounded.

Sorkatti did not look well. Her skin was sallow, and she coughed as she tried to breath. Her hair was flat and unkempt. But she was alive. Our Nubian princess brought back from the dead.

Gallio too was much thinner than I remember. His face grimaced as he moved. He had been hurt badly; it was obvious. But he also was so glad to be back with us. They had just about given up hope too.

We all gathered around the fountain with our extended family who were all curious about this magic—people raised from the dead. Truth told; they looked a bit like corpses.

Deborah made sure they were comfortable and had both wine and bread. When they were situated and ready, they told us their harrowing tale.

If you remember, the Roman soldiers who had kidnapped Sorkatti and the two young bedouin slaves from our ship, 'escorted' them in chains to an important Roman agent named Faadicha. He was Egyptian, tall, thin, and very black. His disposition was very severe and unnerving.

As Sorkatti and the two sickly teen bedouin slaves stood at attention, barefoot on the cold granite floor, the Egyptian and the Centurion held a side conversation. It was animated with raised angry voices. Sorkatti could hear only some of what they discussed.

They were very uneasy, Sorkatti observed. It seemed they had no idea how to deal with situation and so they were conspiring together how to move forward in a way that neither would be blamed.

Apparently, their last voyage had suffered even more losses, and they were very concerned this could not happen again—not on their watch. There were serious consequences if they didn't get this one right. One of them mentioned a Nichomachus Flavianus, apparently the Proconsul of Rome in Alexandria. They were clearly terrified of him and what he might do. He was not a compassionate person to say the least.

The Centurion was arguing it wasn't his fault. The Egyptian's eyes grew wide and retorted he was not going to be whipped this time.

In the end, as we feared, they decided the only way to move forward with minimal consequences from Flavianus was to substitute Sorkatti for the two sick bedouin.

We were shocked. In what world would that be a reasonable outcome? Sorkatti took a moment to gather herself. She clearly had many emotions to work through still. She took a deep breath, wiped tears away from her eyes and continued her story. We were spellbound.

Sorkatti looked to the ground as she described to us the next part.

The Roman Centurion commanded the two guards to forcefully strip her naked spinning her around so the Egyptian could rudely inspect her body. The Centurion spit, but Faadicha shrugged his shoulders and nodded in minimal approval.

Sorkatti said she never felt so violated. Didn't they know who she was? Didn't they know this is not done? But what could she do? She was naked, in a room with four men, two heavily armed. She could only cry. She had no one who would rescue her. No *karim*.

They locked all three in a small dark brig, smaller and viler even than the one on the ship. She argued for healing ointment of some kind for the slaves—and water, and clothing to replace her torn ones. She got the ointment.

Unbeknownst to her, Gallio had followed her to the Egyptian's compound. He was not allowed beyond the heavily guarded gate. Gallio expected this. He was no stranger to how the Romans, and it appears, the Egyptians, wielded power.

In his role as Marcus Gallio's estate manager, he had to do business with many bureaucrats, some who had authority, others who wanted it. While it is better to have more power, or better contacts—some leverage, the same results can happen through relentless noise.

He knew what to do and he worked quickly. He found the head guard and made a humble formal request for an audience with Faadicha. Then you wait. In this situation, you are at the mercy of the person with all the power.

A day past, then two, then a week. Gallio stubbornly persisted. Stubbornly kept making official noise and multiple requests. Still nothing. Gallio was becoming discouraged and wondering if the worst has already happened. Was Sorkatti even still alive?

Finally, after two weeks, he was roughly escorted into the lush office of the Egyptian. Gallio had spent a great deal of time doing some background on the Egyptian. While much was unsubstantiated, Faadicha was likely from the Egyptian royal line, a very distant relative to the crown. But his education and loyalty were to Rome.

His job was similar to mine in Capernaum. As I mentioned earlier, Ptolemais on the Hunt is the first Roman port for all legal shipping headed north in the Red Sea. Faadicha's job was to assess the value of the shipped goods and to calculate the tariff. It is a very important job. He must be a trusted servant, a man of respect and contacts. It also meant he was a very powerful player in the Roman incense trade machine. He is dangerous.

Sorkatti and Gallio guessed he owed his job and loyalty—and maybe his health—to Flavianus, the Proconsul in Alexandria.

Gallio described the luxurious offices of Faadicha in great detail. The vast walls were adorned with ivory, rare animal skins, mounted heads of huge elephants and rhinoceroses. It had lion hide rugs draped on the polished granite floors and elaborate iron candle holders throughout. Faadicha clearly enjoyed displaying his position and wealth. He was a man of some power and worth.

Though angry with the injustice Sorkatti had received, Gallio intentionally followed protocol. He ostentatiously bowed and complimented Faadicha on his status and wealth. Faadicha seemed pleased his worth was noticed, and he nodded in return.

Faadicha was an outwardly impressive man, standing a good 7 or 8 inches above Gallio and was wrapped in a bold colored leopard skin and even wore a crown—of the type of Roman Emperors might wear.

Gallio remained undaunted and asked for permission to speak and to make a request of the lord of the compound.

Faadicha nodded with little emotion—as if bored.

Gallio with a great flourish introduced himself. "I am Marcus Aurelius Libertus Gallio, the servant of Marcus Aurelius, great patrician of Tiberius in Galilee, a friend to Titus, emperor of Rome.

Faadicha was yet unimpressed and showed little concern and even less interest.

Gallio got to his point. "I am the protector of Sorkatti, a princess of the royal house of Nubia," he shamelessly stretched the truth a little bit. "I know she is here because I saw her enter. I have not left your gate since."

He went on to tell of the situation on the ship, "Clearly a misunderstanding," he injected. "I have come to have the Princess Sorkatti set free so we may continue our important journey."

Faadicha listened for a time but cut him off. "You are quite mistaken, freedman." He discerned from his name that Gallio had been a slave. He dismissively shook his head. "I have seen no princess, not on this trip. There were only a couple of very sick teenagers, two unimpressive bedouin who may not last the evening."

Gallio straightened his frame to show he was not intimidated by the tall Egyptian. "As I mentioned, my patron is Marcus Aurelius—a very wealth influential man—known by many in the court of Titus."

He paused for effect. "I can send an official letter to him. I am sure he will pay you whatever you would like to set the women free. What is your price? He will reward you greatly."

"As I said to you," Faadicha retorted impatiently, "While I am a man of business and would be more than willing to entertain such a negotiation, but I know of no Nubian princess, and I am weary of this audience."

He dismissively waved his hands and cried out "Guards! Remove this man."

Gallio resisted. As the muscled guards grabbed his arms on either side, he yelled at Faadicha, "Sir, you dare to dismiss the servant of Marcus Aurelius? This is a mistake; one you will regret. Desist this lie now, or else..."

His voice tailed off as one of the guards slapped the back of his head dazing him.

Faadicha abruptly waved to stop the guards. He slowly walked toward Gallio who now lay crumpled on the granite floor.

"Sir," Faadicha said in a voice sounding more snake-like than human, "I do not know of Marcus Aurelius, or Tiberius. I am not afraid of the Emperor. I _do_ fear the Roman Consul in Alexandria though."

He turned and walked away and issued a final order for the guards. "Flog this man, thirty-nine lashes, then take him to the garbage dump. But be gentle, we do not want some Jewish minor politician upset with us."

To Gallio he said with an evil indifference, "Do not return gelding. There is nothing for you here."

Gallio was stripped to his skin. Then he was whipped and dragged through the main market of Ptolemais on the Hunt and deposited at the dump south of the city. There he was left to die.

Fortunately, he was found by a compassionate stranger who nursed him back to health. It took another month. There was little Gallio could do.

"So, what happened?" I inquired impatiently. "What about Sorkatti?"

They both looked at Obodas. "Our new patron happened," said Sorkatti.

I don't know the entire tale, but when Obodas told us he would send an envoy to inquire about the well-being of our two people in Ptolemais on the Hunt, he did far more than that.

It did not take long for him to locate Sorkatti and Gallio. Fortunately, she was found before the next Roman ship heading south arrived at Ptolemais. Otherwise, she would be headed to India, never to be found.

That was just the beginning. Obodas knew Faadicha. He told us, "He is an evil man who would sell his own mother to India for the right price."

Obodas also knew how to deal with his type.

He immediately sent another servant to Alexandria to gain an audience with Nichomachus Flavianus. It surprised me to hear Obodas was well known and even respected by the Roman Proconsul.

The Romans did not want to do anything to further unsettle the already unsettled relationship with the Nabateans. When he heard a client of Obodas, and also of Gamilah, the Nabatean King's sister, was being held by Faadicha, he immediately ordered her to be set free and to put her in the care of Obodas.

So Faadicha did not know Marcus Aurelius and was not afraid of even Emperor Titus, but he was terrified of Flavianus, and Flavianus was fearful of our *karim* Obodas.

It was Obodas who paid to have Gallio cared for until he could travel again.

As I listened to this story, I laughed out loud. Obodas also was humbly listening but clearly felt very pleased with himself. This tale will be told in his community for many weeks. His status as a Great *Karim* will only grow.

I have recently found out what happened behind the scene. To have Sorkatti released, many favors were promised to Flavianus, in fact a whole series of favors costing Obodas dearly—though he never said anything. He is a *karim*, and we are in his care and protection. There is no money or favor beyond the pale.

I was so focused on Sorkatti and Gallio, I didn't notice for a long while they were accompanied by the two bedouin youth. They still had scars, but they looked like they are on the road to becoming healthy. It turned out, they too were set free, and both wanted to join Sorkatti. She welcomed them with open arms. She is now their *karim*.

And that's not all. They had also been adopted by a scraggly dog, very friendly. He had appeared out of nowhere on the ship to Adulis that Obodas lined up for them. It happened to be a Nabatean triangular-sailed lateen, feared by Rome and Egypt, but in Obodas' care, there was no safer place for them to be.

Oh, the teens names—and our two newest team members—are Shammar and Rashaida.

Sorkatti grinned a little and said, "We named the dog, Herod." That broke the tension in the courtyard, and we all got a huge laugh out of it.

I kneeled down to pet the tail-wagging ugly puppy. "That won't do of course," I said with a grin. "Too risky. It would offend someone. How about we name him Frank—short for frankincense?"

Everyone thought that was a perfect choice.

Now <u>we</u> were in the incense business.

I praise God, our celestial benefactor-patron, but also our earthly *karims*, Gamilah and Obodas. We are well taken care of.

And so back to the Rabboni. Now I can describe what happened on the hillside and on many other occasions.

Jesus willingly and intentionally became the *Karim* of those needy exposed powerless people, people without protectors, without guardians, without someone to care for them. On their own, they carried little or no social weight and were subject to abuse, rejection, injustices, shaming and even harm. Now they had a worthy patron far beyond what they would ever expect or demand. Greater than even Obodas.

Socially speaking, relationships with a patron is equivalent to wealth and power. The clients are not expected to repay the care with coin. The return capital is loyalty and gratefulness. The patron gains honor as the word goes out that they care for and sustain a large body of clients. They gain honor by their level of generosity and care. The clients gain honor based upon the amassed honor of their patron—his or her name—and their own willingness to be loyal and grateful.

In the Greek culture, there is the Euergeton. In Rome, it is the Patronus. In my tongue, we might think of Shepherd, or Savior, the Kinsman-redeemer, the Gibbor or the Righteous King.

Jesus says to the hapless people who came to the hillside some forty years ago now, "You who have come without any previous social standing in this shame honor culture, who have no patron, no kinsman redeemer, no *karim*—you do now."

The Rabboni was, from that point on, their celestial *Karim*. He was casting His lot with them and theirs with Him. They are now part of His eternal people of favor and worth. Now the mourners can dance. Jesus restored the music.

Why would Jesus do that? That is the mystery. It is easiest to say, "Because He says so." But so much more goes into it. This is of course, why Jesus came from Heaven to earth—to make a way for this transaction. This has been his heart from the very beginning and has not changed one iota. He feels mercy towards the helpless, the abused. He is innately the Great Celestial *Karim*.

This was the same passion that moved God to become the *Karim*-Patron-Benefactor for Abraham, for Israel, for David and for so many others. As wonderful as those relationships were, the magnificence of God is now even further expanded. He is the *Karim*-Patron-Benefactor for people like these multinationals in Galilee and now Axum. It is written,

"The LORD your God is right there in your midst. As the Gibbor –the mighty One—he rescues, he delights in you, he makes you quiet with his love, he rejoices over you with singing" (Zephaniah 3:17).

Surely, those former "unenviables" now experienced that very thing. They were then raised up to be "enviables".

Oh, and the crowd was indeed grateful. So many, even most of them showed it by following Jesus—for some it was at great personal cost. From their point of view, where else would one go? You follow honor. Nothing for them anywhere else.

Jesus was not just speaking religiously, or philosophically. He was proclaiming a social and relational transaction in time and place. These societal bottom-feeders are now the honored people of God and inextricably in His favor. Not due to their own innate honorability, or name, or perceived worth, but due to the name of their *Karim*. In a word, enviable.

They will never be the same.

"Enviable are those who were unenviable because God is now their *karim*."

8

Day 242 of the Axum Mission

Often, as Jesus said this first macarism, he would slowly repeat the opening *"Makarioi are the ptochoi"*, carefully articulating each word. Why? Well first, it is a good technique just to make sure everyone heard clearly. But also, in this case, it was because what he said was so outlandish.

Imagine a spectrum of humanity with the *ptochoi* on the one side. You would be hard-pressed to find a better single word for the opposite side of the spectrum than *makarioi*. In Jesus' opening line, we are told the two extreme opposites kiss in his mysterious presence. You can be *makarioi* and *ptochoi* at the same time. Unheard of. And quite confusing at first blush.

At the risk of interrupting the flow, I feel this would be a good time to address another question I am regularly asked.

What language did Jesus speak? I didn't think to be clear in the Gospel. I can tell you the Rabboni spoke many languages. He was very educated and fluent in Hebrew, Aramaic, Greek and even Latin. He was the ultimate communicator and generally spoke the language of the person he was speaking to. That makes it so very hard to translate his comments sometimes, to be sure.

For my missional purposes, with very few exceptions, I write entirely in Greek. It is the accepted language of the world and would be the way to reach the most people. As I write this, I am residing in Axum in Ethiopia. I am learning the native language, well, trying to.

But my point is they speak Greek quite well.

I had to be very careful when translating those things Jesus said in Hebrew or Aramaic into Greek. Sometimes the translation was elusive.

A case in point is related to this Greek word *makarios*. When Jesus spoke the nine (or more) makarisms, he said them sometimes in Aramaic and sometimes in Greek. I had to decide the right Greek word to use.

There are two main Greek options to potentially use: *makarios* and *eulogetos*. Both could be translated "blessed", "happy", "fortunate", "flourishing" and the like. And yet, they are indeed very different.

I should point out every time Jesus spoke the "blessed be's" in Greek, he always used *makarios*. There were other times, in other places when he would use *eulogetos*. This is important to a translator. It is our job to get it right, or at least as close to right as we can be. *Eulogetos* and *makarios* overlap semantically but in the end carry two different meanings.

Eulogetos speaks of a subject actively blessing an object. So, God blessed Abraham. Abraham's life was made better by God. All Jews would agree and say, "Amen!" Often, when God blesses women in the scrolls, they become pregnant. This is a good thing. That is the essence of *eulogetos*.

Makarios more reflects the person who has been blessed. It could be said of them that they are—as a result of being blessed—in a state where they are enviable—i.e., *makarios*. So, using my analogy, when Yahweh *eulogetos'd* women, they often became pregnant—they became *makarios*. Make sense?

When Jesus spoke to a largely Aramaic audience, the word he chose carries the same subtle connotation of being in an enviable experiential state of blissfulness and joy. That's it. *Makarios* comes the closest.

In no way was the Master implying he was teaching rules and principles which, if one did them well, more, or better, they would receive more of some heavenly blessing. That is the other Greek word.

Not at all. Jesus' intent was much closer to the Aramaic meaning, and by the way, the ancient Greek meaning.

The ancient Greeks poets used *makar* primarily of the gods to distinguish them as enjoying a blissful existence as opposed to the baneful existence of mortal humanity. To be *makar* is to be seen as having a home secure against adversity, to be untroubled by wind and rain, to enjoy perpetual sunshine, and enjoy oneself all day long. You need not be a god, just be in a state of divine favor and experience. If so, you were *makarios*. Enviable.

The ancient Greeks poets imagined an experiential divide separating the heavenlies from mortals. Suffering, injustices, and abuse are alien to the gods. The highest experience of honor, glory, joy, and identity are alien to the mortals. Until now, that is.

Think of an outside observer, looking at a person and their context and concluding they are really doing well. They are experiencing a blessed life—it is so clear to all who see. The descriptor to use is *makarios*.

The *makarioi* are humans who from the point of view of observers are living an enviable, divine-esque existence—honored, joyous, fortunate, blissful, in a life-giving community and relations, dancing, happy, an existence free from difficulties, struggles and the accursed everyday experience of mortality. They are in a state of joy previously limited to the realm of the gods.

Yes, we could say they had been subject to divine *eulogetos*, but Jesus was emphasizing their observable state. He wanted to communicate that from his point of view, the unlikely people on that hillside were experiencing —right then—something only the divine deserves. They were experiencing heaven's favor—a little or a lot. The heavens are theirs.

Of course, at first blush and maybe second, this was observably absurd. No one else would look at that gathering and have said they were *makarios*. Only him.

Remember earlier, Jesus had made great pains to heal many in the gathering. All kinds of maladies and afflictions: leprosy, paralysis, deafness, blindness, and even demonic possession. This crowd was wildly needy. They weren't living the life of the gods. Nowhere close. I can tell you the Jews who came would have expected they were being cursed by the Heavens for some reason. The opposite of *makar*.

Jesus disagreed. In his presence, their reality had changed.

By the way, the crowd hadn't come to hear someone tell them they were *makarios*. None of them expected to hear that. They wouldn't have believed it anyway. They knew there was nothing about them to suggest the joy of God might be moving through their lives. And then...Jesus.

You might say, and I agree, these people certainly didn't deserve *makarios*, or earn it, they weren't pursuing it, or reaching out for it. They had long given up. They weren't in a place where they were open for a *eulogetos*.

And yet, Jesus proclaims them as *makarioi*—with no requirements attached—hard to fathom. No one else in their right mind would ever look at this bunch on this hillside and have imagined them as *makarioi*. Other than Jesus.

It would not have been so provocative if Jesus had said *"Eulogeo* are you,"—meaning, "I wish you good life, or health, or honor"—like a good father would say over his son or daughter, or a priest might say "I bless you." That would have been a nice thing to say.

Or if Jesus had used it instructively. "Here is a new path to real *eulogetos* for you. Here is a list of nine things to do and if you do them right and enough, your pain and shame will be diminished a little—and you will feel blessed a little more, you will then experience the favor of God."

But no, Jesus said something far more absurd.

"You long-suffering miserable people <u>are</u> in a state of reception of divine *makarios*. You, here with me now, are in an enviable place—as you are. You came as people without status, rank, or honor. You are now people of the gift of grace. This is not the grace for the deserving alone that has left you out in the cold. This gifting is for the undeserving, a gift from God to an unfitting or helpless recipient. This gift in my hands for you is not a thing, or an idea, or a new set of rules needing to be adhered to, it is a divine dynamic raising the formerly disowned to a position of adoption usually limited to the divine and those in the favor of the divine. Such an indiscriminate gift may look to the undiscerning as foolish or dangerous. But God's reputation is not soiled by your touch, your reputation is lifted. This is an incongruous gift given without regard to the worth of the recipient. This gift is not for you alone. This grace energizes the recipient to action, to begin to love and show mercy to others. It is for you my Kingdom has come, and it will be full of those like you, recipients of this gift, of whom it can be said, 'You are God's, and He is yours'. You are both unenviable and enviable. Come and follow me and we will work out the paradox. You are under my care now."

Well, you can imagine the crowd didn't know how to respond. "Sure, he is a great healer, but what in the world was he talking about? Is the Rabbi so out of touch?"

Witnesses told me <u>before</u> Jesus spoke, they were feeling a wide range of things: hopelessness, anxiety, being marginalized, cynical, despised, unclean, impure, unwanted, like failures, lonely, ugly, depressed, afraid, resigned to a lowest of low status forever, ashamed, terrified—under water, disappointments to God—but they certainly didn't feel enviable. I think of how Sorkatti felt during the abuse by the Egyptian. Or Gallio as he was being flogged. Or the two bedouin youth, first unjustly kidnapped and then left to die uncared for as if animals.

Not *makarios*.

Imagine a mortal life with no divine joy or heavenly value. That was their lot—before Jesus.

In my own conversations with Jesus, I came to understand more of what all of this meant. In the Greek version of the Holy Scrolls I use, this word *makarios* is used two ways.

A person is in this enviable state of *makar* as they live a life pursuing wisdom and understanding, they fear God and depend upon him in all their ways, and they obey the prescriptions of Torah. Our very first Psalm says this.

"*Makarios* is the person who does not walk in the counsel of the wicked or stand in the way of sinners or sit in the seat of mockers. But his delight is in the law of the Lord, and on his law, he meditates day and night."

To put myself in the sandals of the men and women who came desperately to hear Jesus, this would have been discouraging—so very discouraging—if that is what he meant. Such a state of *makarios* would have been way out of their grasp.

For the Jews there, they might have expected this from the Rabboni—or feared he would say this and then tell them to leave and get their act together if they wanted God's *eulogetos*. No good news here for them either.

There is another type of man or woman according to the Torah and the Writings who find themselves in an enviable state of *makarios*. These are those fortunate who have, unbeknownst to them, found themselves rescued by the Lord[1] or they were for some reason chosen by God and brought into His court to live there in honor[2], or those whose sins have been dealt with by God himself, meaning they no longer need to fear God's measuring gaze[3]. What did they do to earn this blessing? Nothing. They were made *makarios* due to His efforts, not their own. It was due to a gift given by the heavenlies or a representative of the Heavens to the undeserving. This is indeed what Jesus meant.

Isaiah speaks of such a *makarios* people. He prophesizes there will come a time in the future when there will be a righteous King who will reign over God's people[4]. Because God Himself puts that King on the throne, God's people thrive.

It will be a time of righteousness and social justice. God's Spirit is poured out and brings surprising life and abundance. The people will no longer live in shame, but secure. They will finally be able to enter rest—something which was alien to the people on the hillside. These are ushered into the enviable state of *makarios* because the King did it all. They can only receive. Not because they have earned anything.

They follow because they are given a new heart with new motivation that considers others more than before and leans into hospitality and mercy. Where before, they looked inward, now there is a new center of orientation. They are beginning to love others over self.

This is what I have come to understand began to happen then and there in Galilee. Jesus was Isaiah's prophesied King. Under his rule, the unenviable become the enviable—a little. These people, from disparate tribes, families, and contexts, became the people of the Rabboni. A new priority began to displace former competitiveness, power struggles, victim mentality, sexism, looking for love in all the wrong places. The celestial dance enjoyed by both Wisdom and the Creator began again in the least likely place and hearts.

Oh, one more thing before I get back to my story. I am aware many of you readers do not have a Jewish background. So, when you hear 'Kingdom of

Heaven', you probably think of a fortress on a rise with a moat and guards with a palace and central throne, and crowns and such. But it is an idiom.

My people have historically veered away from speaking the name of God. Perhaps there is some anxiety and superstition involved, but we mean well. He is to be honored in all things. So, we speak of the 'Name.' But we mean Yahweh Himself. Same can be said of the idiom, the 'Kingdom of Heaven'. Don't imagine a physical Kingdom. We are referring to God Himself. Jesus tells this undeserving remnant, "God is yours." Stunning. Jarring. Maddening for many of the Jewish rabbinic scholars.

If you are not a Jew, you might miss the thing Jesus is saying. So put on your kippah and listen.

Do you know what made the Jews, Jews? Some argue it was circumcision. Some say it was the Temple or the Torah. While those are good answers, the more complete answer is this. They are the unique people of whom Yahweh proclaims, "I am your God, and you are my people."

For reasons of his own, God has blessed us with a unique enviable relationship with Him. It could be shortened to say, "God is ours and we are His" —or even shorter, "the Kingdom is yours."

On that remarkable day, on that hillside and many others afterwards, Jesus proclaimed those people in Galilee—Jews and non-Jews included, faithful Jews and unfaithful Jews, clean Jews, and unclean Jews as the new special people of God, sons, and daughters in good standing. In code, he said, "God is theirs and they are Gods." It was breathtaking.

Let me take it even further. "Enviable are the unenviable because God is yours." Jesus was provocatively saying to this crowd "He is now your mighty One. You are now His beloved."

Unimaginable until this moment in this place in the presence of the Rabboni.

What did they experience? How was this incongruous gift fleshed out in the lives and identities of real people? That's a great question of course. Some, a little. Some, a lot. In my next journal entry, I will attempt to share a few of the real accounts.

1. Dt. 33:29

2. Ps. 65:4

3. Ps 32:1

4. Isa 32.

9

Day 246 of the Axum Mission

Jesus smiled and repeated his first words. "You who came with no one envying your life or story—now you are people truly to be envied. Why? You are now a people of the High God Benefactor, the God of Glory."

There was a moment of silence—people looked at one another for clarification and a sweeping murmur rolled over the slope. All of that was awkwardly interrupted by an aged man just an arm's length below where Jesus sat.

"What did he say?" the broken old cripple far too loudly enquired of his daughter; you know the way a hearing-impaired person might misjudge how loud their voice is. The man was draped in tattered old clothes, his body painfully twisted and bent over, his wispy white hair helplessly blowing in the nearly constant breeze coming from the lake; red open sores covering the exposed parts of his emaciated body. He was not long for this world.

He and his daughter were sitting exposed to the Galilean sun, on one of the large black basalt rocks littering the southern slope. He leaned his tired head on his daughter's shoulder for support—and clearly, his hearing was almost gone.

"What did he say?" he loudly blurted out again, rolling his head slightly toward her face. "Tell me daughter...what did he say? Heaven is what?" For a moment, the crowd's attention was jerked away from Jesus. Only for a moment.

His daughter respectfully shushed him and said "The Rabboni said...," she looked down to the ground in thought wanting to get it right and to make it clear for her Abba. "He said you are *makarios*, Papa. And the Kingdom of Heaven is yours."

The old man blinked his nearly blinded eyes a couple of times probably to try to get a little focus. He rolled his head on her shoulder ever so slightly to look skyward. A peacefulness flowed over his face—his brow unfurrowed for the first time in a long while.

"The Kingdom?" He coughed a couple of times in an unsuccessful attempt to clear ever-present mucous from his lungs. "It is mine?"

"Yes Papa."

He paused.

And then, the most surprising thing. He laughed. "God is mine again?" He cried. Then he laughed out loud again. Not a mocking laugh, but a joyful hilarious one. It started as a deep resonant snigger—but then erupted as a guffaw. If he could, he would have danced.

Jesus, the great Rabboni, paused to intently watch as this scene unfolded as if the old man was an audience of one. He smiled and gazed directly into the face of this broken man.

Shockingly, the great Rabboni slid off the basalt boulder he sat on, took a couple of steps toward the old man, grabbed both of his old shaking hands, and danced with him—actually—for him. They both laughed. It was such an endearing scene. Jesus was fully there, fully engaged. He was like no other Rabboni ever. It was as if to say, "I feel that joy too, old man. That is why I have come. *Makar* is yours, enjoy! Enter your rest."

The old man, for a moment, in the smiling presence of Jesus felt the embrace of God, the arms of heaven reaching around him, hugging him, as he was, not as he should be or could be. He was in the highest possible sense, *lipnay Elohim*, an ancient Hebrew concept of being in the presence of God, but this time not anxious about God's wrath or disappointment but truly knowing God's favor toward him, close enough to see his smile over him, to feel his joy over him. He couldn't help but laugh.

I can testify laughter and gratefulness are most often fingerprints of what worship looks like in Jesus' Kingdom. Laughter and dancing are the most common fruit of a person becoming *makarioi*—blessed or enviable.

To put it another way. In this new Kingdom, the *ptochoi* (the poor in Spirit), those who believed they have no hope for joy, happiness, real intimacy, feeling valued—and who know they cannot and won't be able to dig themselves out of the holes they are in--they are the ones who now find themselves *makarioi*. They dance at last—as they are—not as they should be or should have been. Quite a surprising thing, really.

The *ptochoi* would never ever expect that. They haven't felt the urge to laugh for some time. They had long given up on experiencing *makarios*.

Healing all the physical ailments among the crowd was great, but in the end temporary. Jesus has come to rescue *ptochoi* from their shame and celestial loneliness. Physical healing is great, but it does not accomplish such rest—far from it. Jesus' goal was not just health, but *makarios*.

I know this now to be true. I have said it before, but it is important. You <u>can</u> be *ptochoi* and *makarioi* at the same time. You can be deeply wounded, suffering from ongoing shame, a discard from society, impaired and broken and still be in a remarkable place of the *makarioi* favor of the heavens.

I am sad to report the old man died just a week or so after this audience with Jesus. I know this because his daughter shared the account with me personally. She is now part of my mission team here in Axum. Bernice is remarkable by the way. I do not think we could do this without her. She has single handedly organized our work for the impoverished in the tribal regions of the desert. I taught her accounting and finance and now she runs it all.

Bernice told me she brought her dad that day, at great cost and sacrificial effort, because on top of all his physical issues, he had also been suffering for a long time from a deep malaise. She told me that as a young man, he had great faith in God, but he had some time before, just stopped believing—in fact stopped saying anything at all.

He would wake up in the morning and just silently sit in his chair staring at the barren wall, until it was time to go to bed again. She couldn't remember the last time her father smiled much less laughed—until he engaged Jesus—or better Jesus engaged him.

Jesus' gift for him had changed something in him. Then, until he died, his depression was changed to joy, every day, until his last breath on earth. His last words were about hearing angels laughing over him—and then he quietly was brought to his fathers with a smile still on his face.

In his last few days, he had become a mighty witness, a living testimony of Jesus' unique Kingdom.

10

Day 260 of the Axum Mission

One more story—there are so many—of that day. In a clump of palm trees not far from where the old man now danced was another group of women. One, Callista—whose name means 'beautiful one' in the Greek, just shook her head in derision at Jesus' words.

Callista was not her real name. She was a Jewess, once. She had been married to a righteous man—or so he said. They had a couple of children and lived comfortably in a small village in the Decapolis. There came a time when he grew tired of her and gave her a writ of divorce. She did not see this coming at all. To make matters worse, the synagogue supported him and granted his request. Instantly she was thrown into poverty—a deep drowning structural poverty.

She could not stop the downward spiral. Her family turned away from her. This was an honor-shame culture, and they did not want to share her shame.

What could she do? Because of her divorce, even the few jobs open to women in her village were put out of her reach. She could beg—and would have for her family's sake—but we all know how the righteous-non-shamed others feel about having to see such shame every day. It is so uncomfortable to have such a person hanging around begging every day—a constant reminder of how fast a fall could be. No one wanted the intrusion—or the subconscious threat.

No matter how hard she begged, at the end of the day, she was not able to feed her children. So, she turned to the one occupation that embraces such a shamed one. She moved to a nearby city, one that serviced the Via Maris and became a prostitute.

Her choice? Some would critically and judgmentally say 'yes'. She would say she had no choice. Now there was no turning back. There is no *makarios* for her type. Life is what it is for the unclean. Dramatic clothes and deepening make-up help to cover the decline of her beauty—but there was no relief from the inner nagging shame—the deep ongoing sadness, and yes, the loneliness. She would dance too—if she was paid enough—if it made her more coin—but not because she felt the joy. At first, she didn't relate at all to the crazy outlandish notion of being *makarioi*.

By the way, she expected nothing from God either, other than judgement. Or worse, she expected only to see disappointment in his face. That's what she would do if she were Him.

Do you know the pain of that? *Ptochoi* do. Her life's hole was so deep. Sure, she had dug some, but it was not all her fault. She could see no way out. She would tell you there were days she contemplated taking her own life—but to what end? Just so she would more quickly stand in front of Yahweh as Judge? No need to rush fate.

Sure, Jesus can convince an old foolish man to dance—but she has heard it all before. She will not be disappointed again. She will never be sucked into such emotionalism.

She would tell you she didn't know why she came. Many of her clients had heard Jesus speak and said she might enjoy the show. She told each "No!", but secretly came with two friends and stood back in the shadows of the small oasis.

Do you know what made her shake her head? She had heard the very same word recently from a newer wealthy client. "*Makarios* are you, woman."

Men were all alike. She didn't feel *makarios* then or now. Why would she? She was an object to be used for the pleasure of others—and to be paid for it. That was her value—what the market would bear. Nothing more. Nothing less. Joy? Too expensive for her and her type. The peace of the gods? Absurd—beyond absurd.

But, then Jesus.

As she watched the Rabboni dance with the old man, something cracked inside her. It was more than a feeling, more than an awareness, or a new strength, or even a new hope. She felt something she hadn't known for a long, long time, honor. Jesus didn't walk to her and grab her hands—that wouldn't have gone well—she was still in too much pain—but even from where she was maybe fifty feet from Jesus, she felt the power.

She was embraced—that is how she puts it—by invisible arms. She felt special for a second, her—the prostitute, the shamed wife, mother, and failed Jewess—as she was. Though she stubbornly refused to dance then and there, something inside of her dared to.

How do I know this? She is now my wife. She has no reason to have made this story up.

I get kidded all the time of being a new Hosea, you may remember, the prophet who was commanded by God to marry Gomer, a prostitute—a symbol of God and his pursuing love for the *anawim* (my people's tongue for the *ptochoi*).

First, I am no Hosea. Far from it. And Deborah, oh yes, that is her Hebrew birth name, is no Gomer. Deborah would have done anything she could have to be rescued from her life, from her shame, from her bad choices, from what was done to her unfairly, what was taken from her, the reduction in her identity every time she allowed a man or woman to abuse her so—but she could not.

She didn't have that kind of power. Her life-hole was so tragically deep, so digging further was mere foolishness. She had no time for such foolishness.

She changed that day—or better—was changed—a little. To put a name on the change—let's use *makarios*. And to make a long story short, she sold all she had and followed Jesus. She stayed at a distance for days. Deep chronic shame dies so slowly. She told me for a long time, she wanted to remain anonymous, afraid of how people would look down at her or reject her. She couldn't take that. She still used her Greek name. Until one day, she danced. Deborah danced.

Now? She is one of our most powerful spokespersons for the Kingdom Gospel of Jesus to men and women alike. She has become her namesake, the prophetess Deborah, the great woman Judge of Israel. Her favorite talk starter is "Every saint has a past, and every sinner has a future." She is so right.

When Jesus said "*Makarioi* are the *ptochoi to pneumati*. Theirs is the Kingdom of Heaven", he had their attention. Nothing was more unlikely. Nothing was more improbable. Thank the Heavens, He didn't say,

"*Makarioi* are the *ptochoi* who figure it out, or who work harder, or who choose to follow my principles or teachings, or who bring suitable sacrifices, or say this mantra, or give all to the poor, or who stop their addiction, or who are willing to admit their inabilities, who are open to healing".

No. He said the long-expected Kingdom of God would be made up of rescued *ptochoi* such as us—as we are—but it would not leave us as we are.

This new Kingdom Jesus proclaimed was now right here in the middle of the crowd and surrounding it as well—the former refuse of this world are now embraced by the Heavens. They experience what only God does. Unbelievable, except for one thing. Jesus said so and His power is inexplicable.

It wasn't the words of Jesus that convinced the *ptochoi*—clearly. The *ptochoi* are very resistant to slick talking heads casting out promises of better things. They had been burned before and had quick triggers for boundaries. No, it wasn't just the words.

It wasn't how Jesus said the words. It was Jesus, there, present, his remarkable thick empathy radiating out toward the previously untouchables.

It was also something else. There was a power that flooded across the hillside that day and every day Jesus spoke. It was power making *ptochoi* experience *makarioi*. It made them feel honored and a little bit honorable. It made them feel respectable. It made them feel pure, clean, whole—in a word, enviable—a little. It made them feel less anxious about what God feels toward them. It made them, for a moment, feel God dancing over them, as they were. It made them receive and want more.

Well, forgive me. I am ranting. But I need to stop here to take a breath. In my interviews of those who were there at the beginning—and then later after—*makarios* is one of the words Rabboni used the most.

It is the one word of the Rabboni I hold most dearly.

11

Day 282 of the Axum Mission

With the Rabboni came something wildly new. This, it turns out was always here, but unseen, living deep in the shadows of old hallowed scrolls of my people. But we failed to see or admit it. It is wonderful and disturbing. It is revolutionary. I can see why the powerbrokers in my religion reacted so horribly to it. It is not what they understood about God.

Let me explain. One of the most important stories for young Jews was the faithful work of Eliezer the servant of our patriarch Abraham. Abraham had given him specific instruction to choose a suitable bride for his son Isaac from among his own people, his own tribe. He didn't want to soil his family by choosing from among the unrighteous Canaanites. This was just the way things were done. It makes sense humanly speaking. "Find a righteous bride for my son."

This is a very important charge. I wouldn't have wanted to be in Eliezer's sandals, to be sure. What could go wrong, right?

So, he traveled to his master's homeland and came upon a well.

Now that I think about it, so many of our good old Jewish tales include a well. Surely it speaks of our thirst in so many ways. I digress.

There was Eliezer with an impressive entourage, of camels burdened with gifts, surrounded by skilled and trained guards with swords strapped to their belts—an impressive show of substance and worth—and a well—at the very time in the cool of the evening when young maidens go to collect water for their families.

All young Jews memorize Eliezer's humble prayer. I am old and yet I still can say it well.

"O LORD, God of my master Abraham, give me success today, and show kindness to my master Abraham. See, I am standing beside this spring, and the daughters of the townspeople are coming out to draw water. May it be that when I say to a girl, 'Please let down your jar that I may have a drink,' and she says, 'Drink, and I'll water your camels too' — let her be the one you have chosen for your servant Isaac. By this I will know that you have shown kindness to my master."[11]

It was Rebecca who came and fulfilled the prayer to the letter. She was one of Abraham's nieces and it turns out a glorious and most suitable choice as a righteous and faithful wife for Isaac. In short order, she became the Matriarch of the Jewish people, revered and spoken of as one greatly favored by God. One who was worthy.

This was the first recorded *shidduch* –or the process of 'matchmaking'—in the Torah. That practice remains today among God's people in Judea and even among the Jews here in Axum. No one would want to leave such an important event as marriage to the emotions and lusts of young men and women. Or chance. What a tragedy it would be if the wrong suitor was found for your child?

Ultimately the choice is God's, of course, and yet great pains are taken to investigate to be reasonably sure the union would be righteous and lead to peace and happiness. We want righteous people of faith, not uncircumcised idolater Canaanites—to borrow from our tale.

We have such *shadchans* in every town—even the smallest of villages, who are trained as Eliezer-esque matchmakers. It makes sense. What family wants to besmirch the name and honor of their family by marrying into a family of little or no honor. Honor is very fleeting, hard to build up and easy to lose. How many families have become shamed by an incongruous marriage?

Then the Rabboni came, and proclaimed God does things differently—and this remains so hard for me to get my arms around even to this day. So non-Jewish—so un-kosher.

It turns out God is not looking to wed himself with a worthy bride—or a righteous bride.

No. As evident on this hillside in Galilee, and even before with the calling of the disciples—including my own call—God intentionally pursues a people who are a total mismatch for him, unsuitable brides, even dangerous partners. One might fear God's reputation would be sullied by such union. But hear this—this _is_ His glory.

When He romantically embraced the soiled, those who have no name, his name remains honored. The unworthy becomes a person of stunning unimaginable and unearned worth.

This was what Jesus did—over and over—in multiple and diverse settings. The Rabboni came as the celestial _shadchan_ charged to gather those most unfit and unworthy for the wedding celebration of the Great Celestial King, His Father.

This is why I, a Jew, can go—and want to go—to such far-away places as Axum to tell the unsuitable here of a God who courts and weds to himself the maidens who would never be found in a righteous marriage. I am not sent just to the Jews here. I am sent to all.

God is pleased to wed to himself unworthy people from all tribes and cultures. Not just the high and mighty. In fact, His greatest glory is to find brides among the most desperate and soiled maidens from the most shamed families. He embraces and adores the _ptochoi to pneumati_. This is our God. This is His Gospel for hurting, powerless, and enslaved humanity.

Another point from the Eliezer story. Rebecca was changed by the union, as we can see by the massive show of wealth and glory that was brought as a gift for her family. She was raised from her past social status to something far more glorious. Her name became a great name—not due to anything she did—not based upon her righteousness, or inherent goodness. We know very little about her. Her pre-marriage glory and identity was not important to the story. What was important was who she became due to the marriage.

She became the envy of her tribe and family. From an unenviable maid to an enviable Queen of great status, all based upon her father-in-law's glory—not hers. She became enviable when she became the daughter-in-law to Abraham.

Here is what I am seeing more and more. That is exactly what happened on that hillside. Those people from all over the region, some circumcised, many uncircumcised, the sick, the unclean, the pagans, the atheists, the marginalized, all people—unenviable—"none righteous, no not one"[22] the scrolls proclaim, became highly enviable the moment Jesus uttered his first word.

Is it right to say the event on the hillside was a wedding of sorts? Yes, absolutely. I know how it sounds—and yet—a new union was confirmed, God and his newest unworthy Queen bride.

There, the unenviable were made enviable because God became theirs and they became God's. It is a unilateral wedding vow.

I can now see where the healings fit into the story of the Rabboni and his charge. The healings were not the biggest things that happened that day, as amazing and shocking as they were.

I saw them. People horribly twisted and crippled began to walk. One man hopped up and down in a fit of laughter. Those who couldn't see, most from birth, now saw. People who were violently controlled by unseen powers, invisible demons, became free. Rashes removed; bleeding stopped. Unbelievable things, unimaginable things, each took our breath away.

These unbelievable miracles, as good as they were, were not the big deal of the day. No. They were mere token signs of the vastness of the glory of the Groom. Like the promise-gift Eliezer brought, they were token gifts given by the groom to the family of the bride-to-be to reflect the glory their young daughter is in store for, what is waiting for her in the wedding celebration and union.

To say it differently. If you are impressed by the healings—and who wouldn't be—you will be more than stunned by the marriage and the resulting change of status.

Jesus didn't come to just heal diseases or sicknesses. Those were only the first fruits of the plan. Those were teasers. I am not the first to point out that all those healings were temporary. Such is the human condition. The union they point to is eternal. Amen?

The Rabboni's charge was to consummate the marriage, the transformation in status from little to great worth, beyond what the bride deserved, or her family could ever hope for her.

In a mysterious moment, those unworthy people on the hillside became the beloved bride of God. I saw it with my own eyes.

When the Rabboni first sat before them, the people in the crowd had so little in common with each other. The Syrians would have nothing to do with the Judean Jews. The families from the Decapolis would sit together, drawn by a common worldview and politics. The Judean Jews were concerned about becoming impure if they even touched Galilean Jews. The Nazarenes seemed to be largely attracted to other angry Nazarene Jews.

To be clear, before the Rabboni began speaking, there was very little comradery or fellowship among the people there.

The hillside was divided up by the haves and have nots, the pure and the less pure, the right and the un-right. Though unseen, there were cultural dividing walls, destructive tribalism.

Tragically, they were unwilling or unable to see what they had in common—their mutual need—far outweighed what they had against each other.

After Jesus' proclamations, most of these folk mysteriously became a part of a great new tribe—those who followed the Rabboni. His disciples. Not perfectly—not totally homogenous, don't misunderstand me.

It was as if a huge wall had been torn down. They shared a newly birthed, single priority, to follow Him. Even I could see the birth pangs of something new.

I have heard many stories of new acts of hospitality, awkward to be sure, but new generosity and warmth not witnessed before.

One sad young man had been blind from birth. He came to Jesus helpless and isolated—or better, Jesus came to him. His family had pulled back from him. It was considered in some religious circles shameful to give birth to one considered cursed by God. Rumors swirled around them naming possible sins they might have committed for which God was rightly punishing them. Their once proud family name quickly was kicked to the mud. They did the same thing to their young son. This was not unheard of or rare in our communities. Impurities are to be purged. Face is to be protected.

To survive, he begged, day after day, and barely survived into his teens. As I understand it, he had not heard from his father for over a decade. He was an orphan, without a name, without any hope.

Then the Rabboni. In a moment, in a single touch, his sight became whole. But more than that, he became on that hillside, a person of honor for the very first time. Multiple families embraced him (something previously unheard of for him) and opened their tables for him. His name? Michael. He came unnamed and now his name is resurrected from the dead. He, like me, is a disciple of Jesus.

Jesus unleashed a new power upon our world. He brought the unlikeliest together. Jesus was forming the people of God.

What was promised to the Jews is now offered to all. Jews too. Now, after the Rabboni, there is no one outside the reach of this unbelievable gifting. No one. Including me. Those who enter the marriage now see the world and others differently. We have been changed.

Enough of the personal digressions. There are eight macarisms left to discuss. You will be surprised and moved.

Jesus opened the good news this way. "I tell you the good news, it is these unenviable who are now to be envied, because God is their *Karim* and Husband."

---

1. Gen 24:12-14.

2. Ps 14:3.

12

Day 330 of the Axum Mission

I think this is a good place to clear up another common misunderstanding. A few weeks before the Rabboni's shocking proclamations on the slope there was another event I reported briefly in the Gospel, and I now want to unpack it a little bit more.

After John's arrest by King Herod Antipas, Jesus somehow knew the time for his ministry had come. The long awaited final race was begun.

He had been waiting for His Father's sign before he moved from relative obscurity in the Jewish village of Nazareth to open shop on the wide-open Via Maris. Some advised him to be careful and build up his followers before he makes such a bold move. But alas, the Rabboni only listened to one indistinguishable voice.

Still, his plan was not to go solo. In our community, if you felt the call to ministry, you would pursue a Rabbi, make your case, pull all the strings you can in hopes to become one of the few followers of this or that teacher. There was great honor in being a chosen student of a respected Teacher. This is exactly what Reuben did to become a student of Gamaliel.

Jesus just didn't do things the usual way. He pursued—what would appear to the unwise eyes—the most unlikely, unqualified students anyone could imagine. I include myself in that number.

As I reported in the Gospel, Jesus was actively listening to His Father's voice and walking along the northern shore of the Sea of Galilee, weaving in and out of the many fishermen and boats there. He 'happened' to come across, two brothers Andrew and Peter. Andrew had been one of the many John had baptized weeks earlier and had even become a disciple of John for a time. Peter, well, he was Peter. Neither were educated or schooled in the Torah or Writings. Neither were independently wealthy by any measurement. They were blue-collar fishermen.

But then Jesus.

Jesus stood on the shore, and he yelled loud enough to be heard over the waves, "Hey, you two, become my disciples. You are to become people-fishers."

As Rabboni spoke, he moved his arms like he was casting a net. They have told me his smile was disarming of course. But that is not why Peter and Andrew dropped everything they were doing and immediately followed Jesus.

I should have dug into this more in my first account, but I thought its brevity communicated the vastness of the miracle.

Look, no one in their right mind would just immediately put their nets down and follow. There would be a discussion between the Rabbi and the prospective students. Guidelines would be laid out and negotiated. Money was likely involved. Family would have been brought into the discussion. There would have been fasting and prayers to God for wisdom. At least they would have responsibly made sure the family was informed, the assets put into the hands of a trusted individual and then perhaps a bath to wash off the dead fish smell.

None of that happened. Andrew and Peter went from being career fishermen to Jesus-followers in a heartbeat. Greek philosophers speak of a *causa sui*, an event that causes subsequent events and choices to change their former trajectory. We prefer to speak of a miraculous causal power that changed the direction of two rather unremarkable lives.

Both men would tell you something happened inside of them. At that moment, they wanted nothing more than to be with Jesus. And so, they went. I wish I could explain it more, but, like I said, it was a targeted invasive miracle. The very same thing happened to me.

This was the first time we witnessed the life changing power of Jesus' words. In his Kingdom, this was how disciples were made. It is a miracle—think the parting of the Red Sea.

When Jesus calls, people follow. People for reasons unknown before, want to follow.

The very same thing happened to James and John. Jesus called. They followed. Like the two previous men, they wanted to. It wasn't as if Jesus abused them or belittled them. No, he motivated them to become people of honor, people who were enviable. Sound familiar? They went from unenviable lives to enviable when Jesus spoke. Jesus, the Son of God, became their Patron-Benefactor. They became his clients.

Also, I want to say, the calling to be a disciple did not make anyone perfect, or more righteous, or wiser or feel like their sins were forgiven. I can say that personally for a fact. It just made us want to be a Jesus-follower, step-by-step, loaded with questions, anxieties, and second thoughts. We brought our flaws. All we knew was something special had happened and we were now with him, and he was with us.

This was the very same power that rolled out on the hillside in Galilee. When Jesus proclaimed this mess of humanity enviable, they—many or most of them—would have indeed felt their shame decline a little or a lot. They would have felt honored and loved a little—some for the first time in their tragic lives. They would have felt less unclean, less losers. I saw it. I felt it. This is what Jesus did. They would have felt empowered a little.

That is why crowds flocked to him. Of course, many wanted to be healed. But also, people who were in the presence of the Rabboni, who listened to his words, began to feel honored again, more than they had in a long time. I wish we could package this power, make it into an elixir or a magic talisman. But it was Jesus and His powerful Spirit. It was his gaze, his presence, and his words. It was wonderful.

Why did this need to be cleared up and expounded upon? The very last thing Rabboni said to us before he was lifted into the Heavens was that we should do what he did, going into all the world and make disciples too.

Well, the only thing we knew about making disciples was how he did it.

He said, "Follow me" and people did, and wanted to. After he was gone, we had many conversations about this. How are we going to do that? We can say "Follow me" or even "Follow the Rabboni" and honestly, we didn't expect any results. We didn't have his power. Nobody felt better because we were in the room. Do you know what I mean?

We concluded the Rabboni had told us what to do and how to do it—sort of. He said, "I am with you always."

Here's how we understand what he said now. It has served us well. We do what he did and proclaim the gospel to hurting lost people, we bless the unblessed, and then boldly bid those people to "Follow Jesus." His Spirit then goes forth and does what He does. He makes people—just like us—follow Him.

We understand it is not about us, or how well we communicate, or how reasonable we try to make it sound. No. We are learning to daily rely on the Spirit of the Rabboni to make disciples. We can't do it on our own.

It makes me smile as I have spoken to new disciples of the Rabboni. I have not met one who can describe what happened to them. Only, they were once doing their own thing and living their own lives, and the very next moment, they couldn't help but follow Jesus. They dropped their nets, or their books, or their swords, or their plowshares and nothing was the same. And they have never, ever regretted the change. Me too.

The only common response is something like, "But I still can't understand why me?"

Me neither.

Lest I forget, let me say this over you, the reader, "Follow Him, as you are. You will never be the same".

Back to the hillside.

13

Day 365 of the Axum Mission

It is hard to believe we have been on our mission trip for an entire year. We have grown very close as a team. And we have seen many follow the Rabboni. We are grateful to the Spirit and His workings. Praise God, indeed. Tonight, we are holding another Todah meal to commemorate the year. God has been more than good to us. He is our heavenly *Karim*.

I want to pick up where I left off with Jesus' words on the hillside in Galilee. He said,

> *"Enviable are the inconsolable ('penthein' in the Greek tongue)*
> *because I will bring them close to me and they're under my care,*
> *they will finally experience real comfort."*

Oh, the desperateness of much of the human condition. One of our prophets says even the land itself mourns and all who live in it are wasting away[1].

Alas, in my youth, I was largely blind to the pains and turmoil around me. I was insensitive to it. Sure, I would give to beggars a coin, old shoes. I don't remember if I did it because I really wanted to ease their load. I do not suspect I imagined them at all in any human way. I suspect they did not leave our transaction feeling comforted either. I turned a blind eye to slavery—like our two new team members.

I cared little for the many widows or their children who were perishing for lack of food. I cared little for those who had fallen into debt to the Romans. My job was just, I concluded. They should have known better—taxes are taxes.

I am being honest here. I chose to turn a blind eye to the struggles of so many swirling around me. I was safe.

No one came to me for real comfort. Why would they?

Hear me when I say what I have witnessed—time and again-- something so starkly 'other'—something that truly condemns me in contrast. It shames me, exposes me—and it challenges me.

I have seen the most broken people, people who lived in their pain and sorrows in the fearful shadows of our world—flock to Jesus—come physically near to Him—feeling welcomed—feeling invited to be that close. There, in his presence, they feel comforted by Him.

Our world has people in authority, people whose job it is to bring earthly and emotional comfort to people, many of whom are well-meaning.

There are also those who bring justice to those who have been unfairly treated, abused, robbed, and so bring closure, consolation, vindication, and peace. Of course, all human institutions are flawed and must live within their constraints.

And yet I have seen with my own eyes something astonishing in the presence of the Rabboni.

In the real presence of their new patron benefactor Jesus, such inconsolables exactly experience something remarkable—not perfectly—but real. They feel comforted.

In very few cases does Jesus restore what they lost. It's not about that as much as something new is ushered into their void. Maybe Isaiah speaks about this very thing?

"The desert and the parched land are glad; the wilderness rejoices and blossoms. Like the crocus, it bursts into bloom; it rejoices greatly and shouts for joy. The glory of Lebanon will be given to it, the splendor of Carmel and Sharon; they will see the glory of the LORD, the splendor of our God.

Strengthen the feeble hands, steady the knees that give way; say to those with fearful hearts, "Be strong, do not fear; your God comes, he comes with vengeance; with divine retribution he comes to rescue you." Then will the eyes of the blind be opened and the ears of the deaf unstopped. Then will the lame leap like a deer, and the mute tongue shout for joy. Water will gush forth in the wilderness and streams in the desert. The burning sand will become a pool, the thirsty ground bubbling springs. In the haunts where jackals once lay, grass and reeds and papyrus will grow. And a highway will be there; it will be called the Way of Holiness...the redeemed walk there, and the ransomed of the LORD will return. They will enter Zion with singing; everlasting joy will crown their heads. Gladness and joy will overtake them, and sorrow and sighing will flee away."[2]

For those who are chronically inconsolable this can be a remarkable thing, to begin to see this, to experience this as in the beginning throes of birth.

The people on that hillside, and the many who came into the sphere of Jesus, now know of a Patron-Benefactor who not only rescues the lost, but comforts them, consoles them, and opens a deluge of joy within them.

Who would not find this attractive? Who would not find this wonderful? Who doesn't need this? I desperately need that joy. In fact, I think I am now addicted to it.

Joy can come from a lot of places. But this joy has weight and substance. Not a fake-it-until-you-make-it thing. It can grab hold of the most tragically emptied soul, the one who has suffered abuse and disrespect over and again, the one who has lost everything and cries out that darkness is their closest friend—and it can make them feel hope and joy—a little or a lot. Only in his presence. In fact, due to the presence of his Spirit and power.

I suspect when he first said it on that hillside and in other places as well, it would have been flat out rejected. No one expected such a transaction from some itinerate rabbi.

Then, one after another, the depressed, the emotionally harassed and beat-up, those who had suffered chronic social injustice came and received his compassionate touch. In that moment we could imagine sheep flying like birds, or fish teaching Rabbinic schools—these distressed people laughed.

As I try to explain this to people, I often use the metaphor of two contrasting mountains on display. There is this so-called mount in Galilee where Jesus taught and then there is the contrasting Mount Zion—upon which Jerusalem and the Temple reside—a few days journey south.

I have never ever heard of Jewish visitors to the Temple in Jerusalem who say there they experienced such a comfort, such a consolation. There are no testimonies I am aware of such a transformation on the steps of the Temple.

But up in the north, in this very unlikely place, involving a rabble of disparate many fractured people, there were so many stories of experiencing a new comfort. Something new was here.

I tell you, if you suffer inconsolably from loss, abuse, depression, anxieties of any kind, I beg you, run to Him, the Rabboni. Don't wait until you have your questions answered. Bring your shame, your pain, your unbelief, your rage, your loneliness, your history—just come—and hold empty hands skyward into his presence, into his smile, into his embrace and be ready for anything.

Jesus said,

> *Enviable are you, the inconsolable. because I bring you close and comfort you myself.*

---

1. Hos 4:3.

2. Isa 35:1-10.

14

Day 379 of the Axum Mission

Enviable are the humiliated, they will experience the fulfillment of all the promises of God.

I have spoken to many Jews who were there that day. They told me of their immediate visceral reaction to this proclamation. The land of promise, Jesus said, is now given to these people?

No Jewish Rabbi would ever say such a thing. The promise of the land is one of the most sacred and closely held commitments of God to his people. In the sacred scrolls, God made the pledge to Abraham, and to Isaac.

"I am God Almighty; be fruitful and increase in number. A nation and a community of nations will come from you, and kings will come from your body. The land I gave to Abraham and Isaac, I also give to you, and I will give this land to your descendants after you."[1]

The land. Of course, if you are a Jew, you lament your promised inheritance is no longer yours—at least not while it is occupied by others. But you know, you hope, you pray that sometime, soon, God will defeat the Romans and return the land to the descendants of Abraham.

Now Jesus stands on the hillside and literally gives the land away to a collection of strays and rejects—with seemingly no previous attachment to any promise. You are the inheritors of the land.

It is the same as saying, "Everything God had promised Abraham is now yours." Not just the land. It is a figure of speech that would include the blessings of glory, people, and kingdom.

Is Jesus saying God has had a change of heart regarding Israel? Or that Israel had finally failed to live up to the legal aspects of the promise and now must give up all rights to others? Or is there something else at play here?

I have come to see from trying to piece together the clues in Jesus' words and his ongoing conversations with us, Jesus was proclaiming not an end or a new beginning, but the expansion of the old that had been misunderstood.

God's heart and passion had never been exclusive to just one tribe of people. His bold movement has always been to the larger expression of descendants of Adam and Eve. Oh, of course, he chose to use Abraham, and Israel in that goal. For that alone, Israel is to feel glory and honor, but it was not all about them—ever.

As Jesus gazed into the eyes of one Syrian woman who had been violently raped by some thugs in her home village and subsequently forced into abject poverty and disgrace, and rejected by her former family and tribe, he longed for her to know the glory of God, the abundant love of the Creator toward her, his consolation for all loss she had known here.

She was given the 'land.'

As Jesus held the blinded Jew in his arms who had only known dishonor and the paltry existence of a beggar, Jesus extended to him social value. The blindman inherited the land—not some quarter acre parcel—but that place of honor in Yahweh's Kingdom.

As Jesus cast out demonic battalions from the man who had been stripped of all humanity, he gave him a throne alongside him in this relational Kingdom—never again to be resigned to disgrace and abuse—but to begin to feel love—his peace.

Jesus' strategy is not about a piece of land. It is about a new experience of royalty and honor for those who only have known the opposite, the humiliated, the '*praus*' (in the Greek language).

As I mentioned, in my earlier Gospel, I edited the many beatitudes of Jesus down to these nine. I remain happy with my choices. These first three are so similar particularly in the objects of Jesus' desires. They are ultimately the same person. They are all of us. If you feel beat up, tortured, sad, suicidal, overlooked, oppressed, generally like a failure, falling short of expectations, this is you.

To one degree or another, we all have come to Jesus stuck in the functional wrecks of our lives. We can keep digging to get ourselves out of this bog, but it hasn't worked. It won't work. This world groans. If the truth were known, all of us need a rescuer.

All of us, to one degree or another have experienced loss, injustices, unbearable pain that cannot be consoled—at least not here. We long for comfort—but there is none to be found—not really.

Then there are the *praus*—the Greek word Jesus used, the bullied, the tread upon, the humiliated. What can they hope for? In our world, the strong are victorious, the warriors, the wise, the beautiful, the wealthy, the evil, the bullies, the ones in power. But in Jesus' estimation, according to his calculations, it is the meek who get what the others long for but will never find here. The *praus* find glory in Jesus' eyes, from his incongruous gift to the unworthy.

We are each *ptochoi, penthein* and *praus* –the poor in spirit, the inconsolable and the humiliated to one degree or another. It is of these Jesus' Kingdom is most manifest. He came for the likes of these.

I am one.

---

1. Gen 35:10-12.

15

Day 380 of the Axum Mission

My story? I loved my Abba, but he never told me he cared. He never told me he loved me or was proud of me—not even on the day he died. I came to his death bed, bowed, and kissed his cheek. He could only look away with a vicious repulsion in his eyes. I was the son who brought him shame—no honor, no joy—only shame.

Today, I am so disappointed at my insensitivity that day. I had entered his bedroom filled with Jews in Jewish mourning garb crying out in lament and supplications to Yahweh-- and then there was me, the dying rabbi's oldest son decked out in a white Roman tunic, hair shortened and straight, expensive perfumes wafting amidst the earth tones in the room. It was nothing short of an offensive challenge to my father's honor, his legacy. It was a very public poorly timed slap in his bearded face. I wish I could take it back.

I see now I wanted to make—no, I needed to make a statement of "Look at me, Abba! You were wrong! I have value—just not to you."

God help me. The damage I did on that day alone to my family was irreparable. May I live long enough to reconcile with them. It is my most repeated prayer.

I digress again.

My point is I can see now, and it still makes me downcast, I could never satisfy my abba's expectation for righteousness and purity. No matter what I did, it was never enough. I was never the Jewish son Abba pray to God for. I was never interested in my religious studies--enough. I was not interested in following in his footsteps at the Synagogue—enough. We were just not meant to be that father-son duo.

I am not totally blaming him for my lot. I can see that also now. Yet, because of our conflicts, I was left with a deep hole inside of me crying out for attention—demanding to be touched and filled. We humans have a deep need to be seen as persons of value by those we love. I failed—partly my fault, partly his. I desperately needed a real father.

I wanted to please him so much—and never could. Never knew how. Children should never be expected to assuage their parent's voids. We are terrible God-substitutes.

In my dreams still, I look into my abba's eyes, and see his disgust. I can only remember a few times when he looked directly at my face. I never remember him smiling at me. Ever.

We functional orphans find substitutes, alternative fathers, people, or things to staunch the internal bleeding, to fill the crevices—dampen the pain. It is in our nature.

It turned out I was quite good in math and my skills were recognized by—of all people-- a local Roman magistrate. High praise in fact. I will admit, I had never spoken to a Roman before, not face to face. But he was very complimentary. It felt good to be seen and honored—even by a stranger. He ordered my abba to release me to his care. I would be sent to the best Roman schools to be tutored by the best mathematicians in the region. It was just another in the list of my offenses to my father. But I will say, I was so proud of myself. I felt good for the first time in my young life. And I was free from my father's constant disappointing gaze.

This came at a time when the Romans needed more tax collectors in the region—Jewish ones in particular. Trade along the international highway, the Via Maris had ramped up dramatically, largely because we have enjoyed an extended season of peace in the region. We were seeing increased traffic from trade caravans from the far east carrying silk and spices, gold and precious metals from Arabia and manufactured goods from Rome, Crete, and even further west.

We Galileans benefited directly. The taste for our dried fish extended to all corners of the region. This trade complex was one of the geniuses of the Roman empire. They had successfully shaped a vast bureaucracy to track the goods and exhorting taxes and customs all along the trade line. I would be part of the organization along the northern Galilee province.

Ah, but here's the rub. We would also be the instrument of Rome to receive required taxes from all residents of the region, including Jews, my own family in fact. To them, I was not just a hard-working brother who was making a difference, using his skills and talents, and improving his own lot and creating Galilean fishing jobs. I was colluding with the hated Romans. I was no longer a Jew and intentionally excluded from fellowship, despised, spit at, impure, unclean, and unrighteous. I was even told often I had brought shame to my own family's honor.

I was not a prostitute, but my social standing was no higher. There is an old concept of being cut off from the community due to some vile breach of the Covenant. I was a cut-off one—a *karat* one. My soul was relegated to the grave with the Gentiles.

Still, I made a great deal of money which bought me a nice home in a nice non-Jewish part of town, with nice clothes and nice jewelry. But ironically, it only made me feel worse. Every time I looked into the eyes of my fellow Jews; I saw my father's disappointment. I was financially secure and so dishonored at the same time.

I found no respite for my loneliness from the non-Jewish community either. After a while, I stoically accepted my lot. I was to be isolated, a person regularly shamed by my own people and lonely forever.

"Repent," one of the synagogue leaders angrily barked at me as I received his taxes. "Resign and give the money you gained back to the poor. Then God might forgive you."

Who was he kidding? Even if I wanted to, I could not turn back time. I could not change my former people's opinions of me. I could not remove my shame—or my family's shame. I could not make my deceased father pleased with me. I did not have such soap. I would always be an object of derision—a parable to frighten other young boys to stay in the synagogue. People would never say my name without spitting on the ground. Jewish mothers would turn their children's faces away so they wouldn't even see me pass by.

Then Jesus.

It was not on a hillside. It was on a crowded street near an important highway checkpoint where my tax booth was situated. That was where I spent my day calculating tariffs from the traveling merchants and gathering taxes from the locals.

I had heard of the miracle healer, a Jew, a prophet, but it meant little to me. I knew my place. I was a cut-off circumcised exile among the occupied circumcised. I couldn't imagine I would glean anything from this or any Jew. Only more judgment. I didn't need that. I had enough of to last a lifetime.

But he walked right up to me, stopped me in my tracks and waited until I looked up into his eyes. Until that moment, I hadn't been aware how much time I spent looking at the ground. I suppose looking into people's eyes had hurt me so badly. The dirt was friendlier.

Jesus didn't budge until I saw him, his eyes, his smile at me—at me. He stood in my way. Jesus does that a lot.

"Follow me, Matthew," He commanded. It was not my abba's voice; it was gentle and warm. I was not offended. I didn't feel defensive or challenged. I wasn't sure at all what to say. Did he know me? Did he know my father? Did he know I am hated by so many Jews? Did he know I work for the occupiers? What would my father say about this? Did he somehow speak from the grave? What would I do as a disciple? The math didn't add up for me. This is not how it is done.

"Rabboni, do you know me?" I blurted out rudely, quickly feeling the impulse to look away from his intense gaze. Looking back, I would describe his gaze as deeply interested, curious, even fascinated. Very unnerving I thought.

"Yes, of course. I do know you. Follow me, now."

"You are aware I am only a Jew by birth? I am disowned by my father, my family--unrighteous. I work here as a Roman. I am a tax collector. Do you see how the people spit when they see me? Why would you want to bring such criticism upon yourself? I am not the one to follow you, Rabboni. Surely there are others?"

"Matthew, I have come for you. That is exactly why you should follow me. Come now. You will see."

And I did. It wasn't immediate. I am told I stood there, silent, my head spinning for long moments. Jesus just waited—quietly-- the picture of patience. Awkwardly, not knowing what to say, I invited him to a great banquet at my villa. What does one say in this situation?

I did it big. I invited all my colleagues, Romans, and other rejected Jews. I am not sure what I expected but unfortunately the Jewish religious leaders came as well. I promise you they were not invited. But they came. Not to rejoice over a lost sheep found. They came to disrupt and challenge. Chief of their concerns? They were indignant the Rabboni would eat with the likes of me and my colleagues.

Unperturbed, Jesus stood, looked them straight in their angry eyes and said, "It is not the healthy that need a doctor, but the sick." I swear, he was speaking about them.

"I have not come to call the righteous but sinners to repentance." Then I was sure he was speaking directly to them. They got it, huffed, turned, and left my home. I almost laughed out loud. I knew then something fresh had happened.

What could I say? It made absolutely no sense to me then, but within me was a powerful new compulsion, a desire to follow. Looking back, what I felt was the very beginnings of hope. I was an adult and had never felt it before. It turns out, I was not an anomaly, I was the norm.

I was *ptochoi*, I was *penthein*, suffering a deep loss of a father—the void in my soul of the absence of a father's love and praise, and I was *praus*, without honor in a shame-honor world.

Oh yes, I was unenviable in so many ways, but in a moment of time, I became enviable. How? I had a new King. My patron-benefactor was no longer imperial Rome, but Jesus. I now at last had the adoring Abba my soul desperately needed. I was no longer an orphan. I was the Beloved.

I was no longer cut-off. I was no longer unclean. I was righteous.

It is funny, but now I can begin to see I was just like my abba. He too was desperately lonely. He too was an emotionally needy orphan. He worked so very hard to get his heavenly father's attention, to hear him say "Well done, good and faithful servant."

But in the end, he went to the grave with a deep longing and emptiness. I supposed something in his head caused him to blame me for that void. I see the logic there.

I remain hopeful, as at creation, during his last moments on earth, the Spirit of God hovered over my abba's formlessness and void and spoke life, joy, and peace. It is something the Rabboni would do.

I have re-embraced my father's name and legacy. It is his name on all my manuscripts. I am and remain, Matthew, the son of Alphaeus.

That is why I love Rabboni's words. They are music to me even now.

Enviable are the unenviable, God is theirs and they are God's.

Enviable are the inconsolable, I will bring them close to me and there, they will finally experience real comfort.

Enviable are the humiliated, they are the ones who will experience the fulfillment of all the promises of God to broken humanity.

16

Day 470 of the Axum Mission

Sadly, it has been over three months since I added to this manuscript. A lot has happened. There was a nasty sickness rushing through our village like a flood. It affected the elderly first, with waves of headaches and nausea, the inability to hold any food down. Many perished.

It spread through the poorer neighborhoods next. These were the people who had nowhere else to go. Even though we welcomed them and even pursued them, so many chose to stay in their infected homes and huts. Many more died.

We turned our compound into a free hospital for all our community—and all our energies turned to being healers and caretakers. At one point, we had over one hundred and sixty mats spread out in the courtyard and in the rooms reserved for those who suffered the most.

It didn't take long for the illness to spread even further—no one was untouched. I was down for two weeks wandering between death and life. There were moments I prayed to God to take me to be with my Lord Rabboni. Alas, I recovered, much to Deborah's joy.

Just outside our village there are dozens of mass graves where bodies were taken and covered up to protect the living. Cries of mourning rang throughout the village all day and night.

During this time, we lost many friends. We made new ones. We made some enemies as well.

Haaman is a well-respected shaman in our village. He comes from one of the many tribes in the valley to the south of Axum. He is one of the people I pursued early on in our time here. Obodas suggested I reach out to him—of course requesting an official audience with him. I did and invited him to join us for our Todah meal.

A week later, he came along with his six wives and fifteen children. It was a wonderful time. He seemed interested in the work of the Rabboni. In particular, he really wanted to know more about Jesus' resurrection from the dead.

I will say, at first Haaman was pleased with our outreach and deference. He seemed honored. He was curious about us and our new teachings. Were we a threat? Was our teaching compatible with his beliefs? Who was this powerful shaman –his words not ours—Jesus? There was a bit of a dance—that is until the illness swept through the village.

It was then we came face to face with what it meant to be a shaman. We learned shamans were spirit-inspired priests who can divine the future, diagnose, and treat illnesses while they are in a physical trance. Then the so-called spirits come upon the shaman from the outside and take control of his body and voice. Haaman once described it this way, "The ancestral spirit mounts me as a rider does a horse."

I can still recall the day Haaman arrived in our compound filled with sick men and women scattered on mats from wall to wall. He was in glorious costume, his face covered with a bark cloth mask. He hammered a special drum with a ghostly rhythm and danced between the mats almost uncontrollably, his body consumed with trembling movements and crying out in some arcane native tongue, with high pitched voices he claimed was the only way to communicate to dead ancestors. He believed they had the power of life and death, sickness, and healing. His drum seemed to have power for his work. He cannot seem to connect with the spirit world without it.

Patients tell me something happened to them as he danced over them and beat his drum. It was like they became drunk or faint. Another testified of feeling struck in their gut or as another person said they felt like they were beaten with a hoe-handle.

It seems inevitable the patient would be invited to drink some murky elixir made up of a secret recipe of herbs, plants, and other ingredients. I am told it is a vile combination.

Our team has never had to deal with anything like this. Haaman is unique. If you were to come across him any normal day, he would truly just blend into the community. He is short, very thin, bald and walks as if he has broken some bone which just didn't heal correctly. His eyes are black as black can be yet very bright. He is quick to share a laugh, to greet strangers and to help people.

But when his services are required, Haaman is transformed. He seems to grow a couple of inches in height and stature and in confidence. He becomes bigger than life. A force to be reckoned with.

During the illness, he would enter our compound in full regalia and go from mat to mat pounding his drum, crying out prophecies in the name of the dead ancestors and offering the sick his tonic.

It was very troubling and made me harken back to the time the Rabboni sent us disciples out to cast out demons. It was a frightening time. None of us had ever done anything like it. But it was also a rush. To be honest, I had just never spent anytime wondering about demonic spirits before. That opened an entirely new world for us.

Is this that phenomenon? Or is this some legitimate form of ceremonial healing?

Ninos spoke into that. He is not a doctor, but he has been to many healers for his opium addiction. He was concerned at two levels. First, whether it was actual demonic power involved or not, he pointed out Haaman believes he is a funnel for the influence of dead spirits. That is not in concert with the teaching and spirit of the Rabboni.

Second, and he was very keen on this, the affected people became addicted to Haaman and his manifestations. As best as we can tell, for Haaman and his followers, the dead ancestors are to be feared and cajoled. They are as gods. Well-being, health, stature, blessings, and curses are in their capricious hands to give out. You do not want to dishonor a spirit of the powerful dead ancestors—anything could happen to you or your family. There was a great deal of fear surrounding the darkness.

Haaman's people were definitely less open to hearing about new life in the new Kingdom of Jesus. They risked offending very powerful entities.

Either way, this was indeed a threat to our work and the message of the Gospel, and an opportunity. Deborah reminded us that if she had to bet on one side or another, dead spirits, or the living Rabboni, she would put her coins on Jesus ten times out of ten.

It made us laugh. She was right, and yet, we have another problem.

We needed to proceed with caution. Obodas is also a supporter of Haaman and has benefitted from his efforts. We don't want to offend our *karim*.

Rabboni, give us wisdom. What are we to do? What are we to say?

17

Day 471 of the Axum Mission

I confess. I have taken some editing liberties for my Gospel. Over the months, Jesus said such things to individuals and groups all over the region. He would speak freely in Latin, Greek, Hebrew, and Aramaic. At times I was very faithful to scribble down his very words, at other times relied on memory. But I am very pleased with the nine I included. They do reflect the heart and the expanse of Jesus' many macarisms.

I creatively shaped them into three groups of three for illustrative purposes. The first three I dealt with up to this point describe the brokenness and neediness Jesus found here and intentionally plunged into. These were the undeserved whom Jesus loved so much he came among us and actively, at great risk to himself, reached out to gather and adopt as his sons and daughters—his unlikely followers. We were of fractured humanity, the inconsolable and the shamed who did not have the ability or capacity to rescue ourselves. This is all of us.

The second trinity of macarisms defines the miracle that happens within those people, within me. Jesus pursued us as we were, but we were hardly left the same. To be with Jesus was to be changed to become more of a reflection of him—not by shaming or rule or law—we already had those laws. No, there was a change of our deepest priorities and motivations. I know now this was the prime moving of Jesus' Spirit in us. But then, I was only aware I was different.

The third trinity of macarisms are all about—well—I will wait until we get there.

Then Jesus said,

"Enviable are the ones who are consumed with a voracious hunger and thirst for righteousness. They will know full satisfaction in me."

I must go into a little more depth for you readers who are not from my people. I would say the Ethiopians generally have an innate sense of the core of 'righteousness'.

Romans and Greeks tend to overemphasize the ethical and legal aspects of the word, 'righteousness'. To be righteous in the eyes of the Roman law is to obey the law, every jot and tittle. To not subject yourself to guilt.

While this does express one aspect of righteousness, it can be a bit deceiving. For instance, the person who lives their life without breaking a single law or edict might be guiltless according to a law, but not necessarily righteous. In fact, most likely they are not.

This view of righteousness is a hollowed-out version of the righteousness ultimately manifested by Yahweh alone.

Righteousness is at its heart of hearts relational, other-oriented, and other-focused. It is the singular word capturing both movements of the two great commands, to love God and to love others.

Its greatest expression is a relational rightness with God Himself. To hunger and thirst after righteousness ultimately means you want to experience the pure favor of God toward you--to hear God whisper in your ear, "You are my son or daughter with whom I am well pleased." Those who experience this favor from God are changed and experience it more toward others. So, there is no such thing as an isolated righteousness. Righteousness is a relational dynamic which always moves outward from self to others.

Here is an example I hope makes some sense. In our history, we have had good kings and evil kings. What made the difference?

First, it was their relationship to God. Did they rule dependent upon Him, his wisdom, and His direction? Did they fear His judgment and wrath? Did they rule according to Torah? Did they seek to be loyal to Yahweh and establish his worship throughout the land? Yes, to one degree or another, though none perfectly.

Secondly, the good and righteous King was the one who sought to bring a good and happy life for all his subjects. One featured means was through edicts at the time of their accession to the throne remitting debts, freeing slaves, and restoring the land to its original owners. They desired the prosperity of others over their own, the celebration of rights for all, including the aliens and immigrants, care for the economically desperate and challenged, the widows and orphans. They were aware of the need for social justice and equality. In a single word, they were righteous.

Without such righteousness in the land, there could only be abuse, greed, racism, sexism, violence, injustice, crime, poverty, and harm. Hospitality would be absent. The least in the society would be enslaved or abused against their will. All creation groans in the void of righteousness.

For you astute readers, this likely sounds familiar. Jesus' first sermon were the appropriate first words of a righteous king who is rising to his throne, Hear them in that light.

"The Spirit of the Lord is on me, because he has anointed me to preach good news to the poor. He has sent me to proclaim freedom for the prisoners and recovery of sight for the blind, to release the oppressed, to proclaim the year of the Lord's favor."

This was not some casual script reading. This was the heart of a righteous Rabboni who had seen with his own eyes in his first three decades in the land, the abysmal absence of righteousness, and the harsh cruel and often violent consequences left in the formlessness and void.

He modeled for us a hunger and thirst for an urgent restoration of righteousness in the land, not for his own sake—but for the sake of the *ptochoi, praus* and *penthein* ones. This was his passion. No more and no less. There was no more other-oriented human being ever.

The righteous desire—even at great cost to themselves and their own security and comfort-- to bring about harmony for all. It is the very basis of God's rule for the world.

Let me circle back to the Roman narrow definition of the word. There is the possibility of the person to not break rules but care little for the well-being of others. They do it out of fear of prosecution, fear of God, fear of losing face, or wanting to look good in the eyes of others. But clearly, their focus is on themselves, their security, and their reputation.

On the other hand, the truly righteous man or woman –out of deep concern for the well-being of their neighbors, would also keep laws.

In the end, both groups would do right things, but the motives are wildly disparate.

Please do not hear me laying blame on the violated ones—suggesting they would be more pleasing to God if they only thought less of themselves and more of others. May God forbid.

As I have considered this more, I believe some poor people have been so shredded and violated by the powers of evil, humanly speaking they cannot think of others. They cannot be merciful. They can only be and act like survivors. Mercy for others has been beat out of them.

Their drive is to, at the end of the day, have some semblance of security from the night, some sense of physical thirst and hunger satisfied—even a little, and some buffer to the pains of loneliness. That is all.

Who could expect more from them? I cannot. They have been emptied against their wills. They cannot do righteousness in such a desperate state.

Here is an image. Think of them as empty and emptied amphorae. They were meant to be full of life-giving water--useful. But due to abuse, misuse, and misappropriation, they are only dusty and cracked—soon to be relegated to the garbage pile with the other refuse. They cannot quench anyone's thirst.

You may try to shame them into caring for others—but you are wasting your breath. They won't, they can't. It is not all evil. It is not all their fault.

In the presence of Jesus, as a result of his touch, something happens inside such cracked vessels. They become filled, a little or a lot. They become whole, a little or a lot.

Then they think less of themselves and more toward the well-being of others. They become more righteous. Not perfect—nowhere near.

They begin to feel the needs of others, even though their own voracious hunger and thirst is yet unsatisfied. They move outward—like Jesus.

It is because of Jesus' Spirit in us, not rules, or laws, or shamings, or strings. Jesus' love toward us is without any requirement. We slowly become like him as we are increasingly more dependent upon the Spirit of His righteousness in our being.

These former self-focused *ptochoi* now are feeling the birth pangs of wanting to care for others around them again. Why? To be a bit oversimplistic, because their voracious hunger and thirst is being quenched a little, and the Rabboni's righteous yearning for the well-being of others is filling their hearts—displacing their fears and insecurities. Or as Jesus puts it,

"Enviable are you who are obsessed with fixing all the brokenness and disparity in your own selves, relationships, culture and in the world around you, particularly related to restoration to favor with God. You will experience that and more—I will see to it."

I mentioned this earlier, the Romans have an idiom, "*Incurvatus in se*", the self-turned in upon itself. At an extreme it can describe the self-centered person who only wants more and more power, land, popularity, or influence. But it is also reflective of the person who has been so depleted and emptied they must be self-concerned in order to stay alive.

Jesus has come for both types of broken vessels. Ultimately, they need the same thing. They need to be made whole, and when the filling starts, they begin, a little, to care about others more.

The very same thing can be said about mercy. A sick person who is just doing whatever it takes to survive the day, or the person who has a vile disease they have little power to do anything about, or a person who is controlled by the demonic, or who is feeling lonely and distraught, how can they show mercy? What humanity wells can they draw from? Maybe they have made very poor choices that have marked them and their reputation and have little repair.

Again, it is not all their fault. They can't, they won't be merciful to others. They need a deliverance. They need mercy themselves first. When they receive such a rescuing mercy, then they too can begin to imagine being merciful. They <u>will</u> be more merciful.

Think of this righteousness handed out freely by the Rabboni as relational and societal worth—or significance in the eyes of others. Before the Rabboni arrived and spoke, we were dependent upon fragile and contestable reputations. To save face we had to keep defending our name, maintain it—but somewhere in the back of our minds, we knew that we were in a raging competition and our worth was always at risk of being stolen, undermined or slip through our fingers unaware.

Those people on the hillside had found themselves on the losing end of that struggle. They had little social status based upon attractiveness, purity, health, religious righteousness, holiness, education, sex, citizenship status, ethnicity, or economic worth. They had lost most hope of repair.

Then Jesus came and became their surprising supporter/benefactor and raised their lot singlehandedly. No wonder they followed Him.

One famous Roman philosopher, Cicero, captures it, "By nature we yearn and hunger for honor, and once we have glimpsed, as it were, some part of its radiance, there is nothing we are not prepared to bear and to suffer in order to secure it."

In His presence, the dishonored felt honor and needed the former means of honor less.

After the Rabboni, those former sources of honor that have long shaped our world have been displaced somewhat. Or better, they have been displaced by a superior means of value and worth: Him.

Follow me. Jesus freely offers this new unmerited status to us without regard to our normal source of worth (i.e., family name, wealth, influence, power, religious status, sex, citizenship, attractiveness, intelligence, circumcision, relationship to Caesar, access to incense trade, shipping lanes) and so largely nullifying our former means of significance.

The new source of worth is not incense, but Jesus and relationship with him. This undeserved social status is given freely. The world is turned upside down. And those who formerly benefitted from the old ways hate the change. They have been now exposed as having no true and lasting value.

If you have stayed with me, then this will follow logically. Those fortunate people who now find themselves in the Rabboni's embrace are changed. They have experienced stunning mercy—grace beyond what they deserved—and they begin to want to show mercy to others. So, Jesus could say, those who show mercy will receive mercy. Or he could also say, those who have received mercy will show mercy. It is one and the same thing.

Not to mention the Rabboni's Spirit, a spirit of remarkable mercy for others now abides in the inner being of His followers. In some ways, we will feel His mercy for others and will necessarily choose to act in that spirit.

Jesus said to the crowd, "Enviable are the merciful, for they are the ones who experience His mercy over and over."

Back to righteousness for a moment. Am I suggesting, as some have, Jesus is negating the Torah, and obedience to the Torah? Do we still need to do right?

Yes of course. No one has ever held the Torah up more than Jesus. No one has ever done Torah more than Jesus. He knew no sin.

Jesus clarified the righteousness required by Torah was greater than we imagined. We are not only to do right, but we are also to <u>want</u> to do right. This is the foundation of the great commandment to love our neighbor. How can we say we love our neighbor if we do not want to do right to them?

We are also to have a right relationship with God. But before Jesus, it was unclear how that could happen. Now we know and proclaim that while that status and that loving relationship is beyond our control, it is in the hands and of a God who freely and incongruously gives it to the likes of us. Listen to two passages from the prophet Isaiah.

"Listen to me, you stubborn of heart,

   you who are far from righteousness:

I bring near my righteousness; it is not far off,

   and my salvation will not delay;

     I will put salvation in Zion,

for Israel my glory." (Isa 46:12-13)

This new undeserved and unwarranted relationship is of God's hand given to stubborn unworthy people. Righteousness and salvation are synonymous here, given to those who have not or will not earn it. We do not rescue ourselves. We do not become the brides of God by our own hands. Again,

> I will greatly rejoice in the LORD;
>> my soul shall exult in my God,
>> for he has clothed me with the garments of salvation;
>> he has covered me with the robe of righteousness,
>> as a bridegroom decks himself like a priest with a beautiful headdress,
>> and as a bride adorns herself with her jewels.
> For as the earth brings forth its sprouts,
>> and as a garden causes what is sown in it to sprout up,
>> so the Lord GOD will cause righteousness and praise
>> to sprout up before all the nations. (Isa 61:10-11)

This is what happened to me in Capernaum, and on that hillside to those lost hurting people, the *ptochoi*, the *praus* and the *penthein*. And we were changed. And as Isaiah foresaw, we are sprouting up before all the nations. This is why we're in Axum.

I laugh as I see Reuben struggle with this—less so now. But he still scratches his long straggly grey streaked beard hanging to his chest. For so long, he had fervently held that only individual faithfulness was merited as worthy of God's favor. Though he would admit he never felt he had ever done enough, was worthy enough—in fact the idea of being worthy was anathema to him.

A flock of internal contradictions drove him to depression after the Temple's destruction. But now he sees good standing before God is a function of the death and resurrection of Christ alone. Torah observance is not wrong—no, it is good, but does not—no it cannot-- ever establish a person's worth or standing before God. We are right with God strictly because of the work of Jesus on our behalf alone.

And to expand this, our fresh message to the outies in the cultures where we visit is this, spiritual baptism into the Rabboni frees communities from often harmful, often unfair, and unjust traditional, hierarchical systems of distinction.

Or maybe this is a better way to unpack the Rabboni's words,

Enviable are you who are obsessed with fixing all the brokenness and disparity in your own selves, relationships, culture and in the world around you, particularly related to restoration to favor with God. You will experience that and more—I will see to it.

And

Enviable are the merciful to others, that tells me that you are experiencing His mercy for you over and over.

Let's continue.

18

Day 490 of the Axum Mission

Te'oma and Ruth had a baby girl four months ago. A beautiful healthy girl they named Tahir. On a few occasions, I have witnessed Ruth holding Tahir up, face to face, eye to eye. Tahir can't get enough of it.

Ruth coos and giggles and smiles at the love of her life resting in her arms, wrapped in a warm cotton cloth. Ruth's eyes light up, she speaks in an indiscernible gibberish only she and Tahir seem to understand. Tahir is mesmerized, eyes locked on her mother's eyes, sometimes smiling, sometimes moaning, but clearly, she would rather be no other place than right there, secure in her mother's arms, awash in her joyous gaze and smiling face.

Ruth's face is shining upon Tahir. Inside Tahir there is some dancing going on undetected. Pure joy—safe, unaffected by anything else going on around her. She seems to know Ruth is there for her.

I think I have previously mentioned the Hebrew idiom, *'lipnay Elohim'*, literally 'in the presence of God,' or right up in His Holy face—that narrow dangerous wonderful place where I can see with my own eyes, by faith, what he really thinks of me right now.

There is a wide spectrum of what we could experience *lipnay Elohim*. God might be angry, or disgusted, or disappointed in me. Or, and this is my hope and the hope of every Jew, God might be so happy to be with me, so pleased, and would rather be nowhere else—like Ruth and Tahir. His face may shine upon us. *Lipnay Elohim,* he might say to me, "You are my beloved child with whom I am well pleased." Who wouldn't want that very thing?

And so, Jesus provocatively threw out to that relationally hungry crowd on that Galilean hillside.

> *"Enviable are the pure in heart, for they really will gaze into his adoring face."*

One of our teachers correctly said the essence of all sin is finding our significance, security and belonging anywhere other than Yahweh and His embrace. Or better, looking into the gaze of lesser gods. *Lipnay* power. *Lipnay* addiction. *Lipnay* reputation. *Lipnay* religion even. *Lipnay* Rome, or Jerusalem.

If we were honest, we chase a variety of gazes, lesser gazes every day—all day in fact.

We are immersed in sinful relations.

I confess, I often look for identity in my ministry, or report of the success of my writings, or some other things like the love of a father figure other than God. All sin.

I should know better. I do know better, and yet, my heart is not pure. It doesn't naturally depend upon the Rabboni alone for my well-being, my worth, my hope, or my joy.

There will come a time when we will see as we are seen. But for now, we stumble along between feeling like orphans to feeling like adored worthy sons or daughters of His.

How can we come close to being pure enough to earn such a favor? I haven't even begun to talk about the added difficulty of the consequences of depending upon lesser gazes and the shame and guilt that consumes us so.

When am I closest to such heart-purity? It is not when I am struggling to do better, to adhere to Torah more strictly, or to scrub off residual shame and guilt on my own. No, it is when I am by faith gazing into his adoring eyes and being passively immersed in my reflection from his gaze.

Purity of heart is a difficult concept. The Rabboni was clearly referring to one of his favorite Psalms. Listen,

Who may ascend the hill of the LORD? Who may stand in his holy place?

He who has clean hands and a pure heart, who does not lift up his soul to an idol or swear by what is false.

He will receive blessing [barukah] from the LORD and righteousness from God his Savior.

Such is the generation of those who seek him, who seek your face, O God of Jacob. Selah (Ps 24:3-6)

Look, this is always the question in the forefront of my people's minds. What do we need to do, to be, to earn God's favor again, to feel his shining gaze upon us? What is the appropriate quid pro quo so God would legally have to give us that blessing the Psalmist refers to?

I don't mean this in an evil or manipulative way—exactly. I am hurting. I have fallen down. I messed up. I have lost face. I am feeling alone. I am a disappointment to God, or Jesus. I need a savior. What do I need to do to begin to feel God's favor? And how much is enough?

It is a legitimate question. It is <u>the</u> question.

Well, I can bring more sacrifices to the Temple (at least when there was a temple). I can tithe to the poor more. I can come to all three celebrations (again—at least when there was a celebration to go to). But is any of that enough? Am I then pure enough?

The Rabboni is raising the question that is clearly on the Jewish people's mind and in the high-level dialogues in the religious scholarly schools.

Who is righteous enough, pure enough, good enough so they can enter the Temple of God (ascend the hill of the Lord) and make a face-to-face supplication to Him (the right of favored sons and daughters in good standing) so that He would look at them and say they were worthy of being heard officially and would grant their request?

The blessing we long for is a gift from the heavens, maybe some healing, or pregnancy, or economic turnaround, or protection from harm. Righteousness speaks about a restoration to favor with God—being made right with God—and knowing it.

When the Rabboni was baptized—I wrote about it in my Gospel--God the Father Himself said, "This is my son with whom I am well pleased." No other Jew received such acclamation of righteousness. Only him. This is what we desperately longed for—and it has seemed well out of reach from our people for generations.

One of our prophets spoke about God dancing over us some day. Listen.

"On that day they will say to Jerusalem, "Do not fear, O Zion; do not let your hands hang limp. The LORD your God is with you, he is mighty to save. He will take great delight in you, he will quiet you with his love, he will rejoice over you with singing." (Zephaniah 3:16-17)

That is what every Jewish boy or girl wants. To be able to go before God and feel his face shining upon us. Nothing else comes close. But this is only for those with clean hands and truly pure hearts.

As a young boy, we memorized Psalm 80. It is to my very point.

Restore us, O God; make your face shine upon us, that we may be saved. (Psalm 80:3)

This experience of pure parental love is related to being rescued by God. Rescued from what? Rescued from the inhuman celestial loneliness and isolation we Jews have felt at least since the exile when God publicly abandoned us to our shame and guilt, his shekinah glory seemingly relinquishing former commitments to us.

Don't get me wrong, we deserved it, we earned it having failed to glorify Him over and over again.

Understand the disgrace and loss of face coming from being disclaimed by God, cast aside like garbage when he turned his face from us and left us high and dry. We became a jilted bride, a cut off people.

There is something inside of every Jew desiring that relationship be repaired and restored. But how? Nothing has worked.

Every Yom Kippur, before the Temple was razed a decade ago, well-meaning Jews would come to the Temple in hopes of witnessing—experiencing-- the return of God's glory. They would gather and repent of sins, theirs and their forefathers and mothers. They would do sacrifices, mikvah baths, tithes—but nothing worked.

The heavens were silent year after year. The people shamed again and again. That was when there was still a Temple. Now? What can Jews do? How can we be made clean when there is no more sin offering?

What is the answer? Who is worthy? The Rabboni said it is those who have clean hands and pure heart.

Clean hands refer to doing no actions that falls out of the dyad, loving God with all our being and loving others the same.

Pure heart ramps things up even further. It's not just about right actions. Our motivations must also be godly. Jesus will unpack this more later in the collection. It is not enough to not kill someone. You must not be angry. It is not enough to pray according to Torah. You must want God's glory over your own.

Clean hands and a pure heart. But none of us, even on really good days make that height, climb that holy hill. "There is none righteous," says the Psalmist. "No not one."

Meaning, no one is worthy to approach God and have any expectations they will feel him smile, or hear him say, "Well done, good and faithful servant." No one.

Until the Rabboni.

Whereas God's blessings are normally thought to be distributed to fitting or worthy recipients, you know, those who have clean hands and pure heart, Jesus turned that on its head.

Now blessings and righteousness are given freely without regard to worth, in fact, in the absence of worth and worthiness. It is given to those who have spoiled hands and impure hearts. This grace is an incongruous gift that isn't related to the recipient's worthiness, rather it creates it. It is a mystery.

Think back to Ruth and her new baby, Tahir. Tahir is awash in Ruth's love, not because she has done anything to earn such a devotion. She just passively receives Ruth's motherly love. Tahir may have soiled herself—yet she still is immersed in the glow of Ruth's gaze. She may squirm and cry, but soon her mother's gaze softens Tahir's anxieties and fears. In her mother's arms, she feels being fully known and adored.

And this attuning gaze is a dynamic of sorts that does something inside the heart of the infant that makes Tahir respond to that love. She coos and giggles back at her mother. Her eyes are ablaze in response.

Is it too far out of line to say this is a precious pure form of worship? Is this unadulterated gratefulness and deep acceptance of an incongruous love? It is a response that feels no need to prove itself anymore, or to manipulate its object.

For us, in this celestial gaze, which we enter into by faith alone, we get empowered necessarily to love God in return and to begin to love others as well. As implied by Psalm 80, it is God who restores and rescues us. He gets all the credit.

Let me say it less subtlety. We do not enter that relationship with the Holy God because we have clean enough hands or a pure enough heart. God forbid.

We bring with us no worthiness—in fact, only unworthiness. But because of the power of that love manifested from our Father's eyes encompassing us again and again, we leave motivated to give up more of ourselves, our demands and embrace other 'unworthys' with the same incongruous love.

This is why we are in Axum.

We want to be amphorae spilling out the love of the Rabboni to others who are also unworthy of receiving the gift.

Who might we hesitate to tell of such a love? Arabs? Berbers? Nabateans? Nubians? Indians? Romans? Jews? No. The Rabboni has come for celestially lonely and disconnected people who long for a connection that makes them feel enough, makes them feel adored and worthy. This Gospel ignores old sources and hierarchies of worth and connection. That is maddening to so many—but to others, it is an elixir of life.

I must say one other thing. We are in no way tossing out Torah or Torah's requirement. The only one acceptable is the one who has clean hands and pure heart. Incontrovertible. And you know, there has only been one person, the Rabboni himself who fit that requirement and who indeed earned (I am speaking humanly of course) the joy and adoration of the Father. Just one.

The only way for the rest of us to enjoy that attuning joy is to be found in Him. In His death and in his resurrection by faith. But then necessarily in him as he is in the loving arms and gaze of His Father. It is a mystery indeed. Such good news, and yet, it is as real as can be.

In that moment--when I get there-- by the power of the Rabboni's Spirit in me, by faith, I am lifted into his presence, my sight is consumed by him and his glory alone, I need no lesser god, surely, he is more than enough. For a moment in time, my heart is pure. I am whole. I am happy. I am content.

Back to the macarisms, there and then, I begin to feel more mercy for those who desperately need mercy and I am a little more concerned for the well-being of those who suffer from social injustices and violence here. *Lipnay Elohim*, I am not thinking less of myself, but I am thinking of myself less.

As I gaze into his adoring face, as I drink in and experience his flood of mercy toward me and am more aware of his passionate concern for my well-being—more than anyone has ever been, I become filled, merciful, and pure in heart. I am enviable.

I will share one side story as an illustration. Though I did not include this tale in my Gospel, which I regret now, I share it often in my talks as a missionary.

The Rabboni surprised us by going through Samaria instead of going around it as most Jews do. We had been in Jerusalem for something and were headed back to our home in Capernaum. We came to a well, and were grateful, because we were very tired and very thirsty.

Jesus sent us into the local village to buy some food. It was awkward for us, being Jews in such a strange place—often an unhospitable place. We Jews just never really got along with our distant cousins.

It turns out, none of that mattered much to Jesus.

When we returned with food, we were shocked he was speaking face to face with a lone woman from Sychar—a Samaritan. Well, we were speechless. This wasn't done, at so many levels for so many reasons.

We came just as she left, in quite a hurry I would add, leaving her amphora empty in the dust by Jesus' feet.

Jesus could only smile—you know, in his endearing way. I loved that about the Rabboni.

One of the other followers, maybe it was Peter, yes, I am sure of it, began to lecture him about the impropriety of such a public meeting. A man meeting a woman alone, it was culturally inappropriate. He was right, of course, so many things could have gone badly.

Jesus just smiled at Peter. He did so love him.

He asked us what we saw when we looked at the woman? Curious and provocative question.

He clarified his question. She wasn't a Jewess. She was a Samaritan, a hated distant cousin of the Jews. He informed us she was very interested in spiritual things, more than many Jewish women or men for that matter. She had shared with him that she is on her sixth husband. One last thing. She had come here for water in the middle of the day, in this punishing heat, long after the time women would normally come to draw from this well. She was very thirsty, the Rabboni emphasized.

"So, tell me, Peter, who is this woman and what is she desperately needing?"

As we sat to eat, we spoke more about the woman. "Maybe", some speculated, "She was a brazen adulterous who lured men into sexual liaisons for gain or power—leaving shattered families in her wake."

Her dress was indeed very colorful and provocative. Her perfume penetrated the desert air even still. It would seem she might be dangerous. If so, it would have been the wise thing, according to the Proverbs to avoid the seductress and her seductive words (Proverbs 7:5).

"Jesus, Rabboni, you of all people should beware of such a danger," one of us commented—no doubt Peter again.

"Well said," Jesus said approvingly, "I know Wisdom, very well. Wisdom says of herself,

"The LORD brought me forth as the first of his works, before his deeds of old; I was appointed from eternity, from the beginning, before the world began. When there were no oceans, I was given birth, when there were no springs abounding with water; before the mountains were settled in place, before the hills, I was given birth, before he made the earth or its fields or any of the dust of the world. I was there when he set the heavens in place, when he marked out the horizon on the face of the deep, when he established the clouds above and fixed securely the fountains of the deep, when he gave the sea its boundary so the waters would not overstep his command, and when he marked out the foundations of the earth. Then I was the craftsman at his side. I was filled with delight day after day, rejoicing always in his presence, rejoicing in his whole world and delighting in mankind. "Now then, my sons, listen to me; blessed are those who keep my ways. Listen to my instruction and be wise; do not ignore it. Blessed is the man who listens to me, watching daily at my doors, waiting at my doorway. For whoever finds me finds life and receives favor from the LORD. But whoever fails to find me harms himself; all who hate me love death." (Proverbs 8)

"Tell me," said Jesus smiling, "Would wisdom abandon this thirsty woman? What if the woman's story was not as you suppose? What if she had lost five husbands to war or disease, or had been wrongly and unjustly divorced? What if she had been given away by her parents for monetary or social gain and was forced to submit to abuse and shame? What if she had become isolated by the other women for reasons not of her own doing? What would wisdom tell us?"

Once more we were speechless, even Peter—a rare treat to be sure.

But to the point, the woman—whoever she was and whatever her story was—had run to her village and risked everything to tell the people about Jesus—what little she knew. Whatever she said, the townsmen sent out a delegation to welcome us there to be treated with great hospitality for two whole days. We Jews, were welcomed among the Samaritans. Many of them became followers of the Rabboni.

What can I say about that woman? She was thirsty for mercy. Her amphora was desperately empty or perhaps, emptied. But in a moment of time with Jesus, *lipnay Elohim*, it became full, no, it overflowed with mercy for the others in her village, many of whom had no doubt treated her so poorly for so long. This is what the mercy of Jesus does. This is what wisdom does. Jesus pursues the disempowered and empowers them.

To answer the Rabboni's question? What was the woman desperately longing for? She needed to find herself rescued and in the loving adoring gaze of Yahweh. Just like me.

This is the heart of Jesus. He was countercultural. He came for those who were unenviable, lost, disenfranchised, and abandoned here—including Samaritan women.

When he touched them, they became people of honor—some for the first time in their lives. When he gazed into their unworthy faces, people with unclean hands and impure hearts, they became enviable.

By the way, I forgot to mention. Tahir in Arabic means 'pure.' In Ruth's arms and eyes, Tahir is experiencing the joy of her name.

Here is another attempt at capturing what Jesus said to those people fifty years ago,

> *Enviable are you who rest dependent in God's arms like a new-born child, you will see his face smiling upon you and know that He is there for you.*

Amen and amen.

19

Day 500 of the Axum Mission

Let me review. The first three macarisms make us see our beat-up needy hearts as the Rabboni sees them. The second set gives us an inside look at how the gaze of Jesus, the touch of Jesus' Spirit begins to heal us and how we change from within.

The third set of three beatitudes opens our eyes to see what changed hearts do. Simply put, we become peacemakers, even though very likely we will not ultimately be appreciated for our sacrifices. This broken world kills true peacemakers. Here is what Jesus said,

Enviable are you who lean into being reconcilers, versus dividers; that tells me that you have the new heart of a child of God.

Do you know just how enviable you are– you the persecuted ones– when others have systematically organized programs to harass and oppress you because you are doing good to others instead of just yourself – reflecting my heart to a beat up marginalized – every-man-for-himself world. Hear this. They can't take the Kingdom of Heaven away from you.

O your enviable situation whenever people unjustly speak disparagingly of you, intentionally harass you, to purposely make up and say evil things about you, they are deceivers, all this is done strictly because you are with me.

I have spoken about this before, but it is worth the time to expand upon it now. Though I wasn't there, I have been told by very good sources what happened on the day Jesus was baptized by his cousin John.

John had been preaching in the Jordan River valley for a time, just a day's walk east of Jerusalem in Judea. "Repent, for the Kingdom of Heaven is near," he bellowed in a deep prophetic voice.

As I have said before, the Kingdom of Heaven was not a reference to a walled fortress guarded by soldiers and run by Kings and courtiers. It is an idiom referring to God himself.

The prophet Ezekiel had a vision at the very beginning of the Exile of the shekinah glory of God abandoning the Holy of Holies, rising up and leaving the Temple and Jerusalem eastward until it could not be seen anymore.

God had departed from the midst of his people. I will not go into the many reasons why—to be sure, it is over my paygrade. To simplify it, the people of God were beset with sins against God and the Torah and were unrepentant.

After the Exile, many Jews returned to the land, rebuilt the Temple and the city, and re-established the worship of Yahweh there.

But the dirty little secret is that the shekinah glory of God did not come back with them. When the architects completed the Temple and the Holy of Holies, they had to leave the holy place empty. There was no ark of Covenant, no mercy seat, no angelic cover. The curtains closed upon a hollow space.

Reuben has confirmed the Sanhedrin knew about this shame but thought it best to not make it public knowledge. They wanted to encourage participation in the temple worship, not discourage it. I get it, but how tragic.

Over five centuries have come and gone. The people of God went from being occupied by Persia, to the Greeks, to a century of unfortunate self-rule—to now being owned and dominated by Rome. And in all that time, the Holy of Holies has remained an empty dusty sarcophagus.

Then John charged the sons and daughters of Israel with the one thing that truly mattered. "You want God's favor again? You want the return of God and His blessings? You want to be sons and daughters of God once more? You must truly repent, individually, and corporately. And you need to do it now. He is near, He is coming, His favor and His wrath are in his hands. What will it be? Now or never."

The wearied Jews got it. It was something to see. They flocked from the North, South, East, and West into the Jordan Valley humiliating themselves, their families, and tribes, publicly confessing their sins, desperately pleading for God to forgive and to remember his promises to Abraham, and to David.

There they were, person after person, baptized by John in the muddy waters of the Jordan. This was like something no one had ever dreamed of.

Well, you can imagine how the religious leaders took that. They were deeply offended. We get a sense that was part of the problem of course, at least from God's perspective.

John's message of how to regain God's favor clearly marginalized the Temple and the Worship there. The priests, Levites, and religious bureaucracy would have taught God would smile and bless the people who brought sacrifices, who gave to the poor according to the Law, who submitted to temple worship.

John mentioned none of those things. He required a total deep personal heartfelt abandonment of all supposed righteousness from everyone without exception. Meaning that nothing the Temple did or could do would gain any favor or forgiveness from God. God required total repentance—the implication being-- before he would return. So, repent of any uncleanness of hand or impurity of heart.

And so, the people did—at least the regular Jews. They came and confessed their unfaithfulness, their sins, their rebellion from God. It was a sight to behold.

Here's the thing most often misunderstood. God rejected the repentances. It still was not sufficient to gain God's favor—to earn his return—to earn the right to be called sons and daughters of God. It wasn't enough.

How do we know? The heavens were silent. None of them were declared to be sons or daughters of God again. God's shekinah glory didn't return. The people only left the river wetter.

Something else happened, something wild, something so very instructive. Jesus came, he was baptized, and <u>his</u> baptism was accepted as sufficient and righteous.

How do we know? God said so. I wrote these words in my original Gospel, "As soon as Jesus was baptized, he went up out of the water. At that moment heaven was opened, and he saw the Spirit of God descending like a dove and lighting on him. And a voice from heaven said, "This is my Son, whom I love; with him I am well pleased." (Matt 3:16-17)

You see, don't you? It was all accomplished. Jesus was Ezekiel's God's-shekinah glory returning. Jesus was John's "Kingdom is near". Jesus was the only one truly worthy, truly pure in heart, righteous enough to be called the sufficient and pleasing Son of God.

What does it mean to be called the daughters and sons of God? It is another idiom capturing what it feels like to be embraced by your good father, to look into his eyes and know, really know, he adores you. He would prefer to be nowhere else than with you. He is dancing over you—as you are.

I did not know that kind of earthly father. But I am learning to be so with my heavenly father. In Jesus, because of Jesus, with Jesus, God now says over me, about me, "You are my son, with whom I am well pleased." Not due to anything I have done worthy, not at all.

Like those many Jews who sincerely came seeking the favor of God again, I can repent and repent, I can be baptized, I can make sacrifices, I can give all of my money to the poor, none of that earns one inkling of God's favor.

But being in Jesus earns it all. He earned it all for me. It is so simple, even a tax collector with an indifferent father can do it. It is so simple even a Priest or Levite could do it.

This being called a child of God doesn't stop there. Jesus was so clear.

There is a dynamic plan moving the Kingdom outward. The heart of God, the passion of Jesus, and for his new sons and daughters is to go and be part of the reconciliation of broken humanity into this new relationship with the Creator God. To offer this incongruous gift to the undeserving of all lands.

If one was to wrap the whole 'Kingdom of God coming' into a single charge, God has given us the ministry of peacemaking, just as God is reconciling the world to himself in Christ, not counting men's sins against them, so we are to take up that cross and commit to such peacemaking. It is the heart and soul of His Spirit in us. We must be his ears and mouth, hands, and feet.

Yet, we know full well what a broken world does to peacemakers. So many of my colleagues and dearest friends, men and women who left it all to follow Him only to perish violently. Then of course, there was what happened to the Rabboni himself. It is unreal the world couldn't see, couldn't embrace him. But alas. This world does not. This groaning creation can't—won't-- abide peacemakers.

And so, the Rabboni added the last two macarisms. These are stark warnings. They are meant to be jarring, unpleasant and prophetic. So be it.

Jesus said, "Enviable are those who are being persecuted because of righteousness."

Or if I may unpack it more,

"Do you know just how enviable you are-- you the persecuted ones-- when others have systematically organized programs to harass and oppress you because you are doing good to others instead of just yourself – reflecting my heart to a beat up marginalized – every-man-for-himself world. Hear this. They can't take the Kingdom of Heaven away from you.

Of course, being persecuted, falsely accused, tortured, unjustly imprisoned, and even murdered is not something to be envied. Hardly. The Rabboni was speaking in Jewish rhetoric.

The enviable, who are such because of being in the singular embrace of the Christ, are the ones who will go and proclaim such a celestial peace to be found in Him. This is what sons and daughters must do, will do. God is theirs and they are God's. They do not subject themselves to such possible harm because they are enviable, they pursue peace and are enviable because they are God's and God is theirs.

"O your enviable situation whenever people unjustly speak disparagingly of you, intentionally harass you, to purposely make up and say evil things about you, they are deceivers, all this is done strictly because you are with me."

"Rejoice and even greatly rejoice because your wages (what you didn't earn but was earned perfectly for you by Jesus—and so it is as if you really did earn them) are vast in heaven waiting for you. Don't be surprised the so-call righteous—the self-proclaimed religious moralists will persecute you— for in the same way they persecuted the prophets who were before you."

We do not rejoice because we suffer unjustly. We suffer unjustly and rejoice because we are a son or daughter of God.

Strangely the persecution seems targeted to the Jesus-followers <u>because</u> they are doing righteousness—that includes actions done for others, selfless actions. That is a very strange thing on the surface.

This persecution Jesus speaks about is not due to struggle over power specifically or differences of opinion in some argument, or even prejudice. No, it is one group angry over another group doing selfless acts for people. A reflection of Edenic love-lost.

Honestly what difference should it make to the offended group? Why would it make them angry? This is the tragedy surrounding Jesus.

He did nothing wrong. He did nothing selfishly. He healed, he fed, he taught, he comforted, he taught fishing lessons—nothing that in a just, reasonable, mentally balanced world would ever cause anyone to want to harm, mistreat, prosecute, much less despise.

He should have instead been given recognition and glory—which he never sought-- had parades in his honor, been given a lecture seat in the Sanhedrin. Like Solomon before him, Kings and Queens should have come to hear him, to gain wisdom. Instead, the world despised him, persecuted him, murdered him.

The Rabboni taught there is a battle between Kingdoms and philosophies, worldviews. One is intentionally pitted against the other.

My suggestion is all conflict stems out of a battle over 'rightness'. Some act like everybody is in competition for limited resources, glory, identity, power, and success. The prize goes to the strongest, the most aggressive, the most attractive. Ultimately its every person for himself. You may do good to others—but ultimately to get points for yourself.

Others, those who are children of God, who have been infected with the Spirit of the Rabboni seek the wellbeing of others.

These two world views are in intense conflict with each other. Jesus, his narrative, his actions, his teachings are a threat to anyone who is trying to be right based upon guidelines other than receiving right as a unilateral gift from God.

It is true--a frightening thing for we who must follow. This is not our home. We are merciful because we are experiencing his mercy in us and through us—we <u>must</u> let it out toward others—nothing pleases us more. But not all who are treated mercifully will be grateful. Some will react murderously. It is the fallen human condition.

Didn't God plead with Cain, face to face, to look up into his face? Multiple times? Cain was the first murderer. No one would have blamed God if he had been justly angry and required Cain's death—a life for a life.

That is not what God did. All the while, Cain refused to look up into God's eyes. He refused a rescue. He even blamed God. See how humanity's hearts hardened against a loving rescue before even a single generation passed?

It is even worse now. But we, the called and rescued children of the living God, continue to enter worldly turmoil, entrenched social injustices, conflicts, dehumanizations of all kinds, not to assuage, or to come to a middle ground of compromise satisfying no one, but rather passes the issue on to future generations.

No, we speak of a God who pursues perpetrators and victims alike, as they are. He has the capacity and power to satisfy longings, repair wounds, speak forgiveness into being, cause justice to be experienced. He alone can make perpetrators feel godly sorrow. He can resurrect the dead. His Spirit yet hovers over our chaos, our formlessness and void and speaks form and life. He brings sabbath in his wake.

Who wouldn't want that? Certainly, reasonable people would welcome such a revolution and reformation. Alas, it is generally not the case. Untransformed *ptochoi* are not reasonable.

It remains a dangerous thing to follow Him. It is unsafe. It is lonely at times. Humanly speaking, there is not much of a need for a retirement plan. Most of us don't live that long.

We remained compelled to walk his path in his sandals. We do this as we lean into seeing him face to face, feeling more and more of his mercy for us and others, experiencing more of his joy. In this world we will know both trouble and dancing. Only for a little while.

This is a good place to remember my friends and co-peacemakers who have passed through such a persecution. Please bear with me. I want to take this moment to honor some of the martyrs for the Kingdom of Jesus, friends, acquaintances, apostles all, people who should not be forgotten—all of whom were mentioned in my Gospel. It appears there are only two of the original disciples of the Rabboni yet alive. John remains alive in Ephesus, as far as I know. There are only the two of us now.

In most cases, we aren't sure exactly how the others perished—only rumors. The Rabboni knows.

James
Simon Peter
Paul
Andrew
James ben Alphaeus
Simon
Jude
Phillip
Thomas Didymus
and most recently, my dear friend Bartholomew

May they each enjoy the Rabboni in Paradise. I will certainly fellowship with them soon.

20

Day 625 of the Axum Mission

"You are the salt of the earth. But if the salt loses its saltiness, how can it be made salty again? It is no longer good for anything, except to be thrown out and trampled by men. You are the light of the world. A city on a hill cannot be hidden. Neither do people light a lamp and put it under a bowl. Instead, they put it on its stand, and it gives light to everyone in the house. In the same way, let your light shine before men, that they may see your good deeds and praise your Father in heaven."

I wondered and prayed how to speak about the next section of Jesus' words. And then, it came to me. This is my wife Deborah's favorite section—and she shares her thoughts quite often—with amazing response from our community.

I thought it would be very beneficial to hear from her, her words—with as little commentary from me as possible.

Normally we speak and give testimony after our weekly Todah meals—our weekly thanksgiving celebration. All are invited from the community, no matter what tribe you are from, what language you speak, or what sex you are. In some quarters men and women are separated. Not at our Todah.

The speaker, usually either Deborah, Reuben or Sorkatti talk about something the Rabboni said or did. It is after our meal, people are full, satisfied, and relaxed. Often, we have a translator who can communicate the Greek into Arabic or vice versa. It makes for a longer event, but no one is going anywhere.

This evening Deborah shared her thoughts in Greek and Sorkatti acted as her translator. They make an amazing tandem. I will only share Deborah's words to the best of my ability. I hope you enjoy i. You will see why I say I do not think our mission would be successful without her.

Without any further ado, welcome Deborah.

"For you who haven't met me and don't know me, I am Deborah, named after one of the great woman leaders of our people. Deborah the warrior was a wise, brave, and effective leader for our people in a time when few leaders could be found—male or female. She was righteous, just and cared for her people. She loved the Lord. And so, she is rightly revered, a light to our people and the world."

"But I am not her. Nowhere close. I am ashamed to say, and this was before I met my husband Matthew, I had cast off my Jewish heritage, to the shame of my ancestors and the God of my fathers—and took on a Greek name and identity. I put on bright colorfully sexually explicit clothing, expensive make-up, and glorious perfumes, I tied my hair up in a provocative way, put on strings of expensive jewelry and ornaments—so alluring to lonely young men in my culture and called myself Callista, the Beautiful one."

Deborah laughed so captivatingly to the growing crowd of men and women alike. She had this gracious way of opening up the hearts of others. She was so transparent and disarming. She paused and gazed over the crowd and continued.

"And I was beautiful. Today, I have put on some weight and my hair has long since turned grey, lines now dance upon my old face, I sold most of my jewelry—but 50 years ago? My beauty attracted a crowd."

"And I sold that beauty to whoever would pay me a couple of denarii—men or women—it did not matter as long as you could pay. I was Callista, the street worker, the prostitute, the whore."

"Callista was not Deborah. She was a very wounded soul. She had been married before—to a man she loved and whom she thought loved her. She had children, two beautiful children, a boy, and a girl—Isaac and Miriam were their names."

"But, her husband, who had sworn to care for her, to cherish her and keep her safe and hold her reputation high among the villagers—he betrayed her, shamed her, and destroyed her reputation—and then blamed her."

"And so, Deborah fell from her glory—so very quickly—like falling into quicksand. It only took a few days for her to be shunned unjustly by her family, her synagogue and village. She went from cherished to despised so, so quickly."

"Callista, the unfairly disempowered, the shamed, the impure one, did the only thing she saw she could do. She started shamefully chasing trade caravans on the International Highway selling her warm body for cold coin. It was terrifying at first. She would cry herself to sleep. Alcohol helped her nerves and her disgrace. But after a time, her emotions, her heart hardened, and she did what she had to do ."

"I know many of you here know exactly what she went through. You too. I know."

"I am not making excuses. I am not justifying my choices. I am just bearing witness to what happened."

"But then, the Rabboni."

"I still am not sure why I went to Galilee that day. Some of my clients thought I would be entertained by this latest Jewish teacher. I declined at first, but my curiosity got the better of me. I also think I wanted to go and hate him—because I wrongly thought he represented the same God who had abandoned me years before—the same religion that had emotionally raped me and degraded me—and caused me so much pain. I think I wanted to be angry."

"So, I brought some of my fellow prostitutes and we gathered together in the shade of a palm tree grove not far from where he sat and spoke."

"I listened. My arms crossed, my eyes furrowed in suspicion and defensiveness."

"I cringed when he referred to us, the entire crowd that had gathered on that hillside—you should have seen them. And he called us enviable? Who was he kidding? Who does he think he is? How could he tell this bunch, so many of whom

I recognized, many of whom were clients of mine—married men and women who were cheating on their families—and tell them they were enviable? There were the blind, the sick, the infirmed, the poor, the impure, the unrighteous. Anyone could see we were a lot of things, but we weren't enviable."

"How dare he tell me that? He doesn't know me, and what I have been put through unjustly, unfairly. Enviable? It enraged me. I could barely stand there any longer—but for some reason—I couldn't move either."

"Then he said this. And I swear, he looked directly at me when he did."

"You are the salt of the earth. You are the light of the world. Let your light shine before men, that they may see your good deeds and praise your Father in heaven."

"Hmm, I knew salt. I am a Jew. We used so much of the stuff. We used it to bake bread, to preserve fish to be sold to the caravan. We used it in just about every offering brought to the Temple. I used it to clean the afterbirth blood off my two children. Salt was a vital product for our people."

"I wasn't vital to anyone. I wasn't salt—I was road dust—that is how I had been cast away and stomped upon by uncaring travelers. You just use road dust."

"I didn't make anyone better. I didn't make Galilee better."

"My namesake Deborah did. Now, she was salt. Her courage, her faith, her giftings and her leadership was sprinkled throughout the tribes for all to see and appreciate."

"I wasn't light either, God help me. My work was done in the darkness, in secret, in shame, in denial and cover up. I wore masks to bring to life the liar Callista and to crucify Deborah day in and day out."

"No one saw my light and bore witness of a God who loves, who rescues, who raises up the broken, who makes the unenviable enviable."

"They only saw a tragic woman clinging for life in a very dark place."

"My namesake? Now she was a lamp set upon a lampstand. She was a city on a hill. People flocked to her and praised God in her presence."

"What did this Jewish rabbi mean to accomplish by telling me I was mistaken about who I am."

"I swear I heard him say to me,"

'You Deborah are salt and will spice up the world. You Deborah are light—and in your light men and women will see God—and will praise him for you as they did your namesake. Follow me, Deborah.'"

"Right then and there, my knees buckled, and my legs fell out from me. I slumped to the ground in a faint, and if one of my dear friends hadn't caught me, I could have severely hurt my head on one of the black basalt rocks."

"In my head, this is what I was thinking. He sees me. He is not looking away. He is not judging me. He sees me, and in his gaze, I feel cared for. I see a man who really does have my back. I am enough. I felt his empathy, his desire to honor me, all those things I had been missing for so long. I somehow knew that in his care, I would be cherished, my former name resurrected. I felt safe. I felt loved as I was—no need for make-up or masks. I felt empowered again."

"He looked behind the protective Callista-mask and saw the pure Jewess Deborah."

"I thought my saltiness had been lost—given away time and again. But I got his joke. Salt cannot lose its flavor. Water cannot lose its wetness. Fish must swim."

"Tasteless road dust can be kneaded into the salt, and it can lose its immediate effect. He invited me to be salt again—to be me. My choices, the bad things I had done and had been done to me did not murder Deborah—only hid her from sight. The Rabboni knew how to do great things with the formerly dead."

"My light, my former light had been long disguised, hidden under a woven basket of sin. But I realized my dead light could be resurrected and re-created. Jesus could do it. Jesus did it."

"That's my story. I stayed at a distance for a number of days, too ashamed I think—also scared. Was this real? I had been deeply hurt before. Nothing has hurt us more than relationships, amen?"

"Eventually, I approached him. My plan was to look him straight in his eyes and ask him a few questions. I had them all planned out."

"When I finally looked into his loving gaze, I broke down. It was all I could do to just fall at his feet and cry—just cry."

"I was blubbering uncontrollably. I confessed a long list of sins and bad choices. I grabbed dirt from the path and used it to roughly wipe off as much of the make-up I could. I felt so ashamed of Callista."

"Jesus? He patiently and silently looked into my eyes and just listened."

"Then I said something—I said something like, 'If you are willing to associate with an impure woman, who has shared her womanhood glory with so many, whose name has been disgraced again and again—if you are willing, I am yours.'"

"All he said in response was",

'Rise my daughter Deborah. Rise up and follow me. You will be like your namesake again. People will come to your renewed light. You will be a light to the world. Welcome back my beloved.'"

"And I did. That was over 50 years ago now. I met Matthew shortly after. He was on his own journey of becoming salt and light. He was so cute. So smart. So inquisitive. I remember when I first saw him, doing some menial errand for the Rabboni. He was a bit shorter than me. Even then he was balding. His beard was well trimmed Roman style. He wore a Roman tunic and spoke Greek very clearly. I fell in love with his vulnerability and desire to serve—Oh and he has a cute dimple that appears when he smiles. He is a real man."

My eyes teared over when she said that, looking directly at me. The audience chuckled. They know both of us pretty well. They know we care. I rose and went to her and hugged her. She was indeed taller than me. So, people laughed as she bent her head down to kiss me on the top of my bald head. She continued.

"Some of you here have been unfairly beat up, betrayed, robbed of your name, your value, your heritage, stripped of power and unjustly tossed away as road dust. I feel your pain. I will not try to justify or whitewash how you have been treated. I am so sorry."

"All I can say is that if you are looking to be restored to honor and face, I can introduce you to a man, Jesus of Nazareth, the Rabboni, who would cherish you as he cherished me. Nothing you have done or said, or not done or not said, or no matter what has been done or said to you—nothing would disqualify you from being lifted up and rescued. He has come to make the unenviable enviable. He has come to empower the disempowered. To give a name of glory to the shamed discarded ones."

"Come. Bring your story. Bring your scars. Bring your shame—your masks. You will not leave the same. He makes road dust salt. He makes the darkness light."

"Since no one is granted this gift on the grounds of their tribe, wealth, purity, family, sex, or ethnicity, no one of you is excluded from His reach. The Rabboni has unleashed a new creative dynamic power, a quality of value, worth and identity sourced in His Spirit that can only be described as "love"—the love you have down deep been longing for but never found to any satisfaction. What I lost, I have more than made up in Jesus."

Deborah paused, looked around, trying to capture every face, looking for new hope, someone smiling, someone weeping. My bride, the warrior judge of new Israel, Deborah.

Like I said, I can't imagine what I would do without her. I am not sure what this mission would do without her. With everything that has happened to her, no one would blame her for being an angry victim, or cynical, or withdrawn. Who would stop her from complaining about all the injustice in her life? But she is the most gracious and kind, other-oriented person I know, man or woman. Hurting and lonely people flock to her and drink in her empathy and compassion.

She is exactly what Jesus meant when he said "You are salt. You are light."

Allow me to expand upon Jesus's words a little. Maybe this will make sense now?

Don't worry, even though you will endure persecution—I've got this. You—that's right—you all are the savory salt needed for this insipid place. You will make a difference, persecution or not.

Imagine if there was a salt that tasted chalky like gypsum—like rock? That would be absurd. No one would touch it. If they did taste it, they would just spit it out. They would just add it to the other road dust. But are not that type of salt. You will make everyone taste better.

Here's another simile. You will enlighten this grey shaded world. As you depend upon me, the true light of the world, people will see. You will not be hidden.

Can you imagine city planners who built their city on the open face of a hill and then tried to hide it? Or that homemaker who carefully fills her lamps with precious oil so that her family can see at night, but then buries it underneath a woven bowl? Foolish, right?

No, a wise homemaker would put it up on a stand where it's light will shine the brightest and the furthest. That is what I have in store for you. I am putting you on a global stage. Anything less would be foolish. So be light. Be salty.

Don't let anything get in the way of people seeing light in you. Here's the joke. They knew you when you were as tasteless as they were, unenviable. You were like gypsum, road-fill. And you didn't shine any light for people's path. You were shadow-dwellers like them.

Then you were swept up into the loving arms of my Father. Trust me, they will see you in action and they will be so surprised at the change, they will have to praise your Heavenly Father.

21

Day 700 of the Axum Mission

The Jewish community in Axum is large and thriving. The synagogue is even larger and more adorned than the one in Capernaum.

This reflects the growth of diaspora Judaism here in Axum. During the persecution of the Jews by King Herod over a generation ago, many Jewish leaders, priests and sages fled the land and scattered north, south, east, and west.

There had always been a burgeoning Jewish community in Alexandria, but the thriving spice trade spread the community out even further to Axum and beyond. There was a new surge of immigrants when the Romans brutally shut down the stunning Temple in Alexandria. That was only a few years ago. Many of the priests and Levites have found their way to Axum.

I will also tell you the Axum Jewish community claims they were founded by the Queen of Sheba after her audiences with King Solomon. It is indeed a great heritage. Some share other stories that the Ark of the Covenant has found its way here as well, hidden in a secret place known by only few. I cannot confirm it.

Here, the Jewish community grew not only in wealth and influence but in numbers. The synagogue ruler Stafylus suspects so many of the locals had become disillusioned with spiritism and were fascinated by the Torah and the stories.

The synagogue leader, or *archisynagogos* is the most eminent among the officials of the Jewish congregation here. He is the spiritual leader of the synagogue and supervisor of the ritual. But he also plays a political, administrative, and financial role in the affairs of the congregation, and is entrusted with the maintenance of the cult building and serves as a representative of the congregation before the King Zoskales and the city leaders here in Axum.

He is a very capable man, and I am pleased to call him my friend. He is very curious about the teachings and the life of the Rabboni Jesus of Nazareth. He had heard many tales, some of which were quite absurd. We have had many discussions, and of course, he and Reuben speak regularly.

I would guess perhaps half of the Synagogue attendees are locals, many yet uncircumcised. They come for a variety of reasons, generally, they enjoy the pomp of the liturgy, the reading of the Torah and of course the discussion of religion or philosophy that occurs every Sabbath.

This popularity has brought Stafylus and the Jews in conflict with many of the tribal shaman in the valley, in particular our old friend, Haaman.

Haaman is not above a great deal of trickery to disrupt the synagogue and many of its good works for the community. Many of the tribal converts have given testimony their families have been threatened by the goons of Haaman—though nothing could be proven yet. Stafylus has officially brought a formal complaint to King Zoskales, but so far, the King has been unresponsive.

The synagogue is gorgeous. There are large double wooden doors intricately carved with stories of the Torah and the Jerusalem Temple. It is surrounded by massive granite columns topped with carved granite arches. As you enter the courtyard, you will see a massive fountain adorned with gardens made up of fresh flowers, other greenery, and herbs. The aroma is breathtaking. Surrounding the fountain are cisterns always filled with clean water, a mikvah bath and seating areas for contemplation and prayer.

To the south, east and west are buildings for education and hospitality. We have many Jewish families travel through this city. The Synagogue sees this as part of their mission and is pleased to provide temporary housing, free room and board for travelers, pilgrims, those who have been displaced from their housing for whatever reasons and just the weary.

There is also a school for our young as well as an academy to train young men in the Torah. The head sage is Rabbi Tarfon. He was a student of the Pharisaic school of Shammai and he immigrated in the years before the Temple was destroyed. He is very capable and has hit it off with Reuben—even though Reuben was trained in the competing school of Hillel.

You may be aware these were the two main Pharisaic schools in my lifetime at least. Shammai was a fierce debater, from a wealthy family in Jerusalem and was known for strict adherence to the Torah—the letter of the law.

Hillel came from poverty, born in Babylon. Rabbi Hillel was known for his compassion and mercy. It was said Hillel and Shammai had many heated disagreements, but never did it affect their fellowship and respect. But unfortunately, their disciples did not follow in their sandals and there have been many heated arguments between them.

Let me tell you one account that will give you an idea of the difference between the two schools. An uncircumcised Gentile came to Shammai and pled with him, "Convert me on condition that you teach me the whole Torah while I stand on one foot." Shammai pushed him away with the yardstick in his hand.

Then the same man went to Hillel with the same challenge and shortly he was converted. Here is what Hillel reportedly said. "This is the summary of the entire Torah. What is hateful to you, do not do to your friend. The rest is commentary. Go learn."

The man overjoyed cried out in tears, "Patient Hillel, blessings on your head, for you brought me under the wings of the divine presence."

It is said Shammai's severity sought to drive disciples from the world. Hillel's patience brought disciples under the wings of the divine presence.

Rabbi Tarfon, a fervent adherent to the School of Shammai, had heard that before and doubted its historicity, but agreed there was some reflection of the differences there.

The Synagogue's main hall is to the north facing Jerusalem. It has more modest wooden doors but once you enter you are surrounded by tall columns which buttress expansive seating areas, of course, the women's section is separated from the men by custom (though there is a serious discussion at the moment about changing that ancient custom).

On the north side is the ark, a large two-door cupboard, where the Holy Torah scrolls are kept. In front of the ark is the Bimah, where the leader stands to read the scripture, or the cantor sings liturgical songs. In front of the Bimah is a candelabra whose flame is always burning.

Most of my team has started to attend Sabbath services here. Reuben has read the Torah on numerous occasions. His reputation and credibility are highly respected in the community.

When we arrived, the synagogue leaders pummeled us wanting news of Jerusalem. They had heard the tragedy of the destruction of the Temple a decade ago but had heard little else. I am so impressed with the depth of knowledge of Reuben. Of course, he was in the middle of all the happenings. He has tried to answer all their questions.

Rueben is my age. As a mere youth, he was chosen to be a disciple of Gamaliel the Elder, the successor of Hillel son's Simeon and quickly rose to be one of the most respected, educated, and skilled sage in the Hillel school of Pharisaic sages. He was impressive apparently. In fact, he was one of the youngest Pharisees to ever be chosen to the Sanhedrin in year 30 and made his reputation during the official trial against Lazarus—I mentioned this earlier.

Today is a very special day on the calendar and minds of all Jews all over the world. Today is Yom Kippur, our Day of Atonement. Ten years ago, Jews would pour into Jerusalem and take part in the seven-day celebration capped off with the sacrifice of the atoning goat by the High Priest.

For Torahic Jews, this was not just a ritual. This was the only way we could be absolved of our annual sins against God. The High Priest laid his hands upon the head of the goat and transferred all our corporate sins to him. Then the sins were judged to be worthy of death and the goat's throat was cut. It is brutal and bloody, but per the Torah and the Oral writings, that is how a Jew can once again become righteous and can come into the presence, *lipnay Elohim,* of our Covenant God in good standing. It covers us with the righteousness of the High Judge. For a moment we have clean hands and a pure heart—not due to anything we've done or not done, said, or not said. But because a substitute has paid the full requirements of justice for our failures. God's just wrath is propitiated—until the next year.

It has been a high privilege enjoyed by our people for generations since the time of Moses. That is until the Roman armies flooded into the Holy City a decade ago and razed the Temple and the Altar and murdered or sold into slavery all the Priests and Levites. Even after ten years, I still mourn the loss for our people.

Reuben has spent a great deal of time and interviews to put some context around that event and the severe transition that has affected Judaism. The Jews of Axum, both men and women have gathered to hear his thoughts on this Yom Kippur.

Here's Reuben's insider look at the swirling and confusing events behind the curtain. Sorkatti will assist me divide Reuben's extensive thoughts into a few journal entries. With Reuben's help we have attempted to capture all of his thoughts here.

22

Reuben Part 1

Reuben was a large man, a head taller than me, full of frame. With his broad muscular shoulders, strong arms, and large hands, he could have been a stonemason or a farmer.

He normally wore a beige wool tunic, two large squares set together. On top was his brown mantle fastened at his shoulder by a common gold pin. His garment was clean but hardly ostentatious. He felt wealth should not be worn.

His face was round, eyes brown and bright, and almost always the thing most noticed by others was his broad toothy smile. He had a full grey beard hanging to his chest which he habitually stroked. He said it helped him think. Maybe we should all stroke our beards more. He is among the smartest and wisest men I have ever known.

Reuben came from a strict Jewish family in Hebron, south of Jerusalem. He and his siblings, seven of them, were taught Hebrew, Greek, and Aramaic from a very young age. Reuben had not only showed great interest in the Torah, but he amazed the scholars at his school with his insightful questions. Soon his Rabbi reached out to the great Pharisaic scholar Gamaliel in Jerusalem, to tell him about this brilliant and precocious child. It didn't take long for Reuben to take his rightful place alongside of Gamaliel in the school of Hillel.

Reuben would regularly teach the gathered Jewish leaders at the Axum synagogue. There were other teachers, but Reuben was quite unique for several reasons. First, he was an excellent Rabbi, skilled at discipleship, having been taught by two of the greatest Rabbis of all Judaism, Gamaliel the Elder and then Rabban Yohanan Ben Zakkai.

Of Zakkai, it has been said no one before had mastered the entire Mishnah, halakhah, madras, astronomy, numerology, language of angels and demons, along with all mystical aspects of creation and constellations.

Also, and this is perhaps the greatest of all reasons these men and women came to listen to Reuben. He was there. He lived during that important danger-fraught time for Judaism and for much of it he served on the Sanhedrin. He spoke as an important eyewitness.

This day, I am guessing there were over 50 Jewish leaders in the large room of the Axum Synagogue complex. All of them know Rueben personally. Many of them had heard his accounts before in bits and pieces, but this was different.

Reuben is going to give a full account of Judaism from the time of Jesus, around year 30, to today. I know how Reuben has struggled to gather all his thoughts. It was not only the story of Judaism's tragic and difficult transition, but it is also the story of Reuben's search for truth.

Here's Reuben. I should note for you who are unfamiliar with Rabbinic Judaism, when authoring a written document, scholars like Reuben will almost always use the tetragrammaton (YHWH) when referring to God's mercy; or Elohim, when more focused upon God's judgment These two names express the totality of God's providence, his two *Middoth* or measures. When he is speaking though, Reuben will only refer to God respectfully as Elohim.

"Welcome my friends and colleagues. May Elohim richly bless us as we struggle to understand His working among our people—His people. Praise be to the Elohim of Abraham, Isaac, and Jacob. Amen."

He had raised his hands skyward to praise God. The crowd stood in agreement and followed with a very hardy "Amen!" Then Reuben paused, looked to the ground, stroked his beard, and took a deep breath. When he felt ready and the group had settled down on the stone benches surrounding him in a semi-circle, he raised his face and began with a typical Reuben smile.

"As you know, brothers, the Sanhedrin was the official religious court of Israel. The court of 71, the Great Sanhedrin met in the Temple in Jerusalem every day except during festivals and the Shabbat in a building called the Hall of

Hewn Stones. In the past, the Sanhedrin limited its recruiting to a combination of the priesthood—the Kohanim—Levites and then, some ordinary Jews who were members of those families having a pure lineage such that their daughters were allowed to marry priests.

"Due to obvious, very public, and vile nepotism and corruption at the highest levels of the Temple in our days, the Sanhedrin shifted its demographic by intentionally choosing more and more Rabbinic sages, the Pharisees—those from both main schools, Shammai and Hillel.

"I can remember still when the High Priest was also the Nasi –the head of the Sanhedrin. But no more. Particularly after the Roman Governor of Judea shocked the Jerusalem community by naming Annas and then Caiaphas as High Priests. That was clearly a public overreach of authority and almost caused a rebellion—and should have. Since that time, the Priests, Levites, and other Sadducees, have, with only a few notable exceptions, largely been shunned from the Sanhedrin.

"Also, the head of the Sanhedrin would have come from Hillel's family. Hillel's son Simeon followed his father, who was followed by his son Gamliel the Elder in the year 50.

Reuben cocked his head, raised his left eyebrow, and smiled. We all knew the story was indeed about to get interesting. Many of the men here in Axum were unaware of the inner workings of the Jerusalem leadership. Few Jews in rural areas or certainly of the Diaspora would dare ask or pay too much attention to rumors—at least publicly—but you can be sure, all were curious.

He grinned as he looked over the crowd. He had their complete attention. He drank a swig of ale, wiped his full beard with his sleeve and pressed on.

"So, normally then, it was assumed Gamaliel the Elder would be succeeded by his eldest son, Simeon ben Gamliel. But something very interesting happened.

"Hillel's best student was universally accepted to be Rabban Zakkai. Zakkai was not a descendent of Hillel, but he was very popular. The Pharisaic leadership was split—very unhealthy."

"At the very same time, Rome was severely pressuring our people to make changes. There arose, mostly from Galilee a populist party of extremist Zealots who referred to themselves as *biryonim*. They were Jews who were committed to overthrowing Rome and re-establishing the Maccabean Kingdom of a half a century before. The *biryonim* believed they could overthrow Rome. They were so wrong.

"The *biryonim* leaders, who most often referred to themselves as King of the Jews were not interested in compromise of any sort. By the time of the destruction, there were multiple armies led by multiple so-called 'King of the Jews' in the besieged city. Rome could not allow them to continue.

"The lines were drawn in the sand. Are you a supporter of the *biryonim*, or not? No middle ground. The school of Shammai were already for the most part supportive of the *biryonim*. Then Simeon, Hillel's great grandson, came out in support of one of the 'King of the Jews', John of Gischala. I will say more in a moment, but that was a very unwise decision by the nominal Sanhedrin Nasi.

"My master, another Hillelite, Rabban Zakkai took a very unpopular stand against the *biryonim* urging for a peace with Rome through compromise. So, as you can see, during the most critical moments in the history of our people, the Sanhedrin was tragically split and functionally had two Nasi—Simeon and Zakkai. I know for a fact Zakkai never wanted such an honor.

"By the way, the Sadducees who by this time owed most of their power, wealth, security, and future livelihoods to Rome stood against the *biryonim*. They urged the confused citizens to throw down their arms and plea for mercy. Certainly, they were concerned a war with Rome could be devastating and end with a crisis related to the Temple. They were right, it turned out."

"You see our choices? Neither were tenable. It did not take long for the massive Roman army to surround the city and give the ultimatum, "Surrender or die".

"Then the *biryonim* sealed our fate. In the year 59, they burned down the warehouses held all of the city's siege supplies. City managers had spent the last year or more gathering so much grain, food, water, armaments, and such that could have withheld a very long siege. In a few moments, it was all gone.

"Now the only remaining option for the population who would face starvation very quickly was open warfare with the powerful armies just outside our walls. It was a fatal error of course. To make matters even worse, the biryonim would murder any who did not support them. They certainly targeted my master Zakkai, but Elohim intervened."

Reuben went on to tell the amazing story of how Zakkai faked his death by asking his nephew and other disciples to put him in a closed casket, pretend he had died and to take him through the gate guarded by *biryonim* fanatics who were always on the lookout for traitors who wanted to surrender to Rome. Zakkai knew it was proper for the dead to be buried outside the city, particularly one of the members of the Sanhedrin. Zakkai was very old and so it was reasonable he could have perished and gone to Paradise. The guards after a long interrogation allowed the disciples to go and bury the corpse.

The students took their master to the Roman General Vespasian. The story is told, and Reuben said. though he couldn't prove it, he believed it was true. When greeting the General Vespasian, Zakkai referred to him as 'Emperor'. Vespasian corrected Zakkai, but at that moment a messenger brought Vespasian the news he was the new Emperor of Rome.

Vespasian asked Zakkai what request he was making. Zakkai said only three.

First, he requested the Romans guarantee the safety of the scholars of Yavneh, where the new Sanhedrin would be located. Second, he wanted Rome's guarantee for the survival of the family of Rabban Gamliel and lastly, that the Romans allow their physicians to restore the health of Rabbi Zadok, who had fasted for forty days to pray for the safety of the city and the Temple. All these were granted to Zakkai.

Here's the truth, if it wasn't for the bravery and passion of Rabban Zakkai, Judaism would likely have been destroyed, wiped off the land, like spilled milk is wiped clean by a swipe of a cloth. The leaders either killed or sold into slavery by the Romans. Reuben paused to let the audience absorb that shocking statement.

In a moment, Reuben continued. "As I have thought about it for over a decade now, it is fair to suggest there are five Jewish 'paths' proposed to enter the Kingdom of Elohim and to earn his favor.

"But to be clear, while there are overlaps, they are also great differences—vast chasms as well. And so, a discerning and wise Jew who wants to know Elohim's favor, must pick a path. Likewise, you must pick a path my friends.

"First, the Zealots, the *biryonim*. They believed if our people would just organize and violently throw off our pagan occupiers, then Elohim would return to Jerusalem, his shekinah glory would re-enter the Temple and Israel would be returned to world leadership. They failed. The hordes of the Roman army either slaughtered or transported remaining *biryonim* throughout the realm as slaves.

"This was not the path of Elohim. I can say clearly now, no offense meant.

"Having said that, in those last months and weeks, many Priests and many Pharisees—including Rabban Simon ben Gamliel unwisely joined their ranks. But they are gone as well. They were also intentionally and brutally hunted down by Rome's army and assassins.

"I cannot say this philosophy cannot arise again. History suggests it might. I do believe Elohim will indeed raise Israel up in the last days. But it will be of his doing, not an army of Jews, not through the swords of the *biryonim*."

He paused, looking around to see the faces of his audience. There were no obvious questions, so he pressed on.

"The second path to Elohim's favor would be the one proposed by the Sadducees and the priestly party. This institution was ordained by Elohim himself in the Torah. They—to their credit fiercely held to the written text as best as humanly possible—every jot and tittle. Their philosophy of how Israel can propitiate the wrath of Elohim against sin and idolatry involved the prescribed offerings at the Temple. Particularly on Yom Kippur, our Day of Atonement, all of Israel would gather with soiled hands—due the just wrath of Elohim—and the High Priest would make a substitutionary offering for all— two goats, one slaughtered to pay for sins and one to be 'karat'—cut off from fellowship with Elohim in our place—so we could be his sons and daughters in good standing again. Amen?"

The audience responded with a bold "Amen!"

"Setting aside the tragic well-known corruption at the highest levels of the Sadducees and the Priesthood, nevertheless, they were faithful in the sacrificial offering for Israel. And I know so many of you here in Axum have family that served in the Temple—who tragically perished when Rome destroyed the Temple. I am so sorry for your loss."

He looked intentionally around the room again until he caught the eye of one person in particular.

"I also know some of you were faithful priests who served at the Temple in Alexandria."

He nodded in sincere deference. "But that too has been shut down by Rome."

"We Jews who embrace the Torah must also embrace the Temple and the sacrifices. All Jews, even you who are newly circumcised have benefited from the Temple and its sacrifices. I will come back to that.

"Allow me to make a few points. First...,"

Reuben said, pausing as he choked down his emotions and tears. He looked down at the dirt, wiped his sleeves over his swollen eyes to deal with the tears beginning to flow. In a few moments of struggle, he began again.

"...First, this is the dirty little secret. You likely do not know this. Even most of the Jews in Jerusalem did not know this. Ever after the return of our people from exile, and the Temple and worship re-established, something was just not right. The Holy of Holies was an empty shell, void of the Shekinah Glory of Elohim."

He paused again. Clearly the audience was shocked at this revelation. You could hear multiple side conversations reverberating all over the room, some people were shocked, others indignant. Everyone was listening to this disquieting news. He waved his hands over the crowd to get their attention again. Reuben knew this would be controversial. Yet he knew it would all become clear.

We will pick up Reuben's thoughts in the next journal entry. They are well worth the time.

23

Reuben Part 2

Reuben had to bring the audience back to order. Cleary, people were shocked.

"Please brothers and sisters, let me finish. For those of us in the know, though we elected to not make it public for many reasons of course, the Holy of Holies was empty and has been for a long time. When Moses' Tabernacle was completed, the shekinah glory of Elohim came upon it as was witnessed by all who participated in the worship. The same was observed when King Solomon completed his temple. But nothing of the sort was witnessed when the Second Temple was completed. There was no ark, no seraphim. In fact, many believe the ark of the Covenant is somewhere here in Axum, isn't that correct."

A few quietly nodded in agreement. Reuben took note of those who did, he would pursue that more later.

"How was it dealt with? The decision was made long ago that the High Priest would follow the Torahic prescription for all offerings <u>as if</u> the presence of Elohim were indeed there. I understand their dilemma. There were no prescriptions in the Torah about what to do if Elohim's glory ever departed. So, they continued to do what they were told.

"Those sacrifices repeated endlessly year after year did not make perfect those who drew near to worship. It is impossible for the blood of bulls and goats to take away sins and the resulting guilt, shame, and sense of isolation from Elohim.

"Let me ask those of you who are priests. How is any Jew to gain the favor of Elohim?"

He paused and looked around the audience.

You may have many answers, of course, but chief among them would be the faithful participation in the Temple worship.

"But what if there is no Temple? What could the Sadducees and priests say when the Temple was razed to the ground, again? Where could our people go to atone for their sins? Where would one go to repent and confess their sins, to find atonement. There are not more cleansing baths, no sacrifices, no priests, corrupt or not, and no Day of Atonement. Never again will we hear the High Priest say, 'It is finished!'

"The Romans had not only destroyed the Temple, but also pursued and assassinated as many priests as possible. Those few who did either joined Rabban Zakkai at Yavneh or fled the land before the destruction or like the Zealots, were sold as slaves.

"I have had these discussions with the very few surviving Sadducees I could locate. They had little theology of the afterlife. They had minimized all oral tradition. Their whole narrow focus had been on the Temple. And now, there is nothing. For all practical purposes, there is no more Sadducean party. Their lands and wealth have been confiscated. The Temple implements looted, smashed, or melted down. For you who have embraced this path to favor with Elohim, again, I am so sorry for your loss.

"Then there was the third path to Elohim's favor, represented by the many monastic sects of separatists—some have referred to them as the Essenes. The Romans were no less brutal in their pursuit and destruction of these groups as well.

"These well-meaning Jewish brothers and sisters pulled away largely due to the ongoing politicization and corruption in the Temple hierarchy. They were so sure that when Elohim returns, he will be searching the land for the spiritually pure. So numerous communes of "pure-ones' multiplied in the wilderness. Very strict rules, vows of poverty and submission to leadership. In their mind, Elohim would see their efforts to be righteous and reward them with eternity in Paradise.

"In fact, the men of one such commune, Qumran, were buried facing East so when the Messiah came in the clouds and their bodies resurrected, they would be the first to see his glory.

"I am told by a very good and credible source their obsession for purity ironically led to the death of many in the Qumran community. To create a holy and pure environment, the men were required to go outside the commune to relieve themselves. As they re-entered the city, again, they were to cleanse themselves from their impurity by bathing in a pool at the gate.

"Then someone noticed that many were suffering fevers, convulsions and other stomach afflictions leading to an excruciating death. It turned out the pool—or better the so-call cleansing bath was spreading vile uncleanness. All their careful efforts at remaining ritually clean were unknowingly causing a deep fouling. Such are the well-meaning plans of humanity that demand the purity belonging to the Heavens alone.

"Alas, now, the Essenes are gone too."

He paused and looked around the room in silence. "Their communities are wastelands—not from the hand of Elohim, but of man. I have walked down the streets of Qumran. There is nothing left. May Elohim eventually raise them up.

"Let me say some things about the fourth path to God's favor proposed by my people, the Pharisees. As I said, in those last days, we Pharisees had splintered into several disparate camps. It was not our finest hour.

"There was the pro-war camp, those Pharisees who believed we must fight to free ourselves from our Roman occupiers. Unfortunately, they aligned themselves with the *biryonim*. And you know the story, they too were annihilated alongside the Zealots, a bloodbath. I was not there, but the stories I heard from eyewitnesses are shocking. The school of Shammai is gone. The pro-war Pharisees are gone.

"Before this time, Pharisaism had known two complementary yet often competing schools: the precise House of Shammai, known to some of you here in this very room—and the more moderate House of Hillel. But that changed in a moment of time. All that remains from the carnage are those few Hillelite sages who were allowed free passage to Yavneh by Emperor Vespasian. Since that time, only a decade ago now, the survivors of the school of Hillel are reshaping Judaism largely in Zakkai's image.

"Yohanan ben Zakkai in Yavneh assumed the liturgical authority formerly vested in the Temple priest to determine the proper calendar. He also now exercises judicial and legal authority earlier held by the Sanhedrin. All of this is with Rome's approval. Before, Rome tried to rule the people through the King, then through a Roman prelate, and even the Sanhedrin. Now, they are satisfied to allow limited rulership by the Hillel Rabbinic school at Yavneh.

"While some Jewish leaders complain, there is nothing that can be done. This is a new era for our people. The Rabbinic school in Yavneh under the remarkable leadership and vision of Zakkai has become the legitimate successor and heir to the old Sanhedrin's authority in post temple Judaism.

"Let me be clear. For my entire lifetime, Judaism was made up of competing often charged voices, the Sadducees, the Separatists, the Zealots and two main schools in Pharisaism, Shammai and Hillel. Now, the very few survivors of the school of Hillel are the sole definers of Judaism. Now they, virtually all alone determine how the Torah and Oral traditions are to be interpreted and applied to Jews in Judea and in the diaspora. It is now customary to speak of Rabbinic Judaism, as we largely have cast off the soiled moniker Pharisaism. So be it. The theological future is guided by a small official Rabbinical school of those largely trained in Yavneh by Zakkai.

"If you have not heard, Rabban Zakkai retired not long ago and joined his ancestors shortly afterwards. His legacy at Yavneh was then reconstituted as a more formal Sanhedrin under the leadership of Rabban Gamaliel II. But Judaism has dramatically changed. His influence will go on for a long time.

"I was among the disciples of Zakkai who left Jerusalem along with him. It was one of the hardest decisions I ever made. I still have memories of the many friends and family who condemned us as cowards and traitors, Roman sympathizers. I have a scar on my shoulder from a brick thrown by someone in the streets as we exited the doomed city protected by a cohort of Roman soldiers. It was a painful walk of shame I will never forget."

Rabbi Tarfon graciously asked Reuben a question—maybe the only right question at this point in Reuben's narrative.

"Were you right? Did you do the right and Elohim-honoring thing? What are we to learn from this tragedy?"

Reuben paused, took a deep breath, as if stalling to get his emotions at rest and his thoughts together. This was so personal for Reuben. This was his question as well.

"Bless you Rabbi. You are a man of great wisdom. That is the right question. Not so much 'Did I and those other Pharisees do the right thing', but what are we to learn from this crisis of faith? I think I have an answer. Be patient, I beg you. He continued.

"A month or so later, my teacher Rabban Zakkai, blessed be he, walked through the ruins of the Temple with some students. I was there.

"When he saw the Temple was destroyed, he stood and rent his garments, took off his *tefillin*, and sat weeping, as did we pupils with him. One of my colleagues, Rabbi Joshua said to the teacher, 'Woe is us that this place has been destroyed, the place where atonement was made for the sins of Israel.' That is the question, for without the Temple practices no one would ever enter the world to come.

"Rabban Zakkai paused for a moment, sadly shook his head, and said, 'No, my son, do you not know we have a means of making atonement that is like it? And what is it? It is deeds of love, as it is said, 'For I desire kindness, and not sacrifice.'

"This is my theological problem with Rabban Zakkai's reformation. Kindness, prayer, and Torah reading have officially replaced the sacrifice as the way to gain God's favor for Jews.

"It is now taught, 'Just as the sin and guilt offerings made atonement for Israel in the past, so now charity and kindness will make atonement for the nations of the world.' As it is written in the prophet Hosea, 'I desired mercy, and not sacrifice.'"

Many side-comments erupted throughout the common room. This was shocking and provocative—a massive cultural change for Jews. It would take time to digest it all.

"Please, let me continue," Reuben pled with the unsettled audience. "Of the five proposed Jewish ways to enter the favor of Elohim, three have been eradicated from our world—granted glory only in stories and history books. That is those paths proposed by the Zealots, the Essenes, and the Sadducees.

"The fourth proposed path, Pharisaism has been rebirthed and renamed as the new sole guide for Jewish theology in this new era of Rabbinic scholarship. I haven't even mentioned the new emphasis on the deeper mystical teaching of Zakkai, where Torah students in their studies long to explore the mysteries of creation and might find the path to pass from earth with its violence and selfishness through the seven heavens to where the Holy One sits enthroned—like Ezekiel's vision of the heavenly chariot. But that is beyond our topic for this evening."

There was a knowing chuckle in the audience. This new teaching of mysticism was very appealing in some quarters. Many of those who had fled Alexandria when the Romans skuttled their Temple, were very aware of that movement.

"I am told that near his end, Rabbi Zakkai began to weep profusely. The disciples asked the Master why he wept. He replied: 'If I were being taken today before a human king who is here today and tomorrow in the grave, whose anger – if he is angry with me – does not last forever, who if he imprisons me does not imprison me forever, and who if he puts me to death does not put me to everlasting death, and whom I can persuade with words and bribe with money, even so I would weep. Now that I am being taken before the supreme King of Kings, who lives and endures for ever and ever, whose anger is an everlasting anger, who if He imprisons me imprisons me forever, who if He puts me to death puts me to death forever, and whom I cannot persuade with words or bribe with money – nay more, when there are two ways before me, one leading to Paradise and the other to Gehinnom, and I do not know by which I shall be taken, shall I not weep?'

"If the greatest teacher in Pharisaism and in its replacement Rabbinic Judaism, cannot be confident he will be with the Lord for all eternity—what is there for us? For how are we to be confident we will ever show enough acts of kindness, or enough prayer or enough Torah study to tip the scales?

"I will say, with great personal sadness, I have come to the conclusion that this fourth Jewish path has little now to offer to us brothers and sisters. It is familiar, to be sure. But ... I said there were *five* Jewish paths. Yes?"

24

Reuben Part 3

Reuben continued his emotional teachings.

"I realized I had fallen into deep emotional darkness. No doubt, I was mourning the loss of the Temple, of so many friends, and even Judaism as I knew it. I struggled to sleep, to eat, to pray. It was as if, for a time, as the Psalmist said, 'Darkness was my closest friend.'

"I now have come to see how much I depended upon the Temple and the sacrifices to wash me clean from my sins—to remove my sense of guilt. Without it, I was afraid of my very soul. I stopped praying because I was afraid to look up into Elohim's eyes. I was lost.

"I fell into more darkness as Yom Kippur arrived. This was my first Day of Atonement without any atonement. Deep despair attacked me. I became more and more aware of many of my shortcomings, my pride, stubbornness, jealousy, unbelief, lust just to mention a few. I am not proud of my emotions. I am being honest with you, my friends."

Reuben smiled endearingly. We could all relate. Each of us had been there in our own way.

"But what could I do? Where could I go? In what world did Elohim look upon a sinner with any mercy apart from sacrifice?

"I arose early to wander the streets of Jerusalem. The sun was rising in the East and shone brightly on the Eastern gates. I had hoped that if I traversed the exact location where the Temple stood, stood on the piles of rock that were once the altar—I could then find a way to pray—I could cry—I could confess and yes, Elohim might hear me. But alas, nothing-- not that the heavens were silent—they were critical and condemning.

"Suddenly there was a sharp pain in my chest, sweat beaded upon my brow, my breath was arrested in my mouth. I thought I was dying. I imagined Elohim was angry I dared to stand on His defiled altar—defiling it once more with my unclean hands and impure heart. I doubled over in pain for a long time. I know now I was experiencing a panic attack. But then, I believed Elohim's wrath was upon me—for I was unrighteous.

"At that moment, I felt no *chesed* for others. I felt no mercy for others. I felt nothing other than self-pity—and yes, self-condemnation."

He paused, took another deep breath, wiped the tears from his eyes and looked out at the crowd that was intensely listening, aware this was something special.

"I fainted –right there. For how long, I cannot say. I awoke to some arguing that was occurring between some teachers on the Temple stairs not too far away. It was, by the way, the same stairs where I had first sat to listen to Rabbi Zakkai teach his disciples.

"I rose carefully and stumbled over to the group—far enough away I would not be noticed.

"The one man, Thomas was his name, was teaching the Rabbi Jesus of Nazareth was the true Messianic King. But this King was not the King for the worthy but for the unworthy. He had come to be the champion for the unlikely and unrighteous. He started saying the 34th Psalm verbatim.

"Would one of you be willing to say the Psalm now? I do not think I could make it through without weeping more. Keep in mind as you read, I was the afflicted one, the terrified one, the ashamed one, the one strangled by troubles, broken-hearted and crushed in spirit."

A few people volunteered and Reuben gladly pointed to Rabbi Stafylus. The Rabbi rose and began to proclaim the Psalm by memory. He said it with a flourish.

"I will extol the LORD at all times; his praise will always be on my lips.

My soul will boast in the LORD; let the afflicted hear and rejoice.

Glorify the LORD with me; let us exalt his name together.

I sought the LORD, and he answered me; he delivered me from all my fears.

Those who look to him are radiant; their faces are never covered with shame.

This poor man called, and the LORD heard him; he saved him out of all his troubles.

The angel of the LORD encamps around those who fear him, and he delivers them.

Taste and see the LORD is good; blessed is the man who takes refuge in him.

Fear the LORD, you his saints, for those who fear him lack nothing.

The lions may grow weak and hungry, but those who seek the LORD lack no good thing.

Come, my children, listen to me; I will teach you the fear of the LORD.

Whoever of you loves life and desires to see many good days,

keep your tongue from evil and your lips from speaking lies.

Turn from evil and do good; seek peace and pursue it.

The eyes of the LORD are on the righteous and his ears are attentive to their cry;

The face of the LORD is against those who do evil, to cut off the memory of them from the earth.

The righteous cry out, and the LORD hears them; he delivers them from all their troubles.

The LORD is close to the brokenhearted and saves those who are crushed in spirit.

A righteous man may have many troubles, but the LORD delivers him from them all;

he protects all his bones, not one of them will be broken.

Evil will slay the wicked; the foes of the righteous will be condemned.

The LORD redeems his servants; no one will be condemned who takes refuge in him."

"Thank you, brother, Amen," Reuben affirmed. "So, who then does the Psalmist say the Lord will hear? Who then will the Lord deliver from their troubles?"

"Believers—those who seek Him," some said. Others said, "The righteous". Still others, "Those crushed in spirit" and "His servants, the ones who take refuge in Him."

"Yes, I concur, but answer me this. Are those different people or are they the same ones?"

There was silence as people pondered the question.

Finally, one person, an elderly man who was known for his patience and great wisdom said with a gentle wave of his hand. "Surely they are all referring to the righteous, for they alone have standing before Elohim's throne."

"Well said brother. But what is it to be righteous then? Is a man righteous if he commits sin of any kind? If we say no, we have disqualified us all—for all sin. Is a woman righteous if she has gone to the Temple and brought the prescribed sacrifice and openly confesses to Elohim her transgression? If we say yes, once again, we condemn us all because she can no longer find her rightness in that way. There is now no more altar.

"This was the heated debate that was ongoing on the Temple steps by the Offal Gate that morning.

"Finally, I could take it no more and I yelled at the top of my voice, 'Well then how is one to become righteous now there is no more Temple—no more sacrifice?'

"Thomas looked over to me and exclaimed, 'Yes, my brother, that is the question on this holy day, Yom Kippur. Come join us, you are welcomed here.'

"Thomas pointed to the steps just below him and then he waved his arms over the crowd motioning all to sit on the same steps and continued, 'That is the question for we Jews, yes? What does Elohim have to do with the unrighteous? I have wondered and concluded there are three ways for Jews to be blessed by Elohim—to be made righteous. The first one is as we have understood for a long time.'

"Thomas went on to quote from the Psalmist, 'Blessed is the man who does not walk in the counsel of the wicked or stand in the way of sinners or sit in the seat of mockers. But his delight is in the law of the LORD, and on his law, he meditates day and night.' (Psalm 1)

"'The first way is just that.' Thomas smiled. He was a tall thin frail looking man. His clothes were common. His eyes were quite close together making his face feel even thinner and sharper. But he had a confidence about him. An inquisitiveness. A boldness to enter difficult topics. That is what I cherish about my now friend Thomas.

"My new friend continued, 'Clearly, per the Psalmist, the righteous are the ones who do not sin. Ah, but that condemns us all, doesn't it? As another Psalmist says, 'There is none righteous, no not one.' Amen?'

"He continued in rational rabbinical logic. I appreciated that very much. He was speaking of the two paths that influenced the Pharisees and the Separatists.

"'Then there is the righteousness that comes from the Temple sacrifices. And so here we are on Yom Kippur, but look, there is no one. There are no priestly choirs, no offerings, no prayers, no 'It is finished.' Here we are. We can only mourn. We can only cry out. But let us also ask the next question, 'Has Elohim relinquished us to carry our own sins from this point on?' If so, we are all doomed to Gehenna, surely.'

"Thomas rubbed his beard in a very familiar way. It did make me smile, reminding me of someone else.

Reuben paused as many in the audience chuckled at his endearing habit. Then he went on with his story.

"Thomas said, 'But now, praise Elohim there is another righteousness that is from the hands of Elohim alone and is cast upon unworthy sinners. Hear the Prophet Isaiah speak of this righteousness from Elohim Himself that necessarily brings in its wake transformation given to the unworthy—not the worthy.'

"See, a king will reign in righteousness and rulers will rule with justice. Each man will be like a shelter from the wind and a refuge from the storm, like streams of water in the desert and the shadow of a great rock in a thirsty land. Then the eyes of those who see will no longer be closed, and the ears of those who hear will listen...till the Spirit is poured upon us from on high, and the desert becomes a fertile field, and the fertile field seems like a forest. Justice will dwell in the desert and righteousness live in the fertile field. The fruit of righteousness will be peace; the effect of righteousness will be quietness and confidence forever. My people will live in peaceful dwelling places, in secure homes, in undisturbed places of rest. Though hail flattens the forest and the city is leveled completely, how blessed you will be, sowing your seed by every stream, and letting your cattle and donkeys range free." (Isa 32:1-20)

"Thomas queried, 'Answer me this. From where does this special righteousness flow? And for what reason?'"

"There was a long silence. So, I broke in.

"This is evidently a righteousness from Elohim that is a covering over the people of Elohim. This is our hope in the coming Kingdom of His Messiah. When the Righteous King comes, all his people will be blessed—the righteous and the unrighteous alike. I imagine it is accomplished by the King's righteous spirit being poured out upon His people."

"'Yes, I agree my new friend,'" Thomas said with a nod. 'And that King has surely already come and even now his righteousness is pouring out—along with his Spirit—upon us, we who were unworthy and ill-prepared.'

"My head was spinning but something about what Thomas said was resonating deep inside of me. "I assume you are referring to the Rabboni Jesus?"

"'Yes, of course. You have heard of him?' Thomas asked."

"I ignored his question and got back to the main issue."

"What about the sacrifice required for righteousness? Jesus, supposedly being a Torahic Rabbi would know of what I speak. Is there righteousness apart from sacrifice? Are you going to say with the Rabbis that Elohim now desires mercy, not sacrifice?"

"'Yes, and no,'" Thomas responded, 'So it is said by the prophets. And again, in the Psalms, 'Sacrifice and offering You did not desire; My ears You have opened. Burnt offering and sin offering You did not require.'

"Thomas continued his train of thought. 'Let me suggest that indeed the Law required sacrifices to be made for a time. But they were only a shadow of the cleansing that was ultimately required to make us worthy to climb the Holy Hill. Let me put it another way. Sacrifices of animals could never make the unrighteous righteous. All the worshippers since the time of Moses who participated in Yom Kippur, left the Holy City still feeling guilt and shame. Why? The burning carcasses of goats can't cleanse us from our legal guilt before Elohim –or even begin to scrape away our shame and guilt that burdens us so. So,' he went on shrugging his shoulders slightly for effect. 'How do we reconcile the Torah prescriptions and our desperate need for a righteousness worthy of Elohim? Here is my answer. Elohim, our ultimate High Priest provided for us, the unrighteous, a final sufficient and effective sacrifice, His own Son, Jesus. Jesus willingly became the once for all-time final Torahic sacrifice for our unrighteousness. By his singular sacrifice, we are made righteous—meaning we are now made acceptable to Elohim, honorable, and of great value. We are reconstituted in Christ and now draw our life and identity from him. Whereas good gifts are normally thought to be distributed to fitting or worthy recipients, this embodiment of the grace of Elohim is given without regard to our worth. It is an unconditional gift that does not match the worth of its recipients. It does not applaud our righteousness—but initiates it.

"We Jews previously thought practicing the Torah was integral to our standing before Elohim, but we have come to see, in the wake of the death and resurrection of Rabboni Jesus, all Torah observance points to Jesus and is fulfilled by Jesus. This does not accuse the Torah of wrongdoing or fault, may Elohim forbid.'"

"Thomas continued, 'Remember Abraham? His favor before Elohim was established apart from the Torah. His righteousness was poured out upon him by the creative proclamation of Elohim. His worth and standing with Elohim was based upon the work of Elohim alone. The pouring out of Elohim's spirit upon the unrighteous, not the righteous is the fulfillment of Torah. It is the fulfillment of Elohim's promises to Abraham. Elohim is pleased to give blessings to the cursed and freedom to the enslaved.'"

We will do one last journal entry on Reuben's teachings regarding the very important historical changes in Judaism. While I have risked losing some readers in deep and dense weeds, I wanted Reuben's thoughts documented for all diaspora Jews. It has been a confusing and tragic time for the Jewish people.

Reuben does the best I have ever seen putting it all together into a consistent whole.

25

Reuben Part 4

Reuben was wrapping his talk up now. There would be time for questions later, in fact over the coming days and weeks. The participants had dined well and now must digest lest their stomachs become upset.

Reuben stroked his beard unconsciously, "In closing, my brothers and sisters, there are for we Jews, five Torahic paths, each seeking to prepare the way for the coming of the Kingdom of the Lord. Five kosher ways proposed where we Jews can find standing and favor with Elohim—where we would know we are Paradise-bound. Each of them in their own way relied upon Torah.

"Of the five, three are no more, and must no longer be considered. It would be folly. That leaves Rabbinic Judaism and the Way—the latter is the name given to the followers of the Rabboni Jesus.

"I humbly submit it is for each of you to decide where your righteousness comes from in the wake of the rubble that was our Temple. Do you rely on acts of kindness, mercy, prayer, and Torah study? All good things, of course. There is no question we are to be people who embrace all of them. But do you trust they will indeed fill your baskets with the necessary righteousness, the holy hands and pure heart pleasing enough to your heavenly King?

"Think of it this way. When you stand before His holy throne, will you stand in confidence you have done enough—that you are righteous enough?

"Or would you rather receive the righteousness of the Rabboni Jesus by faith, the latter given to the needy, those who need a rescue—to the unrighteous?

"Is this Rabboni Jesus against the Torah? Does he propose the Torah is no longer relevant? He has been accused wrongly for that. In fact, I wondered myself for a time.

"I should say, full disclosure, I was at the court—though it was hardly a legitimate Sanhedrin official congregation. It was during Passover week. I got the word the scribes and the elders had called for an emergency meeting. These were rare but it must have been quite serious to call us away from our families during Passover.

"I was a little concerned when they said we would meet at the house of the former High Priest, the aged Annas not at the Hall of Hewn Stones. This was irregular for a couple of reasons. First, other than at the rites of the Temple, we had little to do with Annas or his son-in-law, the recently appointed High Priest Caiaphas. All of us were disgusted at the corruption involved in their appointment by Rome. They were never consulted any more when there was official Sanhedrin business.

"Secondly, the prisoner was brought in by Roman and Temple soldiers. Very irregular.

"Third, the head of the Sanhedrin, Gamaliel was noticeably absent. To this day, I have heard no explanation and I suspect the court believed he would have stood against them—and he could be very persuasive.

"Fourth, the interrogation was led by the Priests not the Sanhedrin. I had never seen such a sight, silent almost intimidated Rabbinical scholars. Not in my experience.

"Lastly, there was deep fear in the room and anger— even terror. I was aware of the division this Galilean Rabbi had caused in the land. So many were raising him up as the Messiah. Look, he wasn't the first and I was sure he wasn't going to be the last pretender—Messiah. But these men didn't just want him exposed. They wanted him murdered—and that meant Rome needed to be involved.

"Here is my recollection of the interrogation. Someone, either Annas or Caiaphas angrily challenged Jesus. 'If you are the Messiah, you must tell us.'

"Jesus paused, raised his head looking around the room and calmly said, 'I could tell you, but you would not believe. But I will say this,' and I swear he was looking directly at me when he said it, no one else. 'From now on, the son of man will be seated at the right hand of the power of Elohim.'

"The interrogator jumped on that statement and got right up in Jesus' face, yelling at the top of his voice clearly for all to hear. 'Are you saying you are the Son of Elohim?'

"Jesus bowed his head once more. Paused and then said loudly, so he would not be misunderstood. 'Yes, it is as you say.'

"At this, the Priest interrogator rent his cloak with a flourish, and looked around the room to make sure his charge was heard by all. 'This man has spoken blasphemy. There is no need for any more testimonies or witnesses.'

"The truth is they had no legitimate witnesses at all.

"Then the prisoner was cursed at, spit upon and horrifically beaten.

"Looking back, I am ashamed of my participation. This was a travesty and an abnegation of the authority of the Sanhedrin. It is to our lasting shame.

"But I also know now it was meant to be. Without his crucifixion, death, and burial followed by a miraculous resurrection to life again, we would not have any sacrifice sufficient for us. Gentlemen, and ladies, Jesus was the final and completed atonement sacrifice. No more is needed, ever.

"What was Jesus' relation to the Torah? Some would argue he subverted the Torah, teaching the Shabbat was for man, healing on the Shabbat and the like. But I have come to see this was not so, not at all. No one was more Torah-focused than him. Not Gamaliel, not Hillel, and not Zakkai—though those men held Torah to the very highest degree of any persons. Jesus more so.

"Here is what He himself said about the Torah and what he came to do.

"'Do not think I have come to abolish the Law or the Prophets; I have not come to abolish them but to fulfill them. I tell you the truth, until heaven and earth disappear, not the smallest letter, not the least stroke of a pen, will by any means disappear from the Law until everything is accomplished. Anyone who breaks one of the least of these commandments and teaches others to do the same will be called least in the kingdom of heaven, but whoever practices and teaches these commands will be called great in the kingdom of heaven. For I tell you unless your righteousness surpasses that of the Pharisees and the teachers of the law, you will certainly not enter the kingdom of heaven.'

"To be clear, the righteousness we need in order to stand *lipnay Elohim,* in good standing, as daughters and sons about whom the Heavenly King would acclaim, 'This is my beloved child with whom I am well pleased,' can only come from His hand as an undeserved grace. It cannot come from our efforts, even good ones. They are not enough.

"There is so much more to say, I will close with the words of the Rabboni Jesus. It is a quote from the Prophet Isaiah. I am told he read this from the scroll at his home synagogue when he was a young man. 'The Spirit of the Lord is on me, because he has anointed me to preach good news to the poor. He has sent me to proclaim freedom for the prisoners and recovery of sight for the blind, to release the oppressed, to proclaim the year of the Lord's favor.'

"Then he rolled up the scroll, gave it back to the attendant and sat down and said, 'Today this scripture is fulfilled in your hearing.'

"As for me, I have come to believe that on that day, the Kingdom of Elohim began to unroll like a huge scroll in the land of our people. I have become Jesus' disciple. I do not have all the answers. I am not sure I even have all the right questions."

The audience chuckled.

"Yet I follow him. Thank you for your attention and I look forward to our ongoing dialogue. Amen and Amen."

26

Day 756 of the Axum Mission

Eight weeks have passed since Yom Kippur and Reuben's emotional sharing. We have seen a huge increase in Jews who have come to our *Todah* meal, many of whom have already been baptized in our fountain and have become followers of Jesus. This would include many of the Synagogue leadership. Of course, we continue to go to the synagogue on Shabbat. We are gratified and credit the work of our Rabboni's Spirit among his people.

We are also excited to report King Zoskales' wife--well, one of his six wives-- as well as his niece, the Princess Ayana, whose name means 'beautiful flower' are also asking a lot of questions about our faith.

The young Princess is one of the most beautiful women I have ever seen. I jokingly confessed that to Deborah. She laughed out loud and pretended to be angry. She is not threatened by my assessment of other women at all. "The ravings of an old fat Rabbi" she said dismissively—but with a laugh. I love her for that sense of humor—even when it is at my expense. I responded, "What do you mean fat?" She waved her hand and shook her head.

Don't tell her, but Deborah is still the <u>most</u> beautiful woman I have ever known.

Even she admitted she has seen few more perfect women. The Princess is young but certainly of marriageable age. She is quite short even for Axum women. Deborah explained that is why she puts her hair wound high in a colorful bonnet. When in public she always wears very colorful tunics and cloaks that only enhance her beauty. Though fully regal in her comportment, she rarely puts on a scowl.

Sorkatti and Bernice have both spent much time with the two women and are very encouraged by the trajectory. I still have not been able to get an audience with the King. Obodas is not at all encouraging that meeting. He is not willing to tell me exactly why. For now, I submit to his guidance as our *karim*. But I pray to God that the Spirit of the Rabboni would make a path and open the King's heart to hear the Gospel.

I also want to report the very hall in which Reuben spoke burned down last week. It was the third fire in the synagogue compound in the last month. At first, we thought it was accidental or due to lightning strike. Some of the tribal leaders are suggesting the gods of their ancestors have cursed the Synagogue and are urging—or intimidating their people to avoid it completely.

Just yesterday, we had a fire in our compound as well. The entire southern wall was burned to the ground, and fortunately no buildings or lives were lost. Te'oma was studying the Torah in our worship area and ran out when he heard screaming. He thought he saw Haaman and a few other tribesmen run off into the woods in quite a hurry.

This is what we have suspected. The Rabboni said there would be persecution as we sought to be peacemakers. And so let it be.

I gathered our team to discuss what we should do. I won't go over all the discussion. At first, there was a great deal of anger. Te'oma and Hanno were furious and demanded we gather an army to go arrest Haaman. There must be justice, an eye for an eye. Truth told, if we had ended the meeting then, it might have been a unanimous agreement.

But God-bless my wife, Deborah. She gently reminded us we did not come to Axum to build buildings or compounds. They are only tools. We came to build new hearts. She was right of course. There is no one, other than King Zoskales we have prayed for more than Haaman.

He truly believes he is a *karim* over his people, and over all tribes in the Axum region. In that light, we are not only interlopers, but leading his people away from their dependence upon the spirits of their ancestors. We can try to convince him of the truth, but none of us came to the truth that way. All of us were dragged into the truth of the Gospel kicking and screaming. All of us needed the transformative power of the Rabboni's Spirit.

That is what currently separates us from him. Not our goodness, or righteousness, or wisdom, or that we are indeed more right than him, or more loving of the Axumites than him. No, Jesus has unilaterally and unconditionally covered us with his righteousness, and we now stand before God, *lipnay Elohim* in good standing as his beloved sons and daughters due to no merit of our own.

This is our hope for Haaman as well—even though it took a while for our hearts to align with the Rabboni's Spirit.

So, we decided to request from Obodas that he arrange an official audience with King Zoskales so we can make a formal complaint. He is the sword of God in this region and should be informed. We wish Haaman no harm but feel the need for an official governmental intervention. The Synagogue leaders have agreed to join our formal complaint.

We wait for Obodas' lead on this. He seems very hesitant to approach the King. I am curious and will pursue that more when we meet.

27

Day 804 of the Axum Mission

I want to get back to the Rabboni's teachings in Galilee for that is my overarching purpose in writing this expanded manuscript.

I believe no section has been more misunderstood or confusing than this one. Six times in rapid succession, he uses the Torah and the Writings as a foil to teach something apparently new. "You have heard…" followed by "But I tell you…"

So, "You have heard that it was said, 'Do not murder, and anyone who murders will be subject to judgment.'

I tell you that anyone who is even angry with his brother will be subject to judgment."

Or "You have heard that it was said, 'Do not commit adultery.'

I tell you that anyone who looks at a woman lustfully has already committed adultery with her in his heart.

Again, "It has been said, 'Anyone who divorces his wife must give her a certificate of divorce.'

I tell you that anyone who divorces his wife, except for marital unfaithfulness, causes her to become an adulteress, and anyone who marries the divorced woman commits adultery.

"Again, you have heard that it was said to the people long ago, 'Do not break your oath, but keep the oaths you have made to the Lord.'

I tell you, do not swear at all.

"You have heard that it was said, 'Eye for eye, and tooth for tooth.'

I tell you, do not resist an evil person. If someone strikes you on the right cheek, turn to him the other also.

Lastly, "You have heard that it was said, 'Love your neighbor and hate your enemy.'

But I tell you: Love your enemies and pray for those who persecute you, that you may be sons of your Father in heaven.

I can say with great assurance this was the Master's careful argument shaped for the Rabbis alone. He used their language, their form of argumentation. In saying these, the Master is shaping a familiar *halakhic* debate, not invalidating the Torah, rather clarifying what the Torah prescriptions mean to real life ethics, morals and conduct of real Jews in the real world. Simply put, halakhahs are designed to teach the ways Jews are to behave.

The truth is that very few of the pained people on that hillside would have been very familiar with the Torah much at all. But they would have been familiar with the traditions of the Jews.

This was clearly for the scholars. Both Hillel and Shammai would smile and nod their respect. I don't doubt Zakkai was made aware of the Rabboni's teachings. I would love to have dialogued with him about it.

I mentioned that this has been the section most confusing for people I have spoken to both in Judea and now here in Axum. If I had known the problems it would cause, I would have spent more time elaborating on the point of Jesus' logic in my Gospel. For that I am sorry, and I plan to make amends now.

This section, and so many others in my Gospel must be seen and heard in light of the Rabboni's amazing sense of humor. He was not a severely serious academic bore who couldn't relate to real people, who couldn't cry with them or laugh with them.

We who were closest with him shared so many moments of hilarity and joy. He was quite a dancer as well. He was able to make a twist of logic that at first might be shocking and even offensive until you would see the smirk on his face and realize he was using exaggeration or the absurd to make a point and to make us laugh.

This was one of those times. Let me try to explain. Remember, he had just proclaimed he was not here to undermine or diminish the Torah. He was here to fulfill it. To be sure, it was not clear what that meant exactly. No other Rabbi would dare say something so out there.

Did Jesus, as many of his detractors claim, disregard the Torah and the Oral writings? Or was he adding some inward ethical and moral dimension, focused on the heart? Or was he setting aside the Torah and Writings in favor of a new teaching?

May God forbid. Let me try to elaborate.

First, Jesus said that not only should we not murder but also not be angry. Right? Who would disagree? Anger can be very destructive—and usually is—and often leads to murder.

We are having to deal with that now. As I mentioned, Haaman and his strongmen have done harm to us, causing us to fear for our well-being and to worry about the loss of earthly things over heavenly things. What would we do if he ramps up his attacks and people are hurt? What if children are hurt?

Would anyone blame us for being angry? Isn't it a normal human reaction?

That is Jesus' point, do you see? Anger is a normal human reaction in this world. Try to not be angry. Go ahead.

What act of will can you rely on? What muscles can you utilize that will shut off anger or rage?

During the rainy seasons in Judea, storms in the hill country inevitably led to dangerous flooding to the east, raging waters instantly fill the dry wadis and rush with little hindrance into the Dead Sea. God help those who are caught in the wadis when the flood comes. It cannot be stopped by any engineered construction. It must pour itself out.

And that is the way with our anger.

Jesus is being absurd of course. You may be sufficiently sinless when it comes to not murdering someone. Good on you. So, you may be tempted to feel righteous. But the Torah demands clean hands and a pure heart if you want to hear God's acclamation, "Well done good and faithful servant." For that, you must not be unjustly angry.

Jesus' punchline? You can't. You won't. That's the joke of course. It is not Torah's fault. It is our sin.

Consider how God dealt with the first murderer Cain. Of course, this was long before Moses and the Torah, but God is eternal. He hates murder. All murder will be dealt with fairly and equally by His court and His standards.

In the wake of Cain's faulty offering, the Lord was very gentle though Cain was angry.

He said to the first born of Adam and Eve, "Why are you angry? Why is your face downcast? If you do what is right, will you not be accepted? But if you do not do what is right, sin is crouching at your door; it desires to have you, but you must master it."

Can you hear the grace offered by the Lord? It is as if he told Cain, "Don't look away, at the ground, look up into my eyes and you will see my care for you, my devotion for you. It is a cure for your anger. That is how you can master it. If you try to do it on your own, death will result."

We all know what happened. Cain's anger and jealously was unquenchable and irrupted in the first anger-born murder. And yet even then God's desire was reconciliation.

The Lord said, "Where is your brother Abel?" Cain replied in his anger and shame, "I don't know. Am I my brother's keeper?"

What might we expect from the hands of the just God who reveres life and hates anger and murder? You would be right to answer, "Death!"

Rather, God's measured response did not involve such a justice. Rather it seemed more of a gracious punishment allowing for future reconciliation, even taking upon himself the mantel of kinsman redeemer for the angry young man.

It is a show of the grace of God, even in the face of murder.

That is God of course. Jesus' point is we are not God. "No one is righteous, no not one," the Psalmist writes and that includes non-murderers.

What is our hope? Exactly the point of Jesus. What we cannot accomplish He can and did.

In our anger, we are reminded we cannot claim to have a pure heart or clean hands and so we must run to Jesus and be reminded he has taken our weakness and covered us with his rightness.

Can you begin to see the pattern of this halakhah argument.

Try not to lust. I cannot explain it, but there is something very powerful in the heart of all men and women as well. It erupts in a moment and cannot be turned off. It is another dangerous and destructive flooding wadi.

It condemns us as sinful flesh but throws us back into the arms of the risen Lord for comfort and a reminder that strictly because of what he accomplished by his death and resurrection, we are righteous and stand before God, under the headship of our celestial *Karim* Jesus as worthy of God's love and favor. We are a righteous bride.

Or consider the very divisive topic of divorce. Why would a man pursue a divorce? Perhaps he is unloving and indifferent? Perhaps there is anger, or selfishness, or lust for another woman? Perhaps it is greed and a desire to protect their wealth from undesirable offspring. Perhaps their pride has been wounded by something their spouse did or said. Perhaps the spouse has been unfaithful?

Can we begin to see the crimes against each other and ultimately against God began long before the divorce—and yet the legal debate almost always is about technicalities.

This would be so if we looked closely at the wife as well.

On the other hand, if the couple is depending upon the Spirit of the Rabboni, and is being filled with his love for them and the other, why would divorce be inevitable, or even preferable? Doesn't God love your spouse? And if so, you are about to hurt someone under the benefaction and a protection of the Heavenly *Karim*. Wouldn't that give you pause?

Jesus was teaching that unless you ran now to the Heavenly King and were filled again with his love for you and your spouse, divorce is most likely, even predictable. It seems to be one of the most common and terrible fruits among broken humanity.

One of our teachers has said nothing has hurt us more than relationships. Then it follows there is no quicker, viler, or greater emotional reactionary response than to being wounded in the relationship of marriage. There is only one power that can diminish such a wadi flood. It is not the act of will of well-meaning pious people, or charity, or obedience to the Torah. It is from the Spirit of the Rabboni alone.

If we do this, depend more on His Spirit and His power, the legal debate about divorce is transformed.

Then Jesus spoke about oaths. So much debate, so many scrolls about the legality of oaths. But Jesus would say keep your word. Do not deceive or lie.

Who has always told the truth? Who has not resorted to disinformation, white lies, comforting deceptions?

Deborah came to me the other day with a new cloak on. She asked me what I thought. I have known her long enough to know what she wanted to hear from me is the cloak was stunning, a credit to her taste and sense of beauty, and that it had a slimming effect on her, made her eyes light up and made her look a decade younger—oh, and wiser as well.

The truth was I didn't care much for the cloak and apparently it was quite costly. In these moments, we have agreed to say one word. "Deborah, it is fantastic!"

She smiled knowingly and winked understanding exactly what I meant. Then she turned and purchased the cloak anyway. I love her dearly.

Why is it we can't be honest? We won't be honest. Cain's first obfuscation was foolish. When God asked him where his brother was, he blurted out, "Am I my brother's keeper?" Hardly the truth. Certainly, if he was thinking rationally, he would remember God knows everything. But he lied.

God's high holy standard is for us to tell the truth. If we did, we would need no Torah to tell us how our uncleanness would be made clean.

God's Spirit in us is the Spirit of Truth. We need regularly to be filled with that Spirit of Truth.

Then Jesus brought up our proclivity for revenge and hatred—so natural among us. Think of Cain. Think of King Saul. Think of what they did to Jesus.

If on the other hand we were filled with the love God feels toward us and toward others, wouldn't we treat each other differently?

Paul, a wonderful colleague, who I spent some time with when he made rare visits to Jerusalem with desperately needed offerings from the growing Christian churches in Galatia, Greece, and Rome, put it this way in one of his letters. Paul wrote to the church in Ephesus, "I pray that out of his glorious riches he may strengthen you with power through his Spirit in your inner being, so that Christ may dwell in your hearts through faith. And I pray that you, being rooted and established in love, may have power, together with all the saints, to grasp how wide and long and high and deep is the love of Christ, and to know this love that surpasses knowledge — that you may be filled to the measure of all the fullness of God."

If we did that, prayed to God that we would be given His power through His Spirit so that we would –right now—and tomorrow and the next day—really feel the massiveness of the love of Christ for us and others, and that our beat up and leaky identity cups would get filled again and again with the fullness of God (whatever that may mean)—wouldn't it be noticeable? Wouldn't we hate less. Wouldn't we be less jealous, less prone to divorce, less needing to lie, less willing to hate our enemies as well?

Of course. Listen, humanly speaking, why in the world would we ever suggest we should, or even could, love our enemy. That is why we call them enemies—because we <u>don't</u> love them and feel justified. Eye for an eye, right?

And yet, Jesus showed us a different source for love. This love of the Rabboni surpassed the love of any other person, man, or woman. It innately loved those who persecuted him, who betrayed him, who denied him worship and recognition—those who used Torah to justify their rage. It loves enemies—for that was all there was.

It loves me.

Can we see now Jesus' *halakhah* wasn't teaching we must understand the inner softer teachings of the Torah, the heart beneath the letter. No. He was arguing there is no one who keeps Torah.

Many have thought we Jesus-followers have been given new prescriptions, a new Torah we must strive even harder to keep—for then we would please Jesus and finally prove ourselves worthy of his charity and devotion. But even though we should do these things, they are good, we won't. We can't.

Can Jesus be any clearer than when he summed up his halakhah his way.

"Be perfect, therefore, as your heavenly Father is perfect."

When he said that, he chuckled aloud. It was laughable. Can you get the joke? Try as hard as you like, and you will get no closer to this perfection. Oh, you likely will rise further than me. But that is a very low bar.

That statement is the essence of the Torah. It is merciless. It rightly condemns unjust anger, lust, selfish mistreatments of spouse and others. It condemns all that falls outside of the command from Torah, "Love the LORD your God with all your heart and with all your soul and with all your strength."

And again

"If you obey the LORD your God and keep his commands and decrees that are written in this Book of the Law and turn to the LORD your God with all your heart and with all your soul. Now what I am commanding you today is not too difficult for you or beyond your reach. It is not up in heaven, so that you have to ask, "Who will ascend into heaven to get it and proclaim it to us so we may obey it?" Nor is it beyond the sea, so that you must ask, "Who will cross the sea to get it and proclaim it to us so we may obey it?" No, the word is very near you; it is in your mouth and in your heart so you may obey it. See, I set before you today life and prosperity, death, and destruction. For I command you today to love the LORD your God, to walk in his ways, and to keep his commands, decrees, and laws; then you will live and increase, and the LORD your God will bless you in the land you are entering to possess. But if your heart turns away and you are not obedient, and if you are drawn away to bow down to other gods and worship them, I declare to you this day that you will certainly be destroyed. You will not live long in the land you are crossing the Jordan to enter and possess." (Dt 30:10-18)

Doesn't the Torah say that it is not too difficult? Yes, but now we know what it meant by that. The only way for us to accomplish the Torah—to fulfill it—is to depend upon the Lord and His Spirit in us. We cannot do it on our own. Look at the history of our failure—we Jews who had the Torah. Even in those seasons when there was concerted effort. We remained condemned by the Torah.

Didn't the Torah also say we need the Lord Himself to circumcise our hearts in order that we may love Him with all our heart and soul? (Dt 30:6)

But now, we who have followed Jesus have come to experience something celestial, something Godly, something birthed from His Kingdom. Here's Paul again. "The fruit of His Spirit is love, joy, peace, patience, kindness, goodness, faithfulness, gentleness, and self-control. Against such things there is no law."

While we agree the Torah is good, and we should love others and God, we won't. Then as we learn our problem is greater than we thought—that we are not to be unjustly angry, or hateful, or revengeful, or lustful, or even hate our enemy—we also learn we are to hold our hands up, not in frustration or even self-condemnation, but in dependence and need of his Spirit and the fruit thereof.

We do not do this in order to earn righteousness, or to prove our godliness, or to be able to make a case eventually before the throne room of God that we of all persons deserve to be ushered into Paradise. No, we are more and more motivated to do good things because we are already children of God with newly circumcised hearts, a child in good standing of whom he proclaims, "You are my beloved child with whom I am well pleased." This is all due to the work of the Rabboni on our behalf.

The perfect work of Torah is a reminder of our need for another righteousness other than our own.

Here is what I tell people, Jesus followers, who still believe they must struggle to achieve the so-called new standards of Jesus. To love more, to be angry less, to hate less, to sacrifice more and the rest.

"God bless you. Please, I beg you, when you crash and burn, come to me, not to be condemned or shamed. Rather I will speak to you of a hope for failures like me. The favor of God, his pleasure with you is not limited by the gift of Torah, but with the singular event, the death and resurrection of Jesus. God cannot be more pleased with you than He is right now. He loves you as much as the Father loves the Son and the Spirit and the Spirit and the Son love the Father. You cannot add to that or take away from it. It may feel that way, but that is a lie. This favored relational status given to you is part of a new dynamic of grace that has decisively altered the world and has already permanently rescued you and me from what my colleague Paul calls "the present evil age. It is time to put away childish things and dance a little. For in that way you show true gratefulness to your heavenly *Karim*."

28

Day 930 of the Axum Mission

I have not been looking forward to this next section of the Rabboni's teachings in Galilee. Why? I am afraid that because of my Gospel, damage has occurred in some circles.

As a neophyte author, I took for granted the readers would be able to read between the lines where necessary. I was sadly in grave error. So, allow me to repair that mistake and spend some extra time in this section that is becoming popularly referred to as The Lord's Prayer.

Jesus said,

"Knowing your reputation-starving heart, be constantly vigilant you don't just <u>do</u> righteousness, so others are impressed. That means less than nothing to God."

Oh my, this section reflects the absolute genius of the Rabboni as a Rabbinical disciple-maker. I am afraid, as I have spoken to so many who have read my concise Gospel, that is it easy to miss the sarcasm and absurdity in the Master's teachings. He is a Rabbinical scholar and was not above using such teaching techniques to make his point. Though, as it often the case, if you were not there, you might miss the subtleties from his body language and facial expressions. I will try to clarify and elaborate.

I want to remind you there are two types of righteousness. They are both legitimate and Torahic. We come into problems when we don't embrace them both—and in the right order.

There is the righteousness that one <u>does,</u> and the expectation is that as one does this righteousness, they are to be compensated. Hear the Psalmist,

Blessed is the man who does not walk in the counsel of the wicked or stand in the way of sinners or sit in the seat of mockers. But his delight is in the law of the LORD, and on his law, he meditates day and night. (Ps 1:1-2)

Then there is the second meaning that is not in conflict with the first at all. I will explain. In a relational sense, righteous most often refers to being considered in good standing—socially acceptable, a person of worth, value and honor.

And so, Abraham was considered worthy of God's blessing long before the Torah laid out a righteous path.

This is the highest role of the legal court. Through the legal proceeding, the innocent party is vindicated and officially—and publicly—<u>made right</u>—meaning they are restored to their social standing and deemed worthy and honorable again. They are made righteous.

This righteousness is not "done" by the innocent party, rather it is bestowed, acclaimed by a person of authority—like a King or a Judge. The person is legally imputed to be righteous.

Jesus goes much further. In the case of a Judge, they are restoring an innocent-worthy party to their former social standing. They are worthy of restoration.

In Jesus' Kingdom, it is the unworthy who are giving righteous standing before God and humanity. No one is granted this gift on the grounds of their collective "doing" of Torah. This right standing before God is given to the most unlikely—like me.

We previously thought practicing the Mosaic Law was critical to our good standing before God, but we now realize, in the wake of the Rabboni's grace, it is nonessential. Why? Because by doing the Torah, no one can be rescued. This does not make Torah-observance wrong or inappropriate. The point is it is powerless to establish my worth or standing before God. This righteousness is a gift for the unworthy alone.

I should say one more thing. The Rabboni was a Torahic scholar, and I will testify, <u>did</u> righteousness to the full. He was the exception to the rule. He kept its precepts and so earned all the blessings due the one who kept it all. He did not turn aside from any of the commands…to the right or to the left or follow other gods or serve them. (Dt 28:14)

And so, it is written of him and him alone in the entire history of our chosen people,

"If you fully obey the LORD your God and carefully follow all his commands I give you today, the LORD your God will set you high above all the nations on earth. All these blessings will come upon you and accompany you if you obey the LORD your God." (Dt 28:1-2)

As we are put "in him" as our King Benefactor, he liberally distributes these blessing to us, though none of us are worthy, none of us can make any claims based upon our success at <u>doing</u> righteousness. Among these many blessings is the love of God for us.

Strictly because of what Jesus has accomplished—by perfectly doing the Torah in all ways and manners—and so earning all blessings— we who are with Him, can now know and feel the height, width, length, and depth of the love of God. In fact, we are made righteous. And so, God loves us as much as the Father loves the Son and the Spirit and as much as the Son and the Spirit love the Father. He can't love us more than he does right now. He can't love us any less. Why? Because it is legally based upon the righteousness of the Rabboni—not our own.

We can sit back, by faith and enjoy, dance, and be grateful. This is Jesus' point. Do you see? If I am in that space, why would I pretend? And if I pretend, I am not in that space experientially.

How then do the two types of righteousness work together? Isn't it reasonable then that a person of good standing and worth <u>will</u> tend to act accordingly? They will then tend to do right because they are right. It is the righteous who do right, not the unrighteous.

How about the opposite? Is it also true a person who does right will become right socially and relationally to the King? Yes, of course, at least theoretically. And so, this is why Jesus shockingly said to all who would pursue only this tact, that you're doing right will have to surpass the Pharisees. In fact, "You must be perfect as much as your Heavenly Father is perfect."

As the Rabboni begins this section in his teachings, the person he is speaking to has already made the wrong choice. He or she is determined to be a righteousness doer.

Jesus is teaching the way of righteousness-doers—and we all understand—for we all tend to be of this bent.

I liken it to an addiction. My conversations with Ninos and his struggle to cast away his longing for opium has only confirmed my thoughts.

Righteousness-doers are addicted to recognition and praise whenever and wherever they can find it and will jump through hoops, even shameful, absurd, and laughable hoops for even one slight compliment, one glance of approval, one pat on the head—by even strangers.

Jesus is speaking, tongue-in-cheek to approval-addicts who leap from pretense to pretense to get approval hits. It would be the same to say to an opium addict, "Be aware that you are addicted. Stop it. Walk away. You will only need another hit."

We all know during such an urge; they are not listening. They will not—at least until there is a power greater than the hit they expect from their substance of choice.

Jesus is not in any way expecting the approval-addict will be convicted and change their behavior. Being acclaimed as righteous, or faithful to God, or religious, or pure are powerful addictions rivaling opium.

As the Master said, your heart is reputation-focused—and that was a gracious understatement.

Was Jesus being indifferent or cavalier? Was he just teasing helpless imbeciles? Of course not.

In context, and we must always see this in context, He had already created in the audience a new addiction. Remember,

"For though you came unenviable—addicted to anything and everything other than the identity glory and worth that comes from a right relationship with God—you are now enviable because you are under the powerful and life-changing benefaction of your Heavenly adoring Father."

I didn't make it as clear as I no doubt should have in my original and concise Gospel. The crowd got the Master's joke. They got the subtle nuance.

They were able to understand this was them before Galilee. Now they were able to laugh at their old foolishness—for all saw the absurdity of being pretenders—and they all were.

Just listen to the genius of the Rabboni as he continues. As you listen, imagine his engaging smirk, and hear the crowd laugh at their former selves. Step into their sandals and imagine yourself feeling more and more grateful to your Heavenly Benefactor for receiving such a hard-core imposter as you—and loving you as if you had always been right with him.

"For instance," said Jesus, "When you do mercy for those in need, Temple-prescribed or not, you don't need a parade. That's for foolish pretenders."

I remember how the crowd chuckled at this. They got it. They remembered. It wasn't long before they did that very thing. His words exposed us all. But it was OK underneath the loving gaze of the Rabboni. He went on.

"There is no place for that anywhere. And what does your reputation with other pretenders really gain you? Tragically little. So, when you give alms, 'Shhh!' Don't even let your other hand know."

Jesus had held up one hand and hid the other behind his cloak as he said this—and a broad smile irrupted on his face. He wasn't trying to condemn us or shame us. Again, we could only chuckle at even the idea your one hand could fool the other. It was funny.

"Do not draw attention to yourself. And your heavenly father, who sees all, even motivations, will more than compensate you."

I can understand so much more now than I could then. The truth is that the greatest of all compensations, and no more is even needed, is that we are now in this undeserved relationship with a Heavenly Benefactor-*Karim* who cares for us like no other. What more could we reasonably desire? And we, the enviable, already have it.

I don't need to go through the many desperate machinations of an addict. I need to believe and rest. Now I see that this leaps out of Jesus' teachings. Not what he said, but what he didn't say, that was nonetheless always there.

Stop it. Stop thinking that doing righteousness will earn you one iota more of God's favor. It can't—because, as Jesus proclaimed to the unworthy crowd--who had done no righteousness to speak of—they are already sons and daughters of God in good standing.

Stop the flailing. Believe and rest. Enter this Shabbat prepared for you by another. Raise your eyes and look into the secure and adoring gaze of the Rabboni.

"In the very same way," Jesus continued. "When you pray, don't be a pretender. Pretenders love to feel admiration from other pretenders. No place for that anywhere—not now. And does that empty praise gain anything of substance? Tragically little. When you pray, find a hidden away closet where no one can see or hear you and then pray to your Father and no other audience. And your heavenly Father, who sees all, even motivations, will more than compensate you."

"Remember in whose audience you are. Your Father already knows everything about you. He is not wringing his hands wondering what you need. So, it is absurd to go on and on babbling like an unbeliever laying vapid word upon vapid word. In so doing you only shame yourself and waste an audience."

"When you fast, don't be like the pretender, who changes their clothes and appearance so others will see and say to them, "Well done good and faithful servant." They get what they get. Instead, don't change your appearance. Isn't your audience your heavenly Father? Will not your Heavenly Father Benefactor who sees all, even motivations, more than compensate you." (Matt 6:2-18)

If you by faith became aware of whose audience you were in, *lipnay Elohim*—meaning, in the very presence of God—andrecalled He is indeed already your permanent heavenly Benefactor, you would necessarily feel a life-giving wave of gratefulness greater than your need, more powerful than your addiction to people's praise. In the presence of this King, you do not need the approval of others as much.

Reuben and I have lamented how my Gospel has unsuspectingly created a new Torah. I should have known better than to tell approval addicts what to do. I assumed the subtle Rabbinical sarcasm would come through and lead to laughter and joy. Yet in so many circles, it has only formed a new law.

Absurdly some believe if they memorized and said these words verbatim-- then they would feel the approval of God or others more. This prayer has become the newest doing-righteousness. Some refer to it as "The Lord's Prayer". May God forbid.

We who heard the Rabboni say it could hear the rhetoric.

"This is how you <u>should</u> pray...," Jesus said—but what he implied and didn't say, is... "But you won't, you don't."

At he began, he looked up to the sky with hands outstretched and pretended to be a righteous Pharisee loudly praying in the public square. He emphasized every word. Everyone got the message. He wasn't commanding an ideal prayer; he was critiquing our hearts.

"Oh Abba," He said so piously in a deep reverberating voice, "Your name is the only one worthy of honor. Not mine. I long for your rule and will to be done in my life to the same degree it is understood and obeyed in the heavens-no matter what—no matter if I respectfully disagree."

To be sure, this is how we <u>should</u> pray. If we meant it and if we knew our place in the creation, of course a wise person would want God—who sees all and knows all—to run the world—and my life. Why would anyone think we knew better what was good for us—or for others? Of course, we would hope God would just keep on being God.

Is that how we pray? Don't we most often come into the presence of the celestial throne hoping God will hear <u>our</u> ideas and accede to them.

"So, God, I know you have so many things to do, but I have an idea that will benefit us both. Check it out. I know you will agree I am right. The good news is it hallows both of our names."

Jesus is humorously suggesting while we <u>should</u> submit to God's lead, live acknowledging He has got this and will only work things together for good for his people, those under his care and benefaction—we don't, we won't. We lack such faith. We squirm under His lead. We regularly question whether he is in control or if he truly cares.

"Give us today our <u>daily</u> bread..."

The Rabboni intentionally emphasized the word 'daily'. Can we be honest? We humans hate depending upon anyone, any institution, any authority. We start very young.

When we are taking our very first steps, we heard our parents encouragingly say, "Look, he's got this. C'mon, you can do this on your own." And when we did, they cheered us and thanked God in the heavens that we had done this on our own. It is a lesson we all learned far too well.

It has been said the only time when my people were truly faithful and grateful to our rescuing God was the few moments after the Egyptian army was drowned in the Red Sea. For a few moments we danced and cheered and laughed.

But then came the daily provision of manna from God. We chaffed under that new yoke. Why couldn't we have storehouses of the stuff? For then we could organize the provision and know we are secure for a month or a year. What is this about daily dependence?

Jesus knows we hate praying this. We would much rather pray for full storehouses of grain or multiple wells overflowing with fresh water. We would prefer security in the form of gold coins hidden away just in case of an emergency or theft.

So, we <u>should</u> say this prayer. We <u>should</u> be at rest in God's benefaction—we <u>should</u> trust him as our gracious Provider. We should really mean, "I am satisfied to depend upon you for all things. I no longer feel the need to store up things to make sure I am secure."

But we won't. We don't.

"God, I trust you so much I don't require more than whatever you put in my hand today." Who is satisfied by such a request?

And no one, absolutely no one, wants to pray the following. How can this one be so misunderstood?

"Forgive me to the degree I have forgiven others. For why would you forgive me if I don't forgive others? Surely if I don't forgive, you will not forgive me either? That is only reasonable." (Matt 6:12-15)

No sane person wants to limit the Father's forgiveness to just the low bar of how much he or she forgives others. May God forbid.

I will speak for myself. I desperately need God to forgive my sins far more than the paltry amount I have forgiven crimes of others against me.

How can people rotely say this prayer, not aware of what they are saying. Praise God he will not affirmatively answer such a foolish prayer.

The good news is that when you were made enviable, when you were made to be a child of His in good standing, all your crimes against God, the world and others have been forgiven. Every single one of them. This forgiveness is not adjusted in any way based upon your history of forgiving or not forgiving others. God loves unforgivers. That's all there is.

The last line of Jesus' so-called model prayer is still a conundrum for me.

"And don't lead me into trials where I may fail—particularly conflicts with the evil one." (Matt 6:13)

I believe this one stands out from the others as important. And yet, the very first thing the Father did after he publicly proclaimed Jesus as his beloved Son with whom he was well pleased was to lead him to be tempted by Satan in the wilderness. This is to say God did this to His own Son for good. Should we not allow for that in our path as well?

Though honestly, I have regularly prayed that my gracious Heavenly Benefactor would not put me in that situation—or at least as rarely as possible.

Having said that, I am reminded of the very first line in this section, "Thy will be done."

The wise child who rests securely in the loving arms of God will submit to any path—somehow comforted that though the path leads through the valley of the shadow of death, he or she is never alone. Their comforter and benefactor is there with them, loving them still.

Reuben and I have had long discussions about this section in the Rabboni's teachings in Galilee. Despite our pushing back, so many have even memorized this prayer and use it in the same way our people often used the Shema.

I understand it on the surface. The Rabboni did said we are to pray this way—and so then, surely, we please him if we do it, exactly, word for word. But this is hardly the spirit in which it was taught.

Reuben uses that analogy and I have used before in this document, of an infant in her mother's loving and caring arms. They lock eyes. The mother smiles and the infant smiles and coos. The mother smiles and coos and smiles again. The infant responds. It is an intimate primal dance laced with love, security, and joy. The mother feels honored and appreciated. The infant likewise. It is a sort of prayer language.

Imagine if that infant was given the miraculous ability to speak and said rotely by memory over and over,

"Mother, who is above me, you are mother, I am not. I will never question your authority. I am OK with feeding from your breast on your schedule. I will not cry when I am hungry. Care for me as much as I care for others."

It is absurd. Would the mother feel loved and adored by such a prayer? No hardly. She felt loved and adored before the miraculous ability to speak. She was honored by the attunement she experienced with her beloved child. Not some memorized words.

Or think of royal lovers.

"O King, you are over me and I will never undermine your authority. I will depend upon your care every day without complaint. Just love me at the level I have loved others. I am satisfied if you do that."

A romance of the ages? I think not. It is laughable. Sad.

I do not ever remember the Rabboni ever praying to His Abba in repetitive memorized words. There was a real joy in relationship. There was intimacy and security. He didn't need to tell the Father again and again that he desired to do His will. He did it. He was grateful, he was filled with joy, he was transparent. There was a wonderful and enviable dance.

In the garden shortly before his arrest, he urgently went before his Father and did so complaining. Speaking of the coming torture, abandonment, and crucifixion.

"My Father, if it is possible, may this cup be taken from me.

But then,

"My Father, may your will be done."

One would think, based upon how this so-called "Lord's prayer" is being religiously used in so many circles that our Lord missed the bet. He should have said

"My Father, who art in Heaven, hallowed by thy name..."

The Rabboni was not teaching a new path of righteousness—how we are to pray that is more right than other words—that this was the sole way pleasing to God and somehow might earn some favor and just might cause him to bless you a little more.

God help us.

How then are we to pray? This is the wrong question. It is likened unto a similar question for lovers. "What should I say to get my partner to love me more?"

If that is the question being asked, that person is expressing insecurities and fears their love is hanging by a thread, by a word, or a sentence. There is no freedom, no true love.

Rather, access love, then speak freely from your heart to the one who hears by their heart.

If you were not worried that your words would undermine the relationship, the conversation becomes life-giving.

So, it is with God. First pray to God for the Spirit of the Rabboni to make you secure in the knowledge and feelings of the height, width, length, and depth of his love for you, as you are—a love that can never change. Then say what you desire.

Enter that dance in gratefulness and joy.

To close this thought, 1 have thought there was only one prayer I would unhesitatingly label as the legitimate Lord's Prayer. If one must memorize and repeat, then let it be this one,

"My Father, if it is possible, may this cup be taken from me. Yet not as I will, but as you will." (Matt 26:39)

29

Day 1058 of the Axum Mission

It was so good to see our Nabatean guardian angel, Gamilah. She is still as beautiful and majestic as ever. But I was surprised to see her dressed down for this journey. My previous audiences with her were much more formal. When I first met her, she had arrived in Jerusalem with a glorious royal entourage, a ten-soldier cohort fully armed all willing to die to protect their Princess. Her robe was regal, her neck adorned with strands of rare jewels and pearls and the precious aroma of rare perfume wafted from her skin.

That visit was just after her father the King Malichus had just perished and her very young brother Rabbel had ascended to the Nabatean throne. Malichus' wife, Shaqilath, had become the functional ruler for all practical purposes until Rabbel came of age.

Gamilah was a very enthusiastic Jesus follower and had virtually single handedly funded our mission to Axum. She has been given the high responsibility for the Nabatean incense trade. Very impressive.

Let me back up and fill you in on what has transpired in Axum since I last wrote.

Early one morning, I got a surprise visit from Obodas. He was so excited to report Gamilah, his *karim* was coming to Adulis. He told me she had a very busy schedule but definitely wanted to spend some time with me there. How could I refuse?

My only concern was the seemingly increasing friction with Haaman. But it had been five weeks, and no one had seen or heard from him. King Zoskales has also been surprisingly silent. Though multiple requests for audience with him has been sent by me and the synagogue ruler, there has been no response. I will confess it has been quite frustrating.

Sometimes things just work themselves out. We continue to pray Jesus would send His spirit to Haaman in the same way he did for me. As we have learned, Jesus has come to rescue people from this groaning creation. People like me, like Gamilah, like Deborah and of course, like Haaman.

I agreed to join Obodas. The plan was to leave the very next dawn. It is a five-day trek to Adulis. Ninos and Mago joined me. I wanted both to come along for several strategic reasons.

Ninos is our trade expert. He made his livelihood on trade caravans from the far east until addiction to opium destroyed his life and dumped him in our backyard in Galilee. He became a follower of Christ shortly afterwards and joined our mission shortly after that.

He will be very valuable on this trip for I suspect Gamilah has come to this region to strategize how the Nabateans can deal with Rome's increasing attacks on their triangular sail ships, the lateens. Clearly Rome wants to monopolize the lucrative spice trade for themselves—and only the Nabateans stand in their way.

I am pleased to report Ninos recently remarried. His previous wife and children were murdered by bandits years ago—that was one of the things that led Ninos to opium to deal with the emotional pain.

About a year ago, Ninos met a beautiful Axumite young woman. Belkis is her name. I am told the name has something to do with the legendary Queen of Sheba who graced the court of King Solomon.

Belkis is quite a bit younger than Ninos. She is beautiful and full of life, very mature for her 16 years. She has the most beautiful black complexion I have ever seen, and her smile lights up any room. His bride is very intelligent. Her family owns the leading trade caravans from Axum to the port of Adulis, so they have many common interests. Both speak multiple languages, and both can negotiate trade covenants with great skill. It was a wonderful marriage service led by the honorable Rabbi Reuben ben Joseph. Belkis is pregnant with their first child.

Mago has grown into a fine young man as well. He is quite tall and has a wild mass of curly black hair making him appear taller still. He has very sharp features and wide eyes—someone said he had a fastidious face.

He is quite clever. He gets his discipline from his mother and his sense of compassion and enthusiasm from his father. His wife, Sophie is also quite gifted, in fact, she is the mirror reflection of her mother-in-law, Bernice—organized to a fault. They are quite supportive of each other and make a wonderful team.

Mago and Sophie are both very interested in the mission and are praying to God about extending this mission to Nabatean ports further south. Mago clearly wants more responsibility. I plan to give it to him on this trip.

When they disciple other young adults, they have proven themselves to be very wise—skilled with the Torah, Writings, and the Oral Tradition. In a previous era, Mago would have been a great candidate to study with the likes of Gamaliel or Zakkai. Their class is widely attended by men and women of the Way, Jews, and Axumites from multiple tribes. I am so proud of them.

For Mago, this trip is a bit of a coming-of-age exercise. Perhaps God will open a powerful new door for Mago. I plan to speak to Gamilah about that.

We joined a medium size caravan very early the next morning. It reminded me of our trek from Jerusalem now almost three years ago. My back started hurting the moment I climbed the Donkey. Someone called it muscle memory. I think it is just old age.

The caravan carried much grain, exotic animal skins, pottery and over three dozen massive elephant tusks—some five feet long. I am told by Obodas the ivory from elephant tusks is in great demand in Alexandria and Rome. It is used for carvings, royal stamps, and expensive jewelry and such. Each tusk weighed as much as a small man.

Obodas told me hunters would stalk a herd of elephants and surround one of the males with ten or more spearman. It is very dangerous. Wounded male elephants have been known to trample grown men.

The precious ivory is then cut off the dead elephant and hauled off for shipping. The carcass of the elephant is left for the buzzards or other wild animals.

Obodas was clearly disgusted with the practice. The idea of hunting these majestic creatures just for their tusks was appalling to him. He said that as a young lad, he had come upon a killing field once just west of Axum where there were dozens of rotting lifeless elephant carcasses littering the open valley. He had vowed to never support the trade.

"But..." he added as he cocked his head and shrugged his shoulders. "King Zoskales loves hunting elephants. On the walls of his private chambers are several massive tusks—a show of his power and wiles as a great hunter."

"Do you see all of those tusks?" He pointed at the line of weary mules carrying only two of them at a time due to their weight. "Every single one of them is his. He has decreed he owns that market. Who will object?"

A couple of things I have learned on this trip. First, King Zoskales is not a man to be trifled with. He came to power in a very bloody coup against the aging predecessor King Bazen over a decade before. Not only had Zoskales brutally defeated the armies of King Bazen, but he also then had the leaders and generals beheaded and their bloody heads mounted on the walls of the Axum fortress for all to see.

The royal family and key supporters of Bazen were then either also violently killed or sold into slavery. He is apparently quite paranoid about even rumors of any uprises still to this day and does not hesitate to jail potential enemies at the very first inkling of something being amiss.

Obodas was first exposed to the wrath of the King when he originally refused to ship his precious ivory. The King had Obodas thrown into the dungeon for a week with little food or water—until Obodas acquiesced and very publicly apologized to the King for any disrespect.

I now feel so bad for pushing Obodas to appeal to the King on our behalf related to our conflicts with Haaman.

Oh, and there's more—something I didn't see coming. Apparently Haaman has the ear of the King.

Years ago, said Obodas, Haaman was ordered to come to the royal court to minister to the King's first wife Etinesh. She was in the throes of a very difficult childbirth. She had a dangerous fever, significant bleeding and was in constant pain—over and above normal birthing pains. The royal doctors could do little. The King was prepared to lose both his wife and his child.

One of the servants suggested the King contact Haaman. Soon, Haaman arrived and went to work. He took out of the room all family idols and replaced them with crude straw-woven dolls made in the shape of men and women, and animals—each representing ancestor spirits of great warriors, healers, and leaders of Axum's past. He then urinated on the door lentil and around the bed where the Queen suffered explaining this would keep away harmful spirits. Then he put on his shaman grab and started to rhythmically beat his drum late into the darkness.

Sadly, the Queen perished nevertheless, but the child, the Royal Prince Addisu survived. The King credits Haaman with the Prince's life and has anointed Haaman as officially the "Friend of the King" --a very high honor.

It appears Haaman enjoys more than the King's ear. Troubling.

I shared my growing concerns with Ninos and Mago. I am very worried. I am worried about the well-being of my family, my friends, our safety and even the entire mission seems to be held only by a thread. Now that I know about the relationship between Haaman and the King, I am beyond anxious.

God bless Mago—my son-in-law and dear friend. In our team, I rely on four people a great deal as active partners for this writing project. There is Sorkatti. She is the true author, skilled at editing and format. She is the one who takes my notes and scratches and skillfully writes them legibly and beautifully on papyrus.

Reuben is my theologian and scholar. Often, we dialogue late into the night about how to best present the gospel of the Rabboni. I couldn't do it without him. His musings on the multiple paths for Jews was invaluable to me.

Of course, my greatest supporter and bulwark is Deborah. She continues to encourage me and to give me space to do this work—even though I know it is a sacrifice for her. She is sold on this effort and has been the wind in my sails –so to speak.

Then there is Mago. He is young, smart, eloquent, spirit-filled, and wise. I have deeply appreciated his thoughts—particularly from a younger perspective as I have worked through the proclamations of the Rabboni on that hillside in Galilee.

It was Mago who kindly suggested this would be a good time for me to press on to the next section in this Gospel manuscript—maybe even God's timing. As he said the words, his eyebrows raised knowingly, and he smirked. I was so reminded of the Rabboni's smirk.

What could I say? When you are right, you're right.

I am exposed. Right now, I am indeed quite worried, in fact, I am terrified. God help me. But it is true. My anxiety is affecting my life—all parts of it.

With all due respect to the Rabboni, birds may not be concerned with reaping or sowing, but they become quite concerned when a hawk grasps them with its deadly talons. That is how I am feeling more and more.

We are born in anxiety and tread in it our entire lives. There is no breath of air that is not laced in the poison. No one is immune. No day passes. To deny is foolishness and false bravado.

Even the Emperor is terrified of assassination, or loss of public acclamation, or whether he will have a male successor, or worse, find his son is a fool.

Shammar and Rashaida, our two young former bedouin slaves are no longer worried about whether their master would be kind or cruel. But now, they worry about being recaptured, or be shamed somehow by others more secure, or will die penniless and alone. They are concerned about their families back home.

Gamilah is concerned about the Roman's usurping the spice market, their traditional source of income and status.

Te'oma and Ruth are quite concerned about the safety of their young child with Haaman and his goons making such mischief.

The owner of our caravan torments himself that the next caravan will be empty, and he will not be able to cover his cost, or he will suffer a new competitor who will steal his clients—or who already has unknown to him.

The Roman ship captains fear the Nabatean pirates. Faadicha, the Egyptian agent in Ptolemais on the Hunt fears the Nichomachus Flavianus, the Proconsul of Rome in Alexandria. Flavinius fears Rome. On and on and on.

King Zoskales is terrified of being overthrown and being exposed as vulnerable. Haaman is afraid of the spirits of his ancestors.

Our Lord Jesus felt excruciating all-too human anxiety and worry as he paused to pray in the Garden hours before his own crucifixion.

We humans fear disease, poverty, loneliness, bad report from others, not being good enough, strong enough, attractive enough, successful enough, secure enough, marriageable enough. We are a fearful people. It is in our nature. Ultimately, we fear death and dying's dread hallways.

It extends even beyond us. Many fear the afterlife and wonder what celestial beings we will stand in front of. Will we be accepted as worthy or fall short? In our language, will we be righteous enough to be ushered into Paradise or be banished into Gehenna. Even the worthy Rabban Zakkai felt such anxiety only moments before his demise.

Undealt with lingering anxiety drives some to drink and other addictions—those things that quiet the voices of our anxiety for a moment or two. Worry drives others to be demanding, critical or condemning. It drives some to strain for more control and power—for then they foolishly imagine they will manage their anxiety better. But honestly, I have never known anyone who feels free of anxiety.

The powerful and wealthy fear losing and the impotent and poor fear never having.

What Jesus is saying in his messages is both welcoming—who wouldn't find this relevant? —but frustrating and maddening at the same time. He doesn't know me and what I am facing; how dare he treat me and my burdens so lightly.

To say "Be not anxious" is a lovely sentiment but it is no better than a sharp rock when one tries to swallow it whole. Anxiety and worry, particularly chronic issues are deeply rooted in our souls and can't be driven away by urinating on our door lintels or banging on a drum.

To be perfectly clear, when we speak of anxiousness and worry, we do not include careful planning, consideration and strategizing to minimize contingencies. Not at all. Even Jesus says builders should figure out the cost of a project before you go for financing (Lk 14:28).

We cross the line into sinful anxiety when we come to lose trust in God as our celestial *karim* and imagine foolishly He is either not big enough to care for us and protect us, or He has determined to abandon us to our own wiles.

In any case, it is the sin of ungratefulness and unbelief. It is an act of shame to not rest in the care of your Great *Karim*. It is a fist raised to the sky yelling "God, I don't believe you have my interest at heart. I do not believe you can or will make good on your promise to cherish me ultimately. I have found you untrustworthy and I relieve you from your commitment."

Anxiety is ultimately unbelief and idolatry. It to our great shame.

I am sympathetic to the person who just cannot fathom that God, our *karim* would allow us—much less providentially direct us into chaos, pain, loss, sickness, persecution, financial devastation, lack of security or control—for no good *Karim* would do that—right?

Though I wish to tell you otherwise, Jesus already said children of God will be persecuted—not if, but when. I can say this now—right now when my persecution is at a relatively low ebb—that in the hands of Jesus persecution is always purposeful, meaningful—even glory-producing—though it may lead to death—even the most shameful death on a very public cross.

We said at the beginning of our Kingdom quest, "God use us for your glory, for the sake of your Kingdom, for the sake of the unrescued—use us no matter what the cost. We are a weapon for your use. Swing us skillfully."

In the experiential joy of our own gracious rescue, we easily forget how God directed His own beloved Son, who was justly worthy of no condemnation or even discipline. He stood close as his willing Son suffered thirty years of deprivation of glory and recognition—for ultimately, he was only recognized by demons. His path to glory was scarred with persecution again and again, and ultimately the shame and suffering of the Cross.

For what high purpose you ask? For eternal life for people like me and so many others. Was it worth it? We seem to think so as we gather to worship God and to thank him for his Son and our salvation.

Let the heat get turned up even a little in my life—and I slide back into being an unbeliever and idolater, my thankfulness dries up all too quickly and I condemn God for apparent unfaithfulness and abandoning me. I cry out with the Psalmist, "Darkness is my closest friend." The latter is a casting of shame on my Celestial *Karim* and Friend.

To repeat. Jesus said we would be persecuted—we who have as our protector benefactor and *karim*, the God of all the universe—the only one who <u>could</u> wave his powerful arms and rescue us from anything—anytime—anywhere.

Yet He prefers to play the long game. Let me give you an idea of the math of God. If my suffering can be used to rescue a thousand Axumites from Gehenna and eternal loneliness—God would no doubt smile.

I have wondered if I was given the choice ahead of time—which I never am—I likely would ask "How much suffering?" I am after all a bit of a coward. But I would like to think I would ultimately agree—along with some stiff ale along the way.

What if it were a hundred lost souls? Or twenty-five? Or ten? Or one? God's math is still conclusive. In heavenly courts that risk is worth the reward. That is how much God desires to rescue the lost humanity.

"But I am not anxious or worried, I am just concerned". You might say—because it would be too shameful to say—and yet still be untrue. Here are some other signs of anxiousness.

In the moment, the anxious cannot worship God, not really. The anxious feel little joy in their salvation. The anxious tend to pray either rotely or only for things related to them and their insecurities.

It is far healthier to admit each of us fluidly drift in and out of worry and ungratefulness to God. In honor-shame cultures like ours, it is one of the greatest acts of shame to not be grateful to your Benefactor and the pinnacle of ungratefulness is to fall away from trusting and depending upon him or her. There is no more shame that a *karim* can experience than for one of his or her clients to strike out on their own—to find security in their own efforts and means.

To the contrary, there is no greater honor for the *karim* than for their client to go to them with anxiety in tow, prostrating before them in his or her need—especially great ones.

For in so doing you are proclaiming that your benefactor is truly great enough, merciful enough and compassionate enough. If you do not go to your benefactor when your need is great and your anxiety is high, you shame both them and yourself.

Remember the Jesus' parable of the magnanimous King and the boneheaded servant (Luke 18)? The boneheaded servant had every reason to be anxious. By all rights he should have been beheaded. He had betrayed the Magnanimous King and proven to be unfaithful and unworthy of his care--worthy of death in fact, or at least dismissal. But the Magnanimous King was also his righteous benefactor and so He himself paid the boneheaded servant's entire debt to himself –from his own limitless treasuries. That is what great King Benefactors do. What was "due" Him in response? Gratefulness of course.

This servant wasn't anything like the King. He was not only incompetent, but a person of shame and ungratefulness. How do we know? First, he never utters the word "Thanks."

Second, he shames his King Benefactor by not acting like him in his dealing with other servants of the King. Disgraceful. By doing what he did, he cast aspersions upon his Benefactor's name and reputation.

What could he have done? He could have invited the other servant of the King to come with him into the presence of their mutual Great Benefactor. What would happen? I have no doubt the King would be honored his servant trusted his grace that much.

Alas, he does not. He is an unworthy, ungrateful servant-- a person of shame.

Even at the end, the Gracious King leaves the door open for the boneheaded servant to have a change of mind. The shamed servant's only hope in the harsh dungeon is to request an audience with his previous King-benefactor.

Again, I know I am correct here. If he did this, his newest debt would be paid, and he would be fully restored as before.

Why? Because this is what excellent King Benefactors do. They are worthy to be trusted and counted on.

Do we have such a Celestial Benefactor King? If you say "yes" and in this moment are filled with His faith and can even partially rest in that relationship, neither anxiety nor worry weeds can drop roots in such life-producing soil. Such abiding produces only gratefulness, freedom, and worship.

If you say "no", you will have no joy in your prayers and only half your heart will be in them. For the other half is already dwelling on tomorrow; already our mind is wandering. Wondering how you will help ourselves in case God does not intervene, and you remain torn between faith and doubt, anxiety, and trust.

Until we rest in our Benefactor's arms at peace the deserted heaven remains peopled with imps and specters. Every cloud fills us with foreboding for lightning may flash from it. Even the horizon is laden with mysteries that evoke tension and anxiety. This person who worries worships false gods, and the false gods plunge him into fresh cares and anxieties.

The Jesus follower who is not experiencing—in the present moment-- the protection and care of the Rabboni can only sink into fears of thieves and moths, succumb to persecution complexes and paranoia, and little sleep.

The opposite of all of this is the peace of God—not something that comes from our heart, not at all, it is a fruit of the Spirit alone. We can never own it—not this side of heaven. We remain totally dependent upon our regular daily access of it from the storehouses of the Spirit who dwells in our anxiety-prone inner being.

I remember something I wrote about in my gospel that illustrates this well (Matt 14). To our lasting shame, this happened after we witnessed the Rabboni do something ridiculous and beyond description.

He fed a very hungry crowd, over five thousand men-- so if you added the women and children as well, it was at least double that, with only five normal sized loaves of bread and two rather small fishes—they were quite pathetic really.

Not only was the crowd satisfied—in fact satiated as if at a great feast-- but there were so many leftovers we weren't sure what to do.

We disciples could only look at each other and shrug our shoulders. There was no way we could possibly explain the miracle, none of us had ever seen anything like it. I tried to explain it to a couple from Samaria and was just mocked as if I was an imbecile. Of course, it was absurd—and yet....

The reason I bring it up is that—again to my disgrace—within a mere couple of hours—I was once again consumed with fear and doubt. What is wrong with me?

The easiest and quickest way for us to return home was on-board a ship in the Sea of Galilee. I am sure I have said how much I hate being on the water.

We were nearing the middle of our journey, and a horrific storm came upon us in what felt like moments. We were helpless—in a small boat—far away from land being thrashed from side to side by the maelstrom.

I will admit it. I was terrified of dying and even more so, being drowned. In that moment, I had lost any trust in the goodness of God. I was an exposed, impotent, and unbelieving orphan.

I smile now as I think about Jesus. This is definitely his sense of humor that we disciples were able to experience on several occasions. He just came casually walking up to the boat on top of the crashing waves. Walking on the surface. I can get seasick just remembering how his body would rise, then fall, then rhythmically rise again—unmoved, calm. In fact, I think I noticed that endearing smirk on his face, like a child who would say to his glowing parents, "Hey look what I can do."

I can't say that is exactly what happened, because I was trembling in fear holding fast to the gunwale along with the rest of the screaming disciples.

Then what did Jesus do? Did he calm the sea? Not yet. Did he give us courage? No. He said—at the top of his voice because who could hear over the thunder and wind?

"Take heart, It's just me. Don't be afraid."

Really Rabboni? I laugh now because I can. What an absurd thing to tell a bunch of terrified men who were surely facing a horrible death. "*Tharseo*" in the Greek. "Take heart!" Really? Is this the right word you would say to horror-stricken people who are about to die? No, of course not.

"Get a grip. Do not be terrified. Do not worry. Do not be concerned."

And yet, I would say that from the lips of Jesus, it was the right thing to say. Only Jesus could say it and it have any real relevance.

Tharseo is a word that in and of itself was impossible in our situation. We had no capacity to pull it off. If you tell me to run faster—I can do it. If you tell me to choose to go down this street versus that one. I can. If you say to get your feet under that heavy object and really lean into lifting it—I may hurt myself—but I can try. But Tharseo???? Not a chance. I can't do it.

There is something in our heart that manufactures fear, worry and anxiety and it seems to need to run its course.

And yet Jesus said *"Tharseo"* —totally knowing that we would not obey—could not obey.

Also, in that moment, saying, "It's me" didn't help much either. It should have. If we really knew his power, his authority over creation (which admittedly we should have after the meal on the mount) and if we really trusted him as our Benefactor and King, it would have meant everything.

In that setting, with our pulse rate skyrocketing, our brains hijacked with alarm, it meant nothing to us.

Then to top it off, "Do not fear."

Again, I can laugh now. I know Jesus was discipling us like a good Rabboni. He had to know we would not obey.

We lacked such trust—in a word, we lacked His Spirit. We lacked faith. And as result, we were crippled in our fear and anxiousness.

My dear friend, Peter often says we should cast our cares upon Jesus. He is correct of course. But how does one do that? Certainly not when fear and anxiety have hijacked our hearts.

I will speak about this again when we talk about how to pray. When we say, "Thy will be done", that is the posture of a dependent client who rests like a newborn babe in the arms of their powerful Benefactor.

Even though the world quakes around her or him, the child rests secure.

How can we become like that child?

Jesus addresses that very thing in this next section of His teachings. Jesus said,

"Why <u>would</u> you pile up your valuable things here on earth. They are so perishable and vulnerable to bugs and thieves here. How could you not be anxious and worried you will be left with nothing to trust in? Wouldn't a wise and discerning person find their security and status from the wealth of the

Heavenly Kingdom? That status is eternal and does not need to be fretted over. For where your value comes from, that is who you are." (Matt 6:19-21)

Yes, but that is what we do. That is the nature of our heart—including our rescued heart. We are prone to trust in those things that seem to give us even a miniscule of value and honor here—physical things. And yes, we want to collect them and store them away. And yes, we worry about losing them—for we innately fear that they are at great risk.

We spend a so much emotional energy, fights, and wars, trying to protect and hold on to very slippery measurements of worth here. It is not wise, but we all do it.

A truly wise man or woman would obviously give that up in exchange for real and eternal markers of value, honor and worth—heavenly ones that are from the hand of God, our heavenly benefactor, those things that are permanent and powerful, that are always in great abundance and can never be diminished. Heaven has no moths. It affords no thieves.

It is clear then if you follow my logic, we should, but we won't.

Truth told, we just are not generally that wise or discerning—and so we are relegated to worry.

Even when our anxiety has been dispelled for a time, like the sea tide that eventually goes out for a few hours, I still do not have the wisdom and discernment to not trust in physical treasures, or my health, or my job, or my security, or my own strength. My conclusion? I am sadly all too human.

I <u>should</u> prefer heavenly honor and name, but I don't. On my own, I cannot. I will not. Let's keep going.

Jesus continued, "The eye is the lamp of the body. If your pure eyes are single-minded, attentively focused on the attuning gaze of your adoring Heavenly Benefactor, your whole body will feel the difference. You will be so full of light, you won't worry. This is the only way to know any freedom from anxiety and care."

"If you have an evil eye," said Jesus, "that desperately strains to compare itself with others and is prone to jealousy, avarice, and coveting, is never at rest, never satisfied, always looking for the gaze of false *karims* that tempt with flattery, your whole body will be full of darkness. If then the light within you is darkness, how great is that darkness! You can only worry and never sleep."

Oh man or woman, prone to worry, prone to look away from the adoring gaze of your Celestial *Karim*, what is it inside you that tricks you to choose the anxious path, risky path of an abandoned orphan?

Why do you choose to wallow in the weakness and infirmity of your will?

Can we be honest? Each of us knows exactly what Jesus meant by the 'evil eye'. That is our norm. That is where he found us. That is what he rescued us from, imperfectly now, but perfectly when we see him face to face.

On the other hand, the 'pure eye' looks to our Heavenly father and finds its peace in that gaze.

Remember Ruth and her baby Tahir? I told you, when they are in that state if attunement, how Tahir's eyes are locked upon her Ruth's gaze. That connection is glorious. It is not forced or manipulated. It is a dynamic in which both feel honored and adored. It is a 'pure eye'.

It is a primal relational dance, where for a moment, both feel rich. Their treasures are stored up into the gaze of the others. They are indeed enviable.

Having said that, this pure eye is hardly our normal posture. How do we put on the pure eye? How do we take away our evil eye? That is the question, indeed. Here is the Rabboni again.

"No one can find their identity and value and worth from two competing sources. You will choose one and despise the other. Earthly sources of identity are often deviously well-packaged and so tempting but in the end are vapid and ineffective. That is the path to failure, anxiety, and worry. Why not throw yourself upon the care of your Heavenly *Karim*?" (Matt 6:24)

Again, how can one like me, who has been addicted to the evil eye—be torn away from its lure?

Jesus again. "So, stop it. Stop worrying about your life, your sustenance, your health, your reputation, your dress, and appearance. You are pursuing the lesser at the expense of the greater." (Matt 6:25)

"Look around. See the birds flying over your worried brow? They don't measure their value over the appropriate sourcing for food or concern for stockpiling seed just in case. That would be absurd. Do you not know your Heavenly Benefactor Husband loves you more than these?"

He went on, "What is the benefit—wise and discerning man or woman—of fretting and worrying over your life? Has it made a positive difference? Has it made you live longer? What about the quality of your life? Has it made you feel joy?"

"Go and watch the lilies dance in the breeze. Are you jealous? You should be."

"Their majesty is unequalled. Not even all-wise Solomon who was regularly dressed in expensive regal garb by an entourage of courtiers rivaled their beauty, or absence of worry. Kings struggle to keep up appearance. All too often, even the wise ones become slaves to fashion and opinion. How about you?"

"Your Heavenly Benefactor is deeply concerned for your security and glory. You need not worry about what others think, how you appear, you do not need compliments or the fretting of keeping up with the Roman wealthy."

"Stop it. Stop fretting over such things here. If you were un-rescued, then worry makes sense. But you? You were set free from this present evil age, and you are in the adoring and loving gaze of your Great Groom. Dance, do not fret." (Matt 6:26-32)

Easy to say, harder to do. Am I right? Jesus might as well say to you like he said to us disciples on that faulting boat ride, "Tharseo." "Take heart" and "Do not be afraid."

Of course, you exclaim, "How? I cannot. My heart is weak and corrupted. I am tragically addicted to security I can touch and hold, I am addicted to fixing it myself. I am addicted to compliments and playing the part of a successful Jew. I am beginning to see I am addicted to anxiousness and worry. God help me. What am I to do?"

Look up, worried one. By faith turn your face into the adoring gaze of your heavenly King. Not only will you begin to feel honored and enviable, but also safe and secure. Amid the swirling storm and vagaries of this fracturing world with more than enough reason to be afraid and worried, you will rest, you will know Shabbat. (Matt 6:33-34)

Here is my prayer and I offer it to you. May you find in it some mechanism to have the murderous arms of anxiousness ripped from you. May it cause you to laugh more, to dance, to be grateful to your Heavenly *Karim*.

"Abba in Heaven, I have told You everything that troubles me; I have told You the ways in which I think I might be helped. But now, I want to draw a line through it all, forget it all and leave it all behind. Now do with me as You will. Your will be done—not mine. Holy Spirit, make me know my Abba's favor. Make me hear him whisper in my ear, "You are my beloved son with whom I am well pleased." Make me come close, *lipnay Elohim*, to see His joyful gaze upon me. Make me feel Your fruit of faith. Make me pure in heart and pure-eyed. Make me pause, powerless in his arms like a helpless infant secure at his or her mother's breast. Give me Your Shalom, the opposite of anxiousness and concern, the peace that surpasses understanding, that makes no sense as the world falls apart around me and I am surrounded by imps and specters that threaten harm. Make me shabbat in you, today.""

30

Day 1062 of the Axum Mission

I couldn't wait to write an update on our trip.

On the third night after we arrived at Adulis, we were surprised to be visited in our rented apartment by five armed clandestine Nabateans. Obodas calmed our fears and assured us we were safe in his care.

We were led down the beach a few miles south of Adulis and climbed awkwardly into two small dinghies and pushed out into the dark waves. In only a few minutes, as our eyes adjusted to the moonless night, we saw the stark shadow of a Nabatean triangular-sailed lateen.

I was reminded how afraid our Roman friends were at the sight of such a pirate ship. I have no doubt they are the cause of nightmares for Roman and Egyptian captains on the Red Sea. But we felt so safe in the care of Obodas. There was no place safer for us.

The ship raised anchor as soon as we were boarded and settled and headed south. Ninos, Mago and I did not dare say anything. On the other hand, I have rarely seen Obodas so talkative. It turns out he was friends with many of the sailors, including the captain, a hard looking fellow, whose word and orders were never questioned.

I have learned since this was a dangerous voyage, first at night, but secondly, the sea was filled with Roman ships whose sole goal was to sink any and all pirate ships they might find. This clandestine trip was solely for our benefit, at the command of Gamilah. We were the guests of honor.

A couple of hours before dawn, we dropped anchor off the coast of an island in the middle of the sea. I could not tell you the name of the island or where we were. I suppose that is how they wanted it, not that I had anyone to tell their secrets to.

We had anchored in the middle of six other lateens each larger than the one we were on. Each of the anchored lateens had lamps lit and sailors high in the riggings. Obodas said they had orders to raise anchor and flee at the first sight of Roman ships.

It was exciting. When we arrived at our port destination in our same two dinghies, we were escorted to a fortress up a ridge from the port.

We were waved in the large fortress gates by two armed and massive Nabateans. We continued to a large hall to the right of a well in the center of the compound. Two other guards opened the great doors and bowed to us.

That is when we first saw Gamilah as she hurried to us and hugged each of us. We could only laugh. None of us were used to this intrigue—or for that matter, having someone want to see us that badly.

Again, in that moment, I felt honored, a person of value and quite secure. In Gamilah and Obodas' care, we were safe—and so very grateful.

Since we were starving from our journey, we were fed—well that's not accurate, we were awarded with a great banquet. There were spice fish of many types, oysters, lamb and a variety of breads and sweets. Mago and I dearly enjoyed the multiple ales, our mugs were never dry. Ninos took advantage of the exotic fruit juices that were provided. I so wish Deborah had joined us. She would have loved the intrigue and would certainly have enjoyed the feast.

Gamilah filled me in on some of the happenings in Judea. She asked if I heard Rabban Zakkai had died. Of course, I had heard that from Reuben.

The Romans have eased off their restrictions and have given the new Sanhedrin, led by Gamaliel II more authority. While the zealots were virtually decimated, there remain some still hidden in the wilderness caves. People are still very much on edge.

The Way is thriving. Missions are active and extending from Spain to the west and China to the east. Paul and Peter have been murdered in Rome. John has been exiled to a barren island off the coast of Greece. Mary remains well cared for in Ephesus.

Gamaliah is of course worried Rome continues to usurp the lucrative spice trades. Not so long ago, they had sent many ships to attack the main Nabateans fleet at Aden and were successful in destroying much of the navy. But the Nabateans are fighting back. This gathering of their top captains was partly to strategize how to press back even more against the larger and slower armed ships of Rome.

"But..." she said raising one eyebrow. "That is not why I asked for you to join us."

"Really," I inquired with a great curiosity. "You know I am happy to assist you in any way I can. I am afraid I will never be able to captain one of your vessels" I smiled.

"Oh my God, my friend, I know that. I would never ask you to be on the water more than you absolutely must. You and I have spoken about your lack of love for the sea."

"I would like you to tell my captains and their sailors about the Rabboni. I know I have sprung this on you, but I assume you can do that—far better than I."

"I would be honored to do that. I truly would. When would you like me to...?" She cut me off.

"Right now, of course. That is why we have gathered this evening. It is to hear you tell of the Gospel of Jesus."

For the first time, I looked around the hall and sure enough, all eyes were upon me and Gamilah.

These were hard men, some old, some young, all with sun-blackened rough skin, scars, unkempt hair—or little at all. These were warriors of seamen...oh, and seawomen (I saw a few ladies scattered at the tables) whose wealth came from the efforts of their hands and their ships. They were those who only knew their lot and obedience to their captain. They also knew death and loss.

I imagined they were people who wondered about the spirit-world, likely believers in luck, or superstition, or the demons.

In these early morning hours, they were just the gathered unenviable—not in upper Galilee but on this island hill, who wanted to hear of something more.

As for me, I knew exactly what to say. I cleared my throat—gazed slowly around making sure I acknowledged every eye at every table, none left out—and like my Rabboni before me, I waved my arms over their heads and proclaimed at the top of my voice,

"Enviable now are you who were formerly unenviable, because now, you are under the protection of a new benefactor King, the creator of the sea and the waves, God."

I had their attention.

It was a special time. The Spirit of the Rabboni had filled me with just the right words to say.

As I ended my thoughts, I closed with an invitation.

In the end, there were forty-five men and women who chose to be baptized in the sea as the sun brightly rose in the East. Mago assisted me and afterwards Gamilah called for another feast to be enjoyed by us all. Now this was a true Todah.

I looked over at Ninos, as we tore a piece off the same loaf. I said with a smile, "Blessed are the pirates, for they are children of the living God." He roared with laughter.

It was a good day.

I will add a couple of other things. Gamilah had asked me if there was anything we needed. I mentioned our problems with Haaman. She was greatly concerned—I was a bit surprised—she was worried and said she and Obodas would speak about it and come up with a plan.

Then I told her of our newest project.

I noticed a few of the sailors had some copies of manuscripts about Jesus. I saw a couple of John Mark's wonderful account, even one of mine.

I told Gamilah we wanted to set up a copy-center in Axum. Publishing is very costly. I know some about it. My Gospel was a papyrus codex, about a hundred pages or so, depending upon who did the copying.

Papyrus sheets are made by pressing together two layers of papyrus, one atop the other, at right angles. Papyrus is made from the papyrus plant, a reed which grows in the marshy areas around the Nile River. Sheets of papyrus were then made into foot high rolls; commonly twenty sheets to a roll—but they could be larger. Most of a scribe's work was done using reed pens dipped in black ink made of a soot-based pigment.

A final book such as my Gospel, or Paul's letters, could cost as much as 2500 denarii to produce—so figure over three-four months wages for an unskilled tradesman—and take a single person at least six months to copy and bind in a codex format.

Scrolls are very difficult to use and transport. We will use the rectangular codex format bound with a stiff, treated leather cover.

A single copy of my Gospel was about a hundred pages and required over five standard rolls of papyrus.

Pens and inks are also quite costly. The good news is standard rolls of prepared papyrus, writing reeds and ink are readily available in Alexandria—for it has been a publishing hub for centuries. Ninos is prepared to go there and hire staff and necessary supplies.

We estimate that a group of twelve skilled scribes—which we can easily hire in Alexandria-- housed in our new scriptorium compound, could produce a couple of manuscripts a month. That doesn't sound like a lot, but it is twenty-four a year. Our plans are to hire mainly Greek scribes, but also scribes who are skilled with both Nabatean and Ge'ez Arabic dialects.

Sorkatti has already agreed to take the lead. Bernice has volunteered to do the books. Ninos will organize the hiring of scribes and the ongoing supply of materials. Mago and Te'oma will do much of the day-to-day management of the scriptorium. As the Nabatean captain ordered as we raised anchor, "All hands-on deck!"

Think about it. If Gamilah could get one manuscript on every Nabatean ship, the Gospel would travel the globe.

Our scriptorium could grow from there. We have plenty of room in our compound to house even twice that number of scribes.

I have a hard time controlling my excitement. This is just the beginning. We have permission to publish John Mark's wonderful account of the Rabboni, also two of Paul's letters to the church in Galatia and Ephesus. Then there is my Gospel and the first volume of this series, The Rabboni. God-willing I am planning to have this second manuscript completed by winter. I wonder if it would be smart to just publish the Rabboni's teachings in Galilee—kind of a mini-codex. I could call it, The Rabboni's Teachings in Galilee. Or perhaps more savvy people could come up with another title that is more memorable.

Gamilah was more than thrilled with the idea and requested we make haste to move our plans forward. Winter was coming and it would be harder to find ink and quills and other materials we need. Gamilah jokingly reminded me I had promised her my first new Codex on the Birth of Jesus in this series. I laughed and nodded my head.

"Gamilah, God-willing, after the winter, Mago and I will personally deliver to you—in the Nabatean Arabic dialect, my original Gospel and both volumes of The Rabboni—and so much more."

Mago grinned and nodded in agreement.

Gamilah waved her second in command over. He brought a sizable bag of Roman gold coins, a veritable treasure.

"Let this be the first of many gifts for your scriptorium. I am so proud of you, Matthew—so pleased and honored you are my friend and are under my care. Same for your entire team. I am your supporter and will do whatever I can so you will fulfill your calling by God."

"Be assured Matthew, you are doing God's work. Be happy."

One last stray thought. One of the things I truly want to do, and I see this as the powerful work of the Spirit in my protective inner-being. I want to be able to gift the first copy of my Gospel in Ge'ez to Haaman. I really do. Not to manipulate a response or a repayment. I know it would be an honor to him—and I really want to do that.

Praise God that He is more than powerful to overcome my normal emotions and fears. I am so grateful to earthly *karims* Gamilah and Obodas. But even more so for my Heavenly *Karim*.

I am reminded of the Psalmist' exclamatory praise to our Great King,

I lift up my eyes to the hills — where does my help come from?

My help comes from the LORD, the Maker of heaven and earth.

He will not let my foot slip — he who watches over me will not slumber;

Indeed, he who watches over Israel will neither slumber nor sleep.

The LORD watches over us — the LORD is our shade at our right hand;

The sun will not harm us by day, nor the moon by night.

The LORD will keep us from all harm — he will watch over our life;

the LORD will watch over our coming and going both now and forevermore. (Ps 121)

31

Day 1066 of the Axum Mission

It is now morning, and I am sitting in a local thermopolia—or café—on the beach in Adulis. Ninos, Mago and I got back very early before sunrise only a day ago. The same care was taken to surreptitiously bring us back to more Roman environs. Obodas stayed with Gamilah on the mysterious island for reasons he wouldn't share, but he arranged for us to join a safe and secure caravan back to Axum within the next few days.

It shouldn't be long, for already a large Roman vessel is being unloaded. Dinghy after dinghy beach themselves as dozens of workers unload them and shove them back into the crashing waves. At this pace, they will be finished by early afternoon, or this evening at the latest.

I suspect we might even start off at first light tomorrow. I am ready to go home. I do miss Deborah.

When we arrived here, the sun was just rising in the east, and we were exhausted. We found our lodging prepaid by Obodas. The proprietor was a lifelong friend of Obodas and had risen early in expectation of our arrival. We crashed on our straw beds, not waking up until well into the evening hours.

I left the lodgings early this morning by myself. Mago and Ninos wanted to enjoy the sights and sounds of the port before we leave. I don't expect to see them until later tonight for our evening meal here.

The last thing Obodas did for us was to volunteer to protect our treasure. He argued he will be travelling with a couple of very large and very mean armed men and so we can rest assured he will not be robbed.

Truthfully, I was relieved for his offer. I have not handled such coins since I was a tax-collector in Capernaum. And then, the coins were not mine. I am so grateful again Obodas is our *karim*. I am not sure what we would do without him.

One of the things I know he and Gamilah will be discussing is what to do with Haaman. It is a conundrum, and they are quite concerned. "For now," Obodas said, "We want to get you and your team back safely to your compound in Axum. The next step will be the next step."

I appreciated his logic and yet, remain worried.

Since I promised Gamilah, she would get the first copy of my second Codex of The Rabboni, I wanted to take the time today to press on. When I travel, I often bring with me scraps of prepared papyrus. They are no longer suited for the codex, but wonderfully suited for me to jot down notes.

I typically hand the scribbles and scraps to Sorkatti to translate and enhance. She is a trusted and skilled colleague. I am always pleased with the final copy. I am totally confident she could run the publishing project all by herself.

As I reread this section of my Gospel, I am reminded of what I wrote about the section on how to pray. It is easy—as I have since witnessed—to read this section out of the context of the nine makarios. It is easy to read these as godly principles and *halakhah* to teach us how we should live in ways pleasing to God, that earn our standing as men and women of Torahic righteousness. It is easy to read Jesus' teaching as some better tips on how to do-righteously.

The confusing thing is that in many ways, they are good things to do. They are what truly Spirit-filled righteous godly men and women would do and would want to do.

I am going to try something different in this section. I hope this is helpful

We should not judge others, Jesus rightly says. But we will. It is the way of beat-up people who are fighting for honor and worth here. Apart from Jesus' work on our behalf, we remain in stark competition for identity. We have learned to make a virtual lifestyle out of judging others. Honestly, it feels good. It is addictive. Some of us are experts.

So even though Jesus says, "Don't you know when you judge someone, they will judge you back. Then you will feel justified to judge them again, and so forth. It will not stop."

Of course, Jesus knows that—even as he says it—it will convince no one.

We still will do it—as the left foot follows the right foot, then the left again. Tell a fish to stop swimming in the water. This is what fish do. Unless they are transformed somehow, they will stay in the water. It is their fish-ness. And so, we are judgers.

I remember that it was here Jesus chuckled a deep resonant chortle signaling he had a joke he was dying to tell us. He picked a young man out of the crowd. I suppose that the way the man was dressed, he could have been a Rabbinic disciple. Jesus rose, walked to him, and said,

"Let's say you observe a nasty pitiful speck in your brother's eye. In fact, you are obsessed by it. You want him to know it is there and...," he paused for effect, "that you see it. You even volunteer to—in your vast mercy—to help him remove it. But a little child tugs on your cloak and says to you, 'Sir, why do you have a log sticking out of your eye?'

The crowd erupted in laughter as Jesus turned and went back to his seat.

"Speck-watchers are pretenders, you see. Wouldn't it be wise, and wouldn't we avoid a great deal of shaming by observant children if we took care of the veritable forest in our own eyes before we help others see their splinters?"

By now, the audience was so comfortable with Jesus' sense of humor. He was criticizing them, of course, they knew it, but for some reason, it caused them no shame. They knew he was for them—more so than anyone else in their lives. It was laughable when he told these stories.

"Do not give vile dogs what is holy and pure, and do not throw your pearls before swine, lest they trample them underfoot and turn to attack you.

Now this was recognizable for each one of us. This was our story.

We have all heard this in one form or another. This is what led us here.

'Don't let these dogs, these impure, these cut-off ones near anything holy. In fact, if you touch them, you are also unclean.'

We knew our place. We were swine, untouchable. To touch us made the so-called clean, unclean. That also made us a source of fear. If enough of the unclean got together and were mad enough and were pushed far enough, we might have an uprising that would leave no one pure.

Somehow, it didn't hurt to hear Jesus remind us of our narratives. Partly it was because Jesus had been accused of being impure himself. He gets us.

And yet, he didn't avoid us. In fact, he alone is the only one who is giving that which is most holy to former dogs. He is casting great heavenly riches upon the former pigs.

This is the singular concise message he meant to give on this hillside scattered with curs and swine. God's Kingdom is for the unworthy and unclean—not the worthy and clean. God welcomes the offal of the world, those who are labeled as unrighteous and makes them righteous. God embraces dogs and pigs. They become sons and daughters.

There was a wave of silence sweeping over the crowd. Looking out over the hillside, it was as if the crowd had been to a great indescribable banquet and were quieted by their satiation.

I want to skip the next section and add it to the parable at the end. You will see a method to my madness.

By now, you are attuned to the rabbinic formula.

"Whatever you wish that others would do to you, do also to them, for this is the Law and the Prophets."

We should do that, but we won't. We should love others with all our heart, minds and being. But that is hardly our record.

Until our cups are filled to the full with the fulness of God, we will tend to be selfish. When I am desperate for a better reputation, or more security, or more friends, or when I feel anxious and worried, I will naturally focus on my own wishes—to the detriment of all around.

When I am satiated, looking into the glowing gaze of my loving Father in Heaven, I am free and even a little more motivated to care for others. Remember the "blessed be's" about being merciful. It is those who are immersed in the mercy of God who will be able to truly express mercy to others.

"Enter," Jesus said as held his open palms on his own chest, "Enter by this narrow gate. There are many other gates, some quite large and ornate. But those gates, which are large enough to accommodate many travelers, despite their appearance lead into courts of destruction. For the gate is wide and the way is easy leading to destruction."

"This gate," he once again smiled and pointed to himself, "Appears narrow and limited and hard but it leads to abundant life."

Then he waved his hands over the massive crowd, again with his engaging smile, and quipped sarcastically, "And look, only just a handful of people use this oh so thin gate."

In no way was Jesus suggesting the gate was restrictive or that it could only hold a limited number of people and that was it. No, in fact, he had just ushered into the Kingdom a large crowd with the expectation of many more to come.

Rather, he was teaching there are so many paths that self-report to bring you into the favor and presence of the God of all Creation.

Some of these paths are indeed easy. They require no life changes whatsoever; they offer no challenge to your current flailing for identity and worth. They are easy in that sense. They do not raise you up from being unenviable to being enviable. They do not offer you honor, but they are paths, nonetheless. And remember, Jesus, the Way, the Truth, and the Life will inevitably lead to persecution.

Lastly, he wagged his finger at the crowd, like a wise elder speaking to their young child.

"Beware of false prophets, who come to you in sheep's clothing but inwardly are ravenous wolves. You will recognize them by their fruits. Are grapes gathered from thornbushes, or figs from thistles? So, every healthy tree bears good fruit, but the diseased tree bears bad fruit. A healthy tree cannot bear bad fruit, nor can a diseased tree bear good fruit. Every tree that does not bear good fruit is cut down and thrown into the fire. Thus, you will recognize them by their fruits."

We humans are easily deceived by lies and liars. In fact, one teacher has said we love lies. We love to be lied to. We can see their fruit as clear as day. We can taste the fruit and yet, we love the lie.

Remember our mother, Eve? God couldn't have been clearer about the fruit of the tree. And yet how long did it take the serpent to deceive our beloved mother in Paradise? She was not suffering from lack of worth or honor. She, uniquely along with Adam, really knew the height, width, length, and depth of the love of God toward her—and yet she succumbed to deceit. How well do you think we will do? Surely Adam would have fared no better.

Here is how I interpret this portion. I still remember the moment that Jesus bid me follow him. It was not a dream of mine. I was fairly satisfied by my livelihood, my security, who I was. I wasn't complaining. It wasn't perfect, as I have shared. I was quite lonely and had many daddy-issues. But I was not looking to change. The fruit on the tree looked quite fine and tasted fresh.

Now I know it was the Spirit of the Rabboni, through His invitation, or somehow related to the invite, who made me long for different fruit—that I could not recognize before.

Now I can look back and see I was gorging on strange fruit. I was also on an easy path leading to very large gates and certain destruction. Many were headed that way until they were grabbed from that well-trod path and cast upon the single path that alone leads to life—and certain persecution.

This is why we are on the mission field. This is why we are in Axum and are excited about what the Spirit of Jesus can wrought.

Haaman cannot see the lie. He cannot. King Zoskales is blinded by the glory of the broad gate and has plenty of fruit that in his ignorance seems to more than satisfy. Even our dear protector Obodas is blinded. I say this with great sadness. I would do anything for Obodas to see.

On our own we cannot make a change happen. Even the master teacher Reuben can't make either see logic and reason. The invitation of Jesus to the unworthy, to the unenviable, to the unrighteous is absurd unless you are on the narrow path. And yet, we continue to proclaim the Way.

32

Day 1073 of the Axum Mission

All told we had been away from home six weeks. It is a five-day harrowing trek from Axum to Adulis.

When we arrived very weary and looking forward to some downtime, we were confronted with horrific news. Our worst fears had come true.

Shortly after we left, I do not think it is a coincidence this happened after Obodas and his house guards left Axum, Haaman returned to his disruptive ways.

First, he and a couple dozen trained warriors, fit with spears and hammers attacked the Synagogue, destroying much of the wall and burning down several buildings. They also murdered a dozen people, men, and women. They attacked on the Shabbat when most of the worshippers were there.

Te'oma and a few of the younger men resisted the attack or attempted to. Te'oma was hit in the forehead by a war axe and had to be in a doctor's care for over three weeks. He lost sight in his one eye and must wear a patch for the rest of his life. But at least he is alive. Some of the other men who resisted fared much worse. Two of his dearest friends were killed by spearmen.

Reuben almost died. He caught a spear in the back of his right leg as he was trying to lead the children into a root cellar. The spear was removed except the broken off tip remained. He suffered from harsh fevers for over a week. The synagogue gathered around him to pray on three occasions. Fortunately, he has survived but has a very noticeable limp and will need to use a cane for some time.

It didn't end there. In retaliation, some men then armed themselves and attacked Haaman's village in the valley, burning it down to the ground. It is thought many perished in the attack, both men and women. Deborah told me that none of our men were involved, but that is of little encouragement.

Axum is on edge and expects retaliation from the many valley tribes who are aligned with each other. Individually, they would not be a threat to Axum and King Zoskales, but together? They are a sizable force.

They say history repeats itself and so it might be in this case. This is almost exactly what happened when Zoskales came to power. I am sure the irony isn't escaping him.

There was worse news. The King's niece, Princess Ayana came to our home in fear of her life. She told Deborah the King raped her, violently, causing her both shame and pain. He commanded she join his harem, which terrifies her. He threatened if she told anyone, she would be tortured and beheaded along with any other she confided in.

Now at least three know. God help us.

I have been officially summoned to an audience with the King—tomorrow. I have no choice, but now, I am not sure I want to go.

I have sent a messenger to take an urgent message to Obodas in Adulis. If we ever needed our *karim*, it is now. Obodas told me he was planning on catching the next caravan after ours to Axum. I hope he is on the way.

My last thought makes me laugh at myself. Have I learned so little? Have I forgotten who my true *Karim* really is? It would appear so.

Of all the things the Rabboni said, only one sentence, one prayer has rushed into my mind and will not leave. I dare not ignore it.

"My Father, if it is possible, may this cup be taken from me."

33

Day 1096-Year 3 of the Axum Mission

Sorkatti here.

It is my sad duty to inform readers my dearest friend and colleague, Matthew Ben Alphaeus went to Paradise to be with his Celestial *Karim* a little more than three weeks ago. I have been avoiding completing Matthew's journal. It was so important he do this project. It is so sad he is not here to finish the race. I will do what I can to give him voice still.

His dearest friend, Reuben took care of all funeral preparations. His body was ritually washed according to Jewish tradition and wrapped and bound with strips of cloth soaked in precious incense.

Obodas made sure the very best and most expensive incense was used. Matthew would have certainly appreciated the gesture.

Poor Obodas is deeply crushed. He feels personally responsible for the death of his friend. He has isolated himself in his family compound for over a week now. We are concerned for his well-being.

Truth told, there was little he could have done—even if he were here.

Shortly after Matthew returned from his trip to Adulis, he received a formal request—command really—to an audience before King Zoskales the very next day. Matthew immediately sent an urgent missive to Obodas who unfortunately had been delayed in Adulis, still some five-day journey away. It would have been a miracle if Obodas would have been at the royal audience or was able to intervene in any way. It was not to be. Again, I do not think anything would have been different.

On the following day, two heavily armed soldiers arrived at Matthew's home and forcibly escorted him to the palace. There was no opportunity for him to refuse.

Deborah shared Matthew was filled with ambivalence. On the one hand, he wondered if this was the opportunity he had been asking God for to speak of the Rabboni to the King. On the other hand, Matthew was also very worried and felt quite powerless.

We know something about what happened in that royal audience. According to Queen Abeba, the elderly and very frail Matthew was ungraciously led into the chamber by his armed escort and forced to stand during the interrogation. His thin arms painfully tied behind his slumping back.

It is hard to understand why such precaution needed to be taken. Why would the King feel in any way threatened by a 75-year-old man—who was unarmed? The latest trip to Adulis had taken a great deal out of the aged evangelist. He was looking even more frail and weak. He was clearly no threat to the king—humanly speaking.

The King's royal vizier, a tiny vile man with a well-groomed beard and arrogant air about him, began the proceedings abruptly saying aloud, "Matthew Ben Alphaeus," he paused for effect. "You are being accused of encouraging insurrection against the King. Do you deny it?"

Matthew was quite confused and tried to get clarification about the charge. "Vizier, did I misunderstand? What insurrection? Who is making the charge? I know nothing about..."

He was rudely cut off by the slight prosecutor. "Enough obfuscation," he roared. "Do you deny it?"

Matthew paused for a moment, looked around the room and seeing no rescuer, he took a deep breath and calmly and clearly attempted to plead his innocence.

"Oh, Great King, I am not, nor have I ever encouraged insurrection against you. I wasn't even in Axum when the attacks occurred—if that is what this is all about. I would like to know who..."

The diminutive prosecutor cut him off again, formally reading a scroll which he grabbed off a table to his side.

"Matthew ben Alphaeus, you are also being charged with causing division within the King's household. It seems you are harboring the fugitive Princess Ayana in your compound and teaching her strange philosophies which are contrary to our culture and King. Is this true? How to you plead?"

What could Matthew say? He <u>had</u> heard from Deborah that the King had raped Ayana—and yes, it was true the Princess was in the compound and had asked for sanctuary.

He clumsily tried to form some explanation that didn't bring attention to Deborah or others. "Oh King," he directed his words to King Zoskales. "It is true the Princess is at our compound...by her own choice...we do not..."

"Enough," barked the Vizier, likely offended that Matthew was ignoring him. His voice reminded Matthew of the yipping of a small stray mutt. "How do you plead? Guilty or innocent?"

Queen Abeba said she couldn't bear to watch any more. She knew what her husband was capable of, and she was terrified of what the King would do to her if he knew she had told Deborah about the rape. She looked away. What else could she have done that would have made any difference at all?

Matthew said nothing for a long time. Maybe there was nothing he could say. Perhaps, he was thinking of how the Rabboni had been silent in the face of such unjust accusations.

The prosecutor was becoming even more agitated at Matthew's unwillingness to respond to the two charges—not that it would have made any difference. This was not a legit trial. The decision had long been made.

He snapped again at Matthew now like a rabid dog straining at the end of his owner's leash. "Do you have anything to say to this court and your King, Matthew ben Alphaeus?" He derisively spit out Matthew's name.

It was theater. It was a show. But now was the right time for Matthew, the disciple of the Rabboni, to play his role. Cue the evangelist one last time. One last invitation. One last call.

Matthew shrugged his shoulders, nodded his weary grey head, and calmly began to speak about Jesus and the Kingdom of Heaven, and the one true God's desire to rescue and honor hurting unenviable people here in Axum and the world. How the Creator God loved the unworthy as much as the worthy, how Kings and serfs were equal in his eyes. He was determined to keep on speaking until he was stopped.

It was then King Zoskales just snapped.

Until then, he had just sat emotionless on his throne, dressed in official Roman garb, his curly black hair adorned with an olive branch wreath. So much irony. The olive wreath is given as a prize for the race winners at the Olympic games. It was never meant for pretenders.

On this stage, there was only one who is about to win his long race. It is not Zoskales.

To everyone's surprise, the enraged King bolted off his throne and with all his might slapped the aged disciple on the left cheek. Matthew doubled over, his thin legs buckled, and knees crashed to the hard granite floor of the palace. Matthew uttered a horrible groan, clearly in great pain. The vicious attack had caught him off guard and rattled him. He hadn't been prepared to be physically assaulted by the King himself. But it wouldn't have mattered. Even in his prime, which was decades ago, Matthew was never a fighter. Now, in his seventies, he was quite helpless. Now he was on the ground, his chest heaving trying to capture a single breath.

The King was not done venting his rage. He relentlessly swung other punches to Matthew's face. There was nothing the aged disciple could do, his hands remained firmly tied behind bis back. He was like a lamb taken to the slaughter.

The latest rounds of blows this time knocked him backward, he felt a sharp pain in his shoulder as his left arm was wrenched out of its socket as his back and head hit the cold ground.

Still the King wouldn't stop. He knelt on top of the dazed man, with his knees pinning down Matthew's frail body. He then put both of his large hands around Matthew's neck, squeezing with all his might.

It was a horrible scene, the maddened King violently strangling the little remaining life out of a helpless old apostle. The King's twisted face was only about six inches from Matthew's. His crazed eyes were wide-open, and he spit as he yelled his final words.

"You cur, you refuse," howled the out-of-control Zoskales. "How dare you disrespect me, undermine my authority. I am the King and I pick who is my harem. I will sleep with whomever I so desire. Who do you think you are?"

It didn't take long for Matthew's life to be stolen from him. He was defenseless. And of course, there was no way for him to answer the King's last question.

But we know who he was.

Matthew was the beloved child of the Living God in good standing—an Apostle. In a word, he was enviable.

Matthew Ben Alphaeus was 75. He perished a faithful servant of the Rabboni. This time he had not run away.

The King left early the next morning to hunt elephants and at great personal risk, the Queen ordered a couple of her trusted servants to collect Matthew's deceased body and bring it to our compound. We are grateful to her, for we know that doing this behind the King's back might jeopardize her safety.

It was late on the second day the interment procession, led by Deborah, the team, synagogue members and many of the other Axumite families who knew Matthew well, brought the body to a nearby tomb Obodas graciously provided. Obodas had arrived the morning after the tragedy and was devastated by the news.

After burial, the group returned to the Matthew's compound where expressions of condolences continued. The mourning went on for seven more days.

At the end of the mourning, the team organized a great Todah meal to remember and honor Matthew. There was an open invitation to all who had been touched by Matthew.

On that Sunday, over 1000 people showed up, fortunately many brought food and drink to share. Most of them were from the synagogue, but so many people joined the celebration from the city and surrounding villages.

The team had unanimously chosen Deborah to speak. She was well aware Matthew had almost completed his second volume of Rabboni. All that remained was an exposition on the Rabboni's final parable. We could not think of a better way to honor our friend and colleague than to complete his manuscript on this day.

Here are Deborah's words.

"I know Matthew would be surprised and honored to see all of you here today. It is a great testimony to him, to my husband to know he touched so many. He would of course say that so much more of the credit should go to his rescuer and King, Jesus. Most of you know his story. Jesus came to Matthew when he was a lonely young man successful in some ways but filled with anger and shame."

"It was this Rabboni Jesus who called Matthew to become an honored disciple, a son of God in good standing, a child of Abraham in good standing. Matthew ben Alphaeus the beloved of the King of the Heavens."

"Many of you know he has been hard at work on a new codex, a journal actually, an expanded exposition of the Rabboni's core teachings on a Galilean hillside some 50 years ago now."

"The Rabboni's teachings on that hillside in Galilee shocked the audience. It was a mixed crowd, not so unlike this one. These were not the great, the religious pure, the powerful, the successful, the righteous. Just the opposite. They were not welcomed in the temples of their gods, or their synagogues.

Many had been cut off from their families and tribes. But they came to Jesus that day and were powerfully and unexpectedly transformed. I was there. I hadn't come with any expectations. In fact, I am not sure why I came, but I had no expectations that if there was a God, he would spend one second of his precious time thinking about me."

"But then Jesus said, 'I tell you the good news, society's unenviable disenfranchised ones are now enviable, because God is theirs and they are God's.'

"And I knew, I really did, I knew he meant me. In a moment, I went from a person of shame and dishonor to being a person who was worthy. What happened? I was embraced by Jesus, or by His Spirit. I was appreciated, cherished, adored, even liked."

"What did I do to deserve that? That's the wondrous thing. I did nothing. Well, that's not totally true."

"Later in his teachings Jesus said something very provocative."

"Not everyone who says to me, 'Lord, Lord,' will enter the kingdom of heaven, but the one who does the will of my Father who is in heaven. On that day many will say to me, 'Lord, Lord, did we not prophesy in your name, and cast out demons in your name, and do many mighty works in your name?' And then will I declare to them, 'I never knew you; depart from me, you workers of lawlessness.'"

"What are we to <u>do</u>? How can we enter the Kingdom of Heaven, and be wrapped in honor and name far beyond what we are due?"

She paused and looked around the faces of the crowd. "We <u>do</u> the will of the Father of course."

"What then is the father's will? If that is the key, what is it. We want to make sure we cross that narrow bridge, right? We don't want to perish and then stand before the throne of the King and hear that we didn't do the one thing."

"The late Rabbinic scholar Rabban Zakkai, some of you have heard of him, right before he died, he lamented he could not be sure if his lot was Paradise or Gehenna. My beloved husband was sure. As the Rabboni told one of those who was crucified alongside him, "This day you will be with me in paradise.""

"If Matthew were here today in body, he would want us to know what we must do."

"Some would say we are to be righteous as defined by Torah. While that would be a good thing of course. The Rabboni summarized the Torah and the Prophets with two commands. We should love God with all our heart and being and love our neighbor in the same way. The world would be a far better place. But we don't, we won't, we haven't. This can't be the one will of God—the key to enter His Kingdom."

"You may say, 'Do unto others as they would do unto you.' Again, we should. We would be better off. But again, we don't, we won't. Not enough."

"We should give to the poor. Raise up the widows and orphans, do justice and righteousness. Yes, yes, and yes. But we don't."

"We should do prescribed offerings. We Jews know that it no longer possible. We should study Torah. We should show mercy."

"Which of these good things are the key?"

"At the end of the teachings, Jesus gives us a parable, so we would not miss doing the one thing. Listen."

"Everyone then who hears these words of mine and does them will be like a wise man who built his house on the rock. And the rain fell, and the floods came, and the winds blew and beat on that house, but it did not fall, because it had been founded on the rock. And everyone who hears these words of mine and does not do them will be like a foolish man who built his house on the sand. And the rain fell, and the floods came, and the winds blew and beat against that house, and it fell, and great was the fall of it."

"I had an opportunity to see Matthew's notes and scribbles on this last section of Jesus' teaching in northern Galilee. This is the last section, Jesus' final thoughts, the way he wrapped up the messages. Matthew understood it more than most. I am here to tell you what he concluded."

"What is it to build your house on the sand—because we don't want to do that, am I right? And what does it mean to build your house, instead, on the rock? And what does this parable have to do with doing the will of God?"

"If Matthew were here, he would say something like this. What does it mean to do the will of God that gains you an enviable relationship with Jesus? That gains you the promises God made to Abraham. That brings you into adoption as a favored son or daughter of his in good standing. What does it mean for you to build your house, your life, identity, worth on a rock?"

"What do we do? Nothing. Well, nothing but believe, receive, accept what Jesus has already done. Only he was truly righteous. Only he fulfilled all of Torah, every jot and tittle. He alone has earned all the blessings promised in the Torah to the faithful one."

"The will of God is to stop trying to earn his favor and instead, to receive it as a gift of grace given to the unworthy, the underserving, the ill-prepared."

"Then what is it to build our hope and house on slippery sand? Every time we try to earn the favor of God, that will not hold any lasting foundational weight."

"It is backwards to how we have been raised to think. We imagined God pursues the worthy. But such is sand-thinking."

"God loves the loveable. Sand-thinking."

"The Kingdom of God is made up of the righteous. More sand-thinking."

"No, Jesus came for the impure, the unclean, the beat-up, the discarded."

"It is the will of God that we—as we are—today—embrace this one thing, to receive this gift of grace. That is all, that is enough."

"It was on the Galilean hillside now fifty years ago something happened inside my messed up confused and lonely brain and I got it. I believed. I still do and am so grateful the Rabboni swept me up in his fishing net. I am so grateful my husband Matthew helped me see more of the amazing gift we have been given."

"I am thinking maybe the greatest honor you could bestow on my husband today, is to honor the Rabboni by accepting his gift today."

Deborah paused choking back a cry. She wiped away the tears that were now really beginning to flow. Moments later she went on.

"Matthew, my beloved, I miss you, all these people miss you as well. Enjoy the Rabboni and I will certainly see you soon. Amen and amen."

Mago rose next. He gained everyone's attention by knocking on the wooden table. One more thing must be done to honor the heart of his late friend and colleague.

"Friends and neighbors, our team, led by Matthew, came to Axum as followers of the Rabboni Jesus of Nazareth. We came here three years ago this week to tell his story and to speak of His good news."

"Good news of what? Have you heard how each of us, each of you, can know and experience the favor of the Creator God, to feel such an honor that can never be removed, never can be fiddled with?"

"Strictly due to what Jesus our Lord did almost fifty years ago now, due to his life, and death and resurrection, people like me, like Reuben, like Matthew and like you can begin to know and experience the reality of the love of the Creator God toward us, as much as the Father loves the Son and the Son loves the Father, as you are."

"What do you need to do to gain such an incredible honor? What heights must you climb for such a gift, or seas must you cross, or shiploads of incense must you bring by caravan?"

"Nothing of the sort. Just look at me. I had nothing to bring. I came empty handed. I said it was good news, right?"

"It was during his early teachings, Jesus shocked the world with stunning news. What must you do? Jesus said to a crowd not unlike this one. "All you need do is ask,"

"...a child could do it,"

"...And it will be given to you."

"And you, and you," he pointed around the audience. "The keys to the Kingdom of God—placed in your unworthy hands."

He smiled.

"Are you circumcised? This is for you. Are you of the Pharisaic school? Sadducean? Essene? Zealot? Greek? Roman? Arabic? Nubian? Nabatean? Man? Woman? Boy or girl? Wife or husband? Are you a freeman or a slave?

Have you been oppressed by power? Or have used power for your own selfishness? Are you wealthy or destitute, sick, or well? Are you alone? Or surrounded by a large family? Have you been beat up, or abandoned? Abused? Treated poorly due to your tribe? Come to the one who alone rescues people like you and me from this present evil age that is so laced by injustices, inequities, and violence."

"All you need to do is just seek," said Jesus, "and you will find; knock, and the Kingdom of God will be opened to you."

"How easy can it be?"

"The Rabboni said all too clearly, 'For everyone who asks receives, and the one who seeks finds, and to the one who knocks it will be opened.' This is to build your house on a rock—the Rock."

"Listen carefully. Jesus said..." he held up his hands, palms out. 'Which one of you, if his son asks him for bread, will give him a stone? Or if he asks for a fish, will give him a serpent? If you then, who are evil, know how to give good gifts to your children, how much more will your Father who is in heaven give good things to those who ask him!'"

"My neighbors and new friends of our dear friend and departed Matthew, hear me. I am here to speak of a wonderful eternity for me and for you. I am here to speak about a God, the God who made the land and the sea, the skies, and the stars. He is the very one who has sent me to bring a solemn invitation to you today."

"Would you come right now into His loving arms and be received as an honored son or daughter of favor? A child in good standing? You? Loved as much as Jesus loved Matthew. It is true."

"Would you come to look up into the Rabboni's adoring gaze and at last hear him say to you, "You are my beloved son or daughter with whom I am well pleased?"

"You may be surprised there is such a Messiah who would welcome you as you are, no matter what you've done or not done, said, or not said. But it is so. This invitation is rock solid and more valuable than the most precious incense."

"Why would you hesitate? This is the nature of his Kingdom. This is the nature of our God. His invitation is not for the pure, the righteous, the faithful.

No, the Rabboni came on behalf of the Creator God to invite those like us, those like you to join him in the eternal heavenly Kingdom. Will you come?"

"You do not come because you are worthy, but because you are not. You do not come to make claim upon such a privilege—but because you have no claim at all. The invitation is for pirates and thieves, slave and free, the orphan and the widow, the shamed and the lonely, the marginalized, the helpless. For that is who we are."

"Come and be a disciple of Jesus. Come. Reuben and I will be in the fountain to baptize each seeker with water per the Rabboni's instruction. All who want to receive such an honor, to be the son or daughter of the Creator God in good standing come."

Sorkatti again. I am so pleased to record we witnessed an amazing outpouring of new faith. We estimate over 450 people, men women, boys and girls, Greeks, Jews, Nubians, Ethiopians, as well as Arabs from multiple tribes and dialects came to be baptized by Reuben, Deborah and Mago in our fountain. It took hours. There was singing and praise and testimonies. But there's more.

During one of the few lulls in people coming forward to be baptized, our attention was starkly arrested by an unearthly clamor—a shriek—coming from immediately outside our compound's gate. It sounded like a wounded animal or a child's squeal. It was Obodas, our *karim*.

As Obodas slowly moved closer to the crowd gathered around the fountain, we saw he was almost naked, stripped down to his loincloth. He was such a sad and deeply wounded figure, crying out in some ancient dialect unable to raise his eyes from the ground. A deep shame had broken him. His body was covered with white chalk—a sign of great mourning in his tribe—his face traced with rivulets formed by his tears as he wept for the loss of his friend Matthew.

Though we had tried to comfort him by telling him there was just nothing he could have done, he couldn't hear it. He had let his dear friend down—had abandoned him and left him helpless before the King. In his own eyes, he had tragically failed as Matthew's *karim*.

But then it became obvious Obodas didn't come for that reason alone. As we watched this thin ragged pitiful white figure walk toward us, shoulders hunched over, eyes on the ground. The crowd seamlessly parted to let him through. Old Obodas climbed right into the fountain and stood in front of a very shocked Reuben. Reuben looked like a giant compared to Obodas. He stood over a head taller and looked down on the top of Obodas' bald head.

No one spoke. All eyes were locked upon him and waiting to see what Reuben was going to do.

Obodas broke the ice, crying out loud enough for all to hear. "I am here to become a disciple of Matthew's Rabboni. How do I do this? I am here to put myself under Jesus' care—I want him to be my *karim*. Can I do that? Am I worthy?"

Reuben's face broke out into a wide smile and said with a chuckle, "Oh my dear friend Obodas. There is so much for you to learn but hear this now. Jesus has come, not for the worthy or acceptable, but for the unworthy and the unacceptable. You more than qualify. Come and be baptized into Him by His Spirit."

Reuben stood by the side of Obodas and gently leaned him backwards into the cool water. He said, "Obodas, in the name of the Heavenly Father, Son and Spirit, I baptize you. Rise up now a new creature—a new disciple of the Rabboni. He is now your celestial *karim* for all eternity."

Obodas bounced up out of the water grinning, showing off all three of his remaining yellow teeth. The crowd cheered and applauded. How we wished Matthew was here to see this. God is good.

Our dear departed friend and evangelist Paul wrote this in one of his letters. It is a strong elixir for such a time of mourning as this. We look forward to someday seeing our friend once more.

"Brothers and sisters, we do not want you to be ignorant about those who fall asleep, or to grieve like the rest of men, who have no hope. We believe Jesus died and rose again and so we believe God will bring with Jesus those who have fallen asleep in him. According to the Lord's own word, we tell you that we who are still alive, who are left till the coming of the Lord, will certainly not precede those who have fallen asleep. For the Lord himself will come down from heaven, with a loud command, with the voice of the archangel and with the trumpet call of God, and the dead in Christ will rise first. After that, we who are still alive and are left will be caught up together with them in the clouds to meet the Lord in the air. And so, we will be with the Lord forever. (Paul's First Letter to the Church at Thessalonica 4:13-17)

34

Final Entry: Day 1276 of the Axum Mission

Sorkatti again.

It has been six months since Matthew joined his Celestial *Karim* and friend in Paradise. I didn't want to end the codex on the last chapter. I do have some more good news.

First of all, we are still here. In fact, we are thriving. Though Reuben calls us a "sacred mess."

At the end of winter, a few months ago, we celebrated the opening of the Matthew Ben Alphaeus Scriptorium. To date we have been able to hire a dozen scribes largely from Alexandria. Ninos has been quite successful acquiring enough papyrus, ink, and reeds for us to have already published our first dozen codices. We are preparing to do even more.

My plan is to focus on publishing Matthew's original gospel for now—in Greek, Nabatean, and Ge'ez Arabic dialects—and something new for us—we want to publish codices in Indos—or you may prefer, Indian. I will say more in a moment.

Almost all the first two dozen Greek and Arabic codices were committed to Gamilah, but the very first Ge'ez translation did go to Haaman per Matthew's final wish. He accepted the gift, that is about all I can say. May God richly bless that gesture.

What else is happening?

All of Obodas' wives were baptized shortly after him. Of course, we understand they did it because he said to. We are discipling each. They come weekly to help us with our Todah meal. We serve over 400 men and women each time. Te'oma and Ruth are in charge but have a large team of volunteers. Te'oma jokes it is not exactly the Rabboni's feeding of the 5000, but significant, nonetheless.

Mago and Sophie have made plans to extend our mission to the Nabatean fortress port of Aden sometime next year. Aden sits at the nexus between the Red Sea and the Erythraean Sea. From there, Mago says, they can reach the world with the Gospel of the Nazarene. This is why we are preparing to publish some of Matthew's gospel in Indian.

Gamilah surprised Mago recently by bringing to Axum a missionary whose native tongue is one of the many Indian dialects. Hunar was on Thomas' mission to the Far East, until Gamilah 'kidnapped' him for this new mission to Aden. Hunar, his wife Sitar, and their four young children have joined our work in Axum and feel called to the new work in Aden.

Hanno would love to join them. If you remember, he is a sailor and feels Aden is the place where he can reach more and more mariners— 'sea dogs' he calls them. Bernice is not convinced. So, Hanno and Bernice are trying to figure out what the Rabboni wants them to do. We would certainly miss them.

Like I said, we hope to send the new team out early next year. So far, nineteen adults have volunteered to join them, representing seven mother tongues—so far.

Bernice continues to serve the impoverished in Adulis. It is striking that in a region where so many are flourishing, so many others are unaffected. Ninos had a set back a little while ago but is now back on the mend. He has plunged into Bernice's ministry and is a powerful spokesperson to those both impoverished and addicted.

We have heard very little from Haaman. I wish I could tell you we are safe from his mischief. We have hired guards for our compound and the Synagogue. We continue to pray for him—but suspect that we have not heard the last from him.

I can report two tribal chieftains from the valley have become followers of Jesus. We are praying for a missionary family who is willing to go and live with them in the valley.

Our two formerly kidnapped bedouin friends, Shammar and Rashaida are being trained as scribes for the Scriptorium. They are very adept students of language, and their handwriting is improving rapidly. I wonder what their story will be at the end of the day. It is just like the Rabboni to set the prisoners free. Amen? Could they become evangelists to the Arabic tribes to the north? Nothing would surprise me anymore.

Reuben continues to dialogue with the leaders in the Synagogue. It seems every week we have one or two Jewish families who are baptized as disciples of Jesus in our central fountain. We continue to pray that the power of the Gospel to believe continues to make disciples there.

I won't tell you there are no conflicts. There are. Reuben is the perfect one to weather that storm. He is gracious, loves Torah and is used to building bridges. It helps that the synagogue ruler Stafylus has become a Jesus-follower—though that is not public knowledge yet.

Deborah has taken the lead as the teacher-evangelist of our mission. She, along with Mago on some weeks, teaches the growing crowd at our Todah celebrations. After all, she was one of the earliest disciples of the Rabboni. She is currently teaching through Matthew's original Gospel. God is blessing.

She still begins most of her talks, "Every saint has a past, and every sinner has a future."

Our dog mascot, Frank is also doing well. He has put on way too much weight. It's his personality. He can charm food from just about anyone. I am supposed to be taking care of him, but he is quite good on his own.

I do have some sad news. Tragically, Princess Ayana was forced to marry her uncle the King. There was nothing we could do. We hardly ever see her anymore. I am assuming it would be very dangerous for her to come to one of our *Todahs*. We understand. Please pray for her. There is a great deal of sadness and shame in her heart.

As for me? I am very committed to the Scriptorium's vision of producing codices of the Gospel in as many languages and dialects as we can. The

Rabboni's words are powerful and life changing. We are considering expanding our compound to accommodate our goals. Gamilah and I communicate regularly. She is excited to underwrite it all.

I am no longer a Nubian princess, but I am more than satisfied being a layperson Jesus-follower in a much larger Kingdom.

A personal note if I may. I am engaged to a handsome and kind Jewish man who owns a bakery here. His family is from Nazareth if you can believe it. We will be joined at the new year. God is good. I suspect Matthew is laughing in Heaven.

One last thing. If you even happen to visit us here, make sure you look at the cornerstone of the Matthew ben Alphaeus Scriptorium. It is solid marble and was donated by Gamilah and Obodas. Rabbi Stafylus led the dedication service and most of the Jews of Axum came to the celebration.

It reads, in Greek, Arabic and Hebrew,

"Enviable are those who were formerly unenviable because now God is their karim."

The Rabboni Jesus

Amen and amen.